Britta Bolt

Britta Bolt is the pseudonym of the South African-born novelist and travel writer Rodney Bolt, and the German former lawyer Britta Böhler, who has worked on high-profile terrorism and security cases. Their collaboration began in 2010, when Britta Böhler, on holiday and reading her favourite crime fiction, felt the urge to turn her past experiences into a novel. Rodney Bolt was at home, writing biographies and travel stories, and dreaming of doing the same. Soon afterwards, they had teamed up to write a crime series set in their beloved adopted city Amsterdam.

BRITTA BOLT

Lonely Graves

MULHOLLAND
BOOKS

HODDER

First published as *Heldhaftig* in the Netherlands in 2012 by De Arbeiderspers

First published in Great Britain in 2014 by Mulholland Books
An imprint of Hodder & Stoughton
An Hachette UK company

First published in paperback in 2015

1

A CIP catalogue record for this title is available from the British Library

Paperback ISBN 978 1 444 78727 6
eBook ISBN 978 1 444 78729 0

Printed and bound by Clays Ltd, St Ives plc

Hodder & Stoughton policy is to use papers that are natural, renewable
and recyclable products and made from wood grown in sustainable
forests. The logging and manufacturing processes are expected to
conform to the environmental regulations of the country of origin.

Hodder & Stoughton Ltd
338 Euston Road
London NW1 3BH

www.hodder.co.uk

For Victor
and for Christopher Chambers,
who gave our hero his name

AUTHORS' NOTE

The City of Amsterdam really does give 'Lonely Funerals' for anonymous corpses found within the city limits, with music, a poem especially written for the deceased, flowers, and coffee. This book, however, is a work of fiction. Our characters bear no relation to the real-life incumbents of similar posts, and our Department of Emergencies and Internment, its structure and ways of working, are entirely fictional. Similarly, although InSec in the book performs a similar function to the Dutch intelligence service (the AIVD), the 'Constitutional Order' section of InSec and its staff are entirely fictional.

DRAMATIS PERSONAE

Posthumus's World

Pieter Posthumus
Sulung Koster and Maya Wesseling, his colleagues at the city
burials department
Alex Tomassi, receptionist at the city burials department

Anna de Vries, owner of *De Dolle Hond* (The Mad Dog) bar
Cornelius Barendrecht, poet
Merel Dekkers, journalist

InSec, the state security service

Onno Veldhuizen, head of Constitutional Order section
Lisette Lammers, leader of investigation team 'C'
Ben Bos, runner
Rachid el Massoui, audio
Ingrid Visser, analyst
Mick Waling, intelligence officer

The Kolenkit Quarter

The Tahiri Family
Mohammed and Karima Tahiri
Aissa (25) and Najib (19), their children
Amir Loukili, a distant relation

'The Amsterdam Cell'
Hassan Mansouri (the supposed leader)
Tarik Alami
Ahmed Bassir
Mohammed Kaddaoui
Karim El Mardi
Khaled Suleiman (a.k.a Fayyad Haddad)

PROLOGUE

A tram thundering over the metal bridge drowns any sound the body makes as it hits the water.

Amsterdam: 10.58 p.m.
A young man. Slender, unconscious, dressed in a traditional Moroccan djellaba. Every muscle juddering.

The slim body slips down to the muddy bed of the Westelijk Marktkanaal, bounces on an upturned lavatory bowl, rolls over, rests a moment, then buoyed a little by air caught under the djellaba and propelled by an eddy caused by a passing boat, bobs just below the surface towards the middle of the canal. It twitches and jerks, as the lungs make violent, involuntary attempts to expel water and inhale air, the jiggling arms briefly giving it the appearance of an underwater swimmer. Within three minutes it is lifeless.

Boudewijn Krijnen, a little the worse for wear after a night's drinking on his new boat with friends, curses and swings the powerful Century motor launch into a U-turn, perilously close to the bank. Confused by a four-way junction of canals, he has come up the side of the Kop van Jut into the Westelijk Marktkanaal, instead of taking the Kostverlorenvaart, which leads to his mooring place out of town. He allows the boat to drift a moment, engine idling, as he checks the SatNav. Then he ups power and heads back to the junction. He hears the engine strain. Gives it a bit more juice. On around the corner and along the Kostverlorenvaart, towards the Nieuwe Meer. Still the uneasy whine persists. Some crap caught in the propeller, he thinks, and whacks up the throttle to its full 90 horsepower. The boat lurches forward, the engine screams back into normalcy, and Boudewijn quickly hits down the throttle, hoping there are no police boats about.

The body is interrupted in its slow progress towards the centre of the Westelijk Marktkanaal by a gently turning propeller, which entangles a sturdy canvas shoulder-bag strap draped around one side of the neck, crossing diagonally over the chest. The propeller, its prey captured, springs suddenly into life, ripping and tearing into flesh, shredding the djellaba, dragging the body around a corner into the Kostverlorenvaart. Then it bites again, with renewed ferocity, slicing through the canvas bag strap and twisting it around a lifeless shoulder and neck, before shooting off into far waters, creating a wash that thrusts the body back along the way it has come, until the impulse wanes and the corpse sinks.

11.20 p.m.
The slow current along the Kostverlorenvaart, from the Nieuwe Meer towards the centre of town, stirs the corpse from time to time, edging it along the bottom, back towards the junction of four canals. Gentle drifts, then a lurch or two, as the wash from a boat or an eddy around some formless underwater bulk moves it this way and that, gradually, off the Kostverlorenvaart into a canal that aims it at the heart of the city.

Midnight
Zeeburg. The far north-eastern edge of Amsterdam. Gigantic motors at the municipal pump-station whirr into action,

creating a rush of water into the city. All the time that the corpse is making its slow underwater journey, water-company workers have been closing sluice-gates around town. An electric whine and a clang, as ten gates slam shut in succession, to make a route channelling clean water through the canals and filth out into the IJ river. The surge from Zeeburg begins, jolting the young man into motion. The water in the city grows a rippling, stirring, writhing life of its own. A quarter of a million cubic metres on the move. For five hours. Strong currents push down a wide waterway, thrust up a narrower one, churn back along another, sending the young man jerking and threshing through the canals, limbs flailing in a manic underwater dance.

About 4.30 a.m.
The corpse ends its journey, twisted up against a bicycle frame, in the mud at the bottom of the Prinsengracht, near the Westerkerk.

8.45 a.m.
The queue for the Anne Frank House is already long. Tourists watch, half bored, half charmed, as the flat barge with the mechanical arm fishes up debris from the canal that runs alongside. Someone screams. Among the bicycles hauled up by the metal claw, a body dangles. Crooked. Nearly naked. Very dead.

THURSDAY
12 MAY 2011

I

Pieter Posthumus was having a rough day. Three bodies before lunch was irksome. More than he got in a week. Usually. And now on the phone some smartarse rookie policeman was chirping out the creaky quip about his surname and his profession. Posthumus let it pass in silence, gave a curt good-bye, and killed the line.

The Department of Emergencies and Internment was an odd strut in the framework of the Amsterdam municipal government. 'Despatches and Disasters', the other workers called it. And Posthumus occupied a curious corner, on the Funeral Team. Amsterdam hadn't seen a major disaster in decades. Not that the department wasn't prepared for one, in these times of terrorist attacks, and especially since the Americans had shot Bin Laden, but 'Despatches' was its main activity. That bit came from the centuries-old obligation on the Burgermeester to take responsibility for unclaimed corpses within the city limits. These days, that mostly meant tramps and junkies, lonely old men and women, people rejected by their families, the odd tourist who dropped dead in the street, or one of the window-girls with false papers. Also – more than once – the victim of some underworld skirmish. The corpse that suddenly nobody wanted to know.

'Quite a batch this morning! Take your pick.' Alex Tomassi spoke in an exaggerated whisper, poking her head around the door of the Funeral Team office. Posthumus grinned. He was the only one there. Alex walked across the room, grimacing at Maya Wesseling's unoccupied chair, and perched herself across the corner of Posthumus's desk, back straight, hands folded on one knee, self-mocking her role as demure secretary. Posthumus's mood lifted instantly. Alex really was a beautiful girl. Her father was from Sicily. That explained the tumble of black hair, the dark eyes – yet she had her mother's double-cream Dutch complexion. Clever, too. He liked Alex.

'*Madam*'s delayed at a cremation.' Alex tossed her head back towards Maya's corner. 'Not, alas, permanently.' Then she nodded across to the other desk in the room. 'Sulung feeling any better?'

'Spoke to him this morning. He said he'll be in tomorrow.'

'So he's watching daytime television while we struggle alone with three new cases? *Really*, Sulung!' Alex gave her wrist a little whack. 'But, seriously, who would you like?'

'Who do you think?' Posthumus tapped the four pens on his desk into a neat block, tips in a line.

'The attic?'

He looked up and grinned again. 'Know me, you do.' In addition to the routine demands of Reception, Alex was Traffic – coordinating the diaries of the three officers on the Funeral Team, keeping tracks on who was seeing a funeral through, and when they would be back, picking the pairs for house-visits (the department rule was 'out together, home together', in case there were valuables or money on the deceased's premises). With both his colleagues out of the office that morning, Posthumus had been fielding calls and drawing up brief case summaries. He'd sent the customary two enquiries for each (by fax, as was still the procedure): one to the population registry, one to the Probate Office. If those revealed no contactable family, it would mean a house-visit – and it was Alex who would be sorting the schedules.

Alex knew who would be where and when, and channelled cases towards one team member or the next. She did this efficiently, and entertained no undue sense of power. But she had her favourite.

Odd that three had come in, in one morning, Posthumus thought, but there was nothing untoward going on. It just happened that way sometimes. It was a mixed bunch. A woman of over ninety, at the Zonhof old people's home. Fairly standard, that one: dementia, friends dead. She hadn't married, so probably no family either. There would be a couple of humdrum phone calls, then a quiet burial with a couple of old biddies from the home.

Next, a solitary man in an apartment out east on the Madurastraat. Neighbours reported the stench. Dead for a week or two, and the place fit to be condemned. 'An absolute *tip*,' the woman from social services had said on the phone. '*Mountains* of rubbish. Boxes everywhere, piles of plastic bags, a complete *avalanche* of papers. You wouldn't believe it!' Oh yes, he would, Posthumus had thought. He knew that sort, all right. Diogenes Syndrome, it was called: decades of hoarding and accumulated mess. A complete nightmare if you had to excavate for a will, a bank statement, an insurance policy – anything that might give a clue as to surviving friends and family or whether there was any money to pay for the funeral. (With all the cutbacks, the city council was getting even stingier about that.) No, thank you.

But the third call had intrigued him. A younger man. Well, late forties, about the same age as he was. A bit of a loner with a history of depression. He had sub-let a little attic apartment, and had hanged himself. There was no note, but apparently that was not uncommon. There wasn't any question of foul play or anything – police had signed off on the case. That had been the perky little copper on the phone earlier. But the apartment owner didn't know of any friends or family. Now *that* was more his line.

'The attic it is then.' Alex smiled.

Posthumus nodded. 'The whole point of the job, for me,' he said. He had not chosen this. Nor, for that matter, had he chosen to leave his previous job with the Conduct and Integrity Unit, the council's professional standards watchdog. Nine months ago, now. It had been a discreet sideways transfer to a less significant municipal department. A banishment after a long-running contretemps with his boss. 'Uncooperative, not a team player,' had been the official verdict. Posthumus simply could not let things go. On corruption investigations in particular, when all other members of the team were satis-fied, had closed a case, were assured that all was above board, Posthumus would often light upon a single odd fact – not even a discrepancy, merely something that did not quite fit into the picture. Too frequently he had gone off on his own, chipped away at something, got nowhere. He caused time-targets to be missed, had a reputation for going on wild goose chases. The few occasions when his doggedness had paid off – a big case involving backhanders for building contracts, which he had blown open long after the unit had laid it to rest – served only to fan his boss's resentment. And in the end, the boss had got his way, and Posthumus was edged off the scene. No, he had not been pleased to find himself on the Funeral Team at Despatches and Disasters, but now that he *was* here, he was determined to make the best of it.

Posthumus pushed his chair back from the desk, stretched his arms above his head. He didn't want Alex to leave just yet.

'Call me quirky, but I really think you can *do* something,' he said. 'With the real aloners, I mean. Or the anonymous ones. Give them one last bit of dignity, a personal send-off, even if there's no one else there to see it. So that it isn't just a Despatch.'

'Well, you're alone in that,' said Alex. 'I think it's lovely, what you do, but you should watch your back.' She cocked her head towards Maya's chair. 'I hear the gossip at the coffee machine.'

Posthumus did not draw the line at simply digging out wills, address books and bank statements. He went further. He rifled through bookshelves, raided CD collections, even read diaries, building up a picture of the people he called his 'clients', so that if no friends or family emerged he could come up with some music, a reading, even a short oration. Something that turned the moment in an empty funeral chapel or crematorium into an occasion a little less purely functional. Maya Wesseling, especially, thought Posthumus wasted time.

He glanced out of the window. One of the department's Smart cars was edging into a parking space below the seventeenth-century canal-house that accommodated their offices.

'Uh-oh. Talk of the devil.'

'I'm gone,' said Alex, swinging her bum off the desk, disappearing quickly through the door and down the flight of stairs to Reception. Posthumus chuckled after her. Alex understood. He'd liked her from the first; when she had not made the predictable joke as they were introduced, but said instead, 'Oh, I had a teacher called Posthumus.' It was a common enough name in Holland, after all. It pulled him up short to think she was, what? Twenty-two? He was almost old enough to be her father. What age would he have had to have been? Twenty-five? Quite old enough. Same age his parents were when his brother Willem was born. Willem . . .

Posthumus was still staring out of the window, gazing vacantly beyond the houseboats to the delicate line of gables on the other side of the River Amstel, when Maya banged into the room.

'It seems we're very busy today,' she said pointedly, without any greeting. Though the Funeral Team were all on an equal footing, responsible directly to the department manager, she liked to see herself as team leader.

'I've sent the faxes. I guess Alex will be in touch when she hears back,' Posthumus replied, picking up the phone. 'I'm just tying up some other loose ends. Something's been niggling me about that Bloemstraat case.' He had been Maya's second on a house-visit a few days earlier. 'There were three keys on the ring we were given for the apartment, right? But we needed only two to get in . . .'

'Oh, for God's sake, Pieter,' snapped Maya. 'I don't know. Storeroom. Bicycle. Can you never just let go? It's done. Family found, they're sorting the funeral. It's nothing to do with us any more. Closed.'

'It was a Yale,' said Posthumus. He turned and spoke quietly into the phone for a minute or two, hung up, and responded to Maya's enquiring stare. 'Nothing amiss. The neighbour's spare, apparently.'

Maya didn't reply, glanced at her watch and went back to checking her emails.

'By the way, she wants it back,' Posthumus added.

2

'They're being fucking *freed*! Let out. The whole fucking litter. Couldn't find enough *bloody* evidence. Just got the call. Jesus bollocking Christ! Lammers, I want you in my office, *now*.' Onno Veldhuizen, section chief of Constitutional Order, stormed out of the staff canteen as suddenly as he had arrived, leaving the double doors swinging behind him. People shot glances at their table. Lisette Lammers looked round at her team, mouthed a silent '*Shit!*' and followed him out, leaving her tuna salad untouched.

The lift had gone. Veldhuizen hadn't waited. Lisette hit the Up button, closed her eyes and leaned back against the wall, slipping her fingers through her hair and tucking a strand behind an ear. She hated that 'Lammers' thing of his. Almost immediately the second lift pinged its arrival, doors opened, and people streamed out on their way to lunch. Nodding the odd greeting, Lisette edged past them, slapped her pass against the sensor and pressed the button for the fifth floor.

At the door to the fifth-floor corridor, it took three strikes at the pass-reader before it grudgingly obliged with a green light and admitted her. The corridor was just a notch above bland: smart, middleweight-corporate. White walls, forgettable prints at regular intervals, a touch of unfashionable olive green on the fittings, brown hard-weave carpet. Unremarkable, like the building itself: six storeys of straight lines, glass and concrete, in one of those nondescript business-park sprawls between Amsterdam, Rotterdam and The Hague. The security wall that edged the street was perhaps the only jarring note. That and maybe one or two too many CCTV cameras, and – if you could see them – the extra antennae on the roof. Otherwise, InSec (or the National Intelligence and Security Service, as it was officially known), slipped seamlessly in among its commercial neighbours.

Veldhuizen's door was open, its lock beeping angrily. Lisette pulled the ends of her collar a little closer together, ran her palms down the front of her blouse, and walked in. Her boss cocked an eyebrow at the door. She closed it. He seemed already to be on a slightly lower boil. It wasn't like him to forget his training and lose it like that. He must have just got it in the neck from the District Attorney. Lisette had the sinking feeling that the dominoes were falling in her direction.

Veldhuizen was a tall man, fit for his fifty-something years, and strong – with a hint of threat when his face set hard, like now. Blue eyes that read you right down to the small print. The section chief was ex-police, not one of the admin types who, more and more, were climbing through the Service. Types like Lisette. She was very aware that her boss saw her as one of the university wets. And a woman. Of course. Being blonde didn't help, either. He gestured her to sit down, and launched straight in.

'The case has collapsed. Fallen apart completely. Not enough hard facts.' For nearly seven months, Lisette's team had been monitoring the group the media dubbed 'The Amsterdam Cell'. Young Moroccans, mainly, who were up to something. Clearly they were. Her team had been meticulous. They had watched as two of their 'targets' swapped trainers and T-shirts for traditional dress, they had monitored sermons in radical mosques, eavesdropped on the targets talking about jihad. Everything pointed to more than simply tough guys looking for kicks. *Pointed to.* That was the problem. They had gathered enough for the DA to authorise a small wave of 'conspiracy to commit a terrorist attack' arrests. He'd done that quickly enough. *He* didn't want to be the one blamed for inaction when the bomb went off. But for some reason it had been insufficient to support his further investigations.

'It seems, when it came to the crunch, he couldn't find enough to back up your report,' Veldhuizen went on. His fingers twitched quote marks in the air. 'Material too murky.'

That pussyfooting language they had to use in intelligence reports! The 'have reason to believes' and 'indications are thats'. But they *knew*.

'We had to make a move, sir. We couldn't hold back much longer,' she said. It was a tricky balance. You gathered all you could – the taps, the tails, the daily observations, the street work, phone trails, internet tracking, purchase-tracing – but you had to pick the precise moment to bring it off, to alert the police, hand over to the DA. And all the time you were as scared as hell; a week, a day too long, and you'd hear the bomb go off. Nothing could be worse than that – except this, perhaps. Lisette could not understand how the material they had so carefully built up had somehow fallen apart in the DA's hands. Now it would be even more difficult. More dangerous.

'Well, you moved too soon.' He sat back in his chair. 'And now I've had a heap of shit poured on me by the DA. Whingeing that now *he* has to take the flak, it will be *his* face on TV tomorrow.'

So *that* was it, thought Lisette. Yes, here came the dominoes. She began to speak, but Veldhuizen shook his head once, and went straight on.

'It's not a complete train crash. Just craply timed,' he said. 'He didn't have enough to hold them, but whatever the DA thinks, they're still targets. So . . . back to the ball game. It makes sense to keep you on the case, and the team as it is.'

Well, at least that was that out of the way, though hardly a ringing endorsement. It wasn't often a woman got to be a team leader. Lisette had a tough task on her hands, and they were a difficult lot, 'Team C'.

'But there is no way we can let this happen again. No sob stories. We need to move forward,' said Veldhuizen. 'They'll be out this afternoon, tomorrow morning latest. They're going to be even more careful now that they know they're being watched, but they're going to be cocky about being released. So get the team on it pronto. You, I want you in here first thing in the morning. Now, I've got to get to The Hague and brief the minister about this mess. And he's not going to be happy. So by tomorrow I want some bright new ideas on a strategy. As far as the rest goes, you'll all carry on as before.' He paused. Those eyes again. 'With one possible change.' He kept his gaze, but Lisette noticed his hand move towards the cellphone lying on his desk. 'But I'll speak to you tomorrow.' He nodded at the door, indicating the interview was over.

'I'll speak to the team immediately, sir.' Lisette knew better than to attempt any justification, or pumped-up assurances. She got up, and opened the door. One of the other team leaders was passing in the corridor.

'Oh, and Lammers.'

Lisette paused at the threshold. 'Sir?'

'Get it right this time.'

Team C were finishing off their coffees when Lisette got back to the canteen – dubbed Café Minus by InSec staff, because of its location on the first basement level and the poor quality of the food. Someone had packed up her salad for her.

'That was quick. Scalding?' Mick Waling smiled. Lisette

found her intelligence officer the most sympathetic of the bunch.

'Pretty much. Look, I think we'd better do this in my office.'

All three got up and followed her out. They were alone in the lift.

'We're going on, then?' asked Rachid el Massoui.

Lisette nodded.

'Still the same team?'

'That is usual practice,' said Lisette.

'*Just* the same?'

Lisette nodded again. She heard Rachid's little reverse sniff. He had his eye on an analyst's job, she knew. Thought himself above sitting at the computer all day listening to tapes, with his psychology degree. He had been miffed when a younger team member, Ingrid, had been promoted to analyst a few months back, leaving him behind. He was thirty-two and due for a step-up, true, but they needed his language skills. Good audio workers were hard to get. Rachid's resentment at the younger woman's promotion was just one of the little fault lines in the team that Lisette had to keep an eye on. Or was it *her* he resented?

Third floor.

'Go, go, *go*!' Ben Bos, at twenty-nine the baby of the team. Bit of a wide boy, saw himself as an action man. Still, he was one of the best runners. Bright. Tough. And he used his head – sensible underneath the bluff, and a skilful chameleon, who got the most unlikely people to trust him. Good at the street work. Lisette was thankful for Ben Bos.

The team filed into her office. Mick took a standard-issue guest chair, back against the wall. Ben propped up against the filing cabinet (how could anyone brushing thirty wear their belt so low?), Rachid still standing. Ben was dancing silently to himself, as if his earphones were still in. Lisette took up a position in front of her desk.

'Well, as you will have gathered, our targets are going to be released. The DA says his investigations haven't thrown up enough to bring any of them to trial.'

'But the police searched the place!' said Ben. 'They *must* have found those DVDs, and the stash of bleach and acid and tacks and shit. And they took the computers, right? What about all the downloads? The radical sermon stuff, and the "How to Make a Bomb, For Complete Friggin' Dummies"?'

'Well, whatever they found, it wasn't enough for the DA,' said Lisette. 'But the point remains they're still targets, so we go on. It's back to basics. This is a setback, not a defeat. *We* know there's something up with that lot, *I* know that you three are as good as it gets. So this time we've got to make it stick. And we've got to do it before anything happens. There's a responsibility here.'

'Pity the DA didn't feel the same, the dickhead,' said Ben.

'This goes with the territory, we know that,' said Lisette. 'If we're successful, no one gets to hear about it, like with Flevopark.' Their previous case: two Albanians about to car-bomb a minister, picked up by Immigration and deported. Swift. No fuss. Hush-hush. 'But if we muck up, a bomb goes off and we get the blame for not stopping it. We don't want that to happen here. The bottom line is that the DA isn't satis-fied, and we must move on.'

'But we've been working *with* them the past few weeks,' Ben went on.

Ten years ago that would have been unlawful, thought Lisette. Now it was all part of a grey area, in the name of effective security, but where did it get them?

'Just can't do their friggin' job,' said Ben. 'Or they just want to get one over on us, more like.'

'We could certainly have provided any necessary clarifica-tion, if they'd asked,' said Mick, his mellow voice suddenly making Ben sound strident. 'We have the same aims, surely. Does seem there's bit of unhealthy competition somewhere, perhaps?'

Lisette did not answer.

Mick's look said: 'Veldhuizen?'

'Whatever the ins and outs, we need to get on with it, and I want to move fast,' she said. 'The targets could be released any minute. They'll probably go straight home – but I'd like to keep a track on their first calls and contacts. And to keep an eye on what goes on after Friday prayers tomorrow. Like the chief said, they're going to be more careful now they know we're watching, but they could be a bit cocky at being released. Is audio still in place on Mansouri?' Hassan Mansouri: twenty-five, the ringleader. Or so all their findings – their apparently insubstantial findings – indicated.

Rachid shrugged. 'If he uses his old phone. Probably won't. Besides, I've been helping Coco out with the backlog on that Belgian case, don't forget, since last week.'

'Don't worry, I'll sort that. All effort is needed here now. Can you get on to Mansouri, just in case. I think we should focus on him and Alami, they're the dangerous ones. You got some ground-team people who can move right away?' This to Ben.

He punched the air feebly.

'Thanks, lads,' said Lisette. 'It'll be good to be already showing some signs of life to the chief when I see him tomorrow. Meanwhile, how about a new case name? Might bring better luck. Ideas, anyone?'

'Mission Impossible,' said Ben. Nobody laughed.

'Investigation Rembrandtpark?' countered Mick. The park some of the targets hung out in. No reaction. 'Kolenkit?' The neighbourhood where three of the cell lived, the 'Coalscuttle', dubbed that after the nickname of a modernist church in the area. It had been named in a survey as 'the worst neighbour-hood in the Netherlands'.

'It's snappy. Sounds good to me,' said Lisette. 'You others?'

'Cool!' said Ben.

Rachid shrugged a 'Whatever'. It was where he'd lived till he was twelve.

'Investigation Kolenkit it is,' said Lisette. She flashed them a rare smile, and walked back behind her desk. 'Let's get going.'

FRIDAY
13 MAY 2011

3

The fawn chinos would work. Those and the brown brogues he'd bought on a trip to London, handmade but edging into old age. Nothing too good. You never knew what to expect on a house-visit, even with all the protective gear. Posthumus didn't own a pair of jeans, nor any trainers other than for sport. He selected a shirt, dressed quickly, knocked back the remains of his wake-up espresso, and spiralled down the metal staircase from his attic bedroom. He crossed to the front window to look out over the canal. It was a beautiful day. One of those gentle Amsterdam mornings, suffused with light. The gables along the Krom Boomssloot each carried the faint wisp of a halo, the sun tinging the curls of stucco pink. He'd grab some breakfast on the way.

Posthumus slipped a jacket off its hanger on the rack just inside his apartment door – a soft, chocolate-brown Zegna he'd picked up for a song at the flea-market. Even in his days as a squatter, back in the eighties, living in one of the big Amsterdam houses commandeered by artists, rebels and motley scruffs, he'd been a natty dresser – teased a bit as 'Prissy Pieter'. These days he bought new, rather than constructing classy outfits from second-hand finds, but he hadn't lost his eye for a bargain.

It took him barely thirty seconds to shoot down the three flights of stairs to the street door, and out on to the canalside of the Rechtboomssloot. A barge laden with bricks slipped silently under the bridge, a golden Labrador in the prow sniffing the morning air. Posthumus relished the fact that nearly half of Amsterdammers walked or cycled to work. He crossed the bridge, and set off briskly down the Krom Boomssloot, which made a T-junction with his own canal. It was odd how quiet this little patch of the city was, even when the Nieuwmarkt – just minutes away – heaved on a Saturday night. At the last bridge he ducked left, turned right again at the crooked old sluice-house, now a café, past the mansion in which a very rich Rembrandt had lived and painted some of his greatest works, and down the steps to where stallholders were setting up on Waterlooplein.

'Morning, *schat*! Gorgeous, isn't it?' Lotti, who from her little trolley provided coffee and breakfast *broodjes* for the flea-market crew. Blousy, bawdy, bleached-blonde and big, Lotti treated him as one of her boys. 'Buried any good-lookers lately?' She winked archly at Dirk, who was hanging out grungy tweed jackets on a rack across the way.

'Ah, we don't get to see the corpses,' said Posthumus, feigning regret.

'Just look at him! Always so smart, and such a nice smile, too. I don't know. I'm losing patience with him. When are you going to pop the question, duckie? I won't wait for ever. I'll be snapped up before you know it, and you'll lose out, I'm warning you!'

'I'm still building up the courage, Lotti.'

'Playing the field more like, you wicked man. You need to settle down. Nice tall guy like you. You're not too bad-looking, you know. Bit skinny, but I'll make do.'

'I promise you, Lotti, when I'm ready, you'll be the first to know.'

'It shouldn't be allowed. You're going to waste, you know. Look! Going grey already!'

Posthumus touched the side of his face. His sandy hair was indeed beginning to fleck around the temples.

'Got something that will stop the rot?' he said. 'I'm starving. Haven't had breakfast yet.'

'Lovely strawberry *broodjes*, just for you, *schat*.'

Soft white rolls, with a fat, red gash of fruit. Early season, but deliciously soggy and sweet, juices seeping into the bread. The coffee tasted like plastic, but it was all part of the ritual. He lidded it after a sip, wiped his mouth with a scrap of paper napkin, nodded a 'goodbye' to Lotti, who was by now gossiping with Dirk, and – so as not to hurt her feelings – carried off the coffee between forefinger and thumb. On past the ugly City Hall building (thank God he didn't have to work in there), and across the bridge to Staalkade, where his department led its detached existence in a modest, spout-gabled canal-house.

Onno Veldhuizen turned off the car engine. He shot quick glances to the mirrors, barely moving his head. The back road into Zoetermeer from Boskoop was quiet. No one in the lay-by. He slipped a phone from the inside pocket of his jacket. A new pre-paid he had picked up at a supermarket the night before. A couple of farm workers with a tractor a few fields away. One cyclist, a woman in a tracksuit, passing slowly on the cycle path. He checked his watch. He could be at InSec in twenty minutes, and still be early. He wanted to time this right. Damascus was an hour ahead, and Friday was the first day of their weekend. So Haddad would be home, not at work. He'd be up and about, finished breakfast, too early for visitors, wife probably in the kitchen. Veldhuizen punched in a number. It wasn't one in the phone's memory. It wasn't written anywhere. But he knew the sequence.

No pick-up of course. No greeting on voicemail. Just a beep. Veldhuizen spoke in English. 'That young man you mentioned in Amsterdam. It's all sorted, but now you can help me out. Phone me on this number. Now.' He kept hold of the phone, and again darted out glances. Mirrors. Fields. Boskoop road. The woman on the bike had stopped, and was sending a text. The phone rang within seconds.

'Yes?' Veldhuizen listened a moment, and his voice softened. 'Hello, you old bastard.' After all, they went back a long way, he and Haddad. Back to the first Gulf War. His first overseas mission for the Service, just after he'd left the police. They'd clicked. Had a lot in common. And, over the years, as they rose through their respective organisations, had on and off helped each other out. He had just done his bit for Haddad. Big time. Now it was Haddad's turn. 'You've heard from him, right?' said Veldhuizen. 'He's OK. The papers are impeccable, I made sure of that,' he went on. 'And the name is the same as on the passport you gave him. From that angle he has nothing to worry about, it all looks above board. Unless, of course, he misbehaves . . . I know, I know. But he's been here before, right? A couple of months for you on that Mostafa case.' Veldhuizen laughed. Sharp. Dry. 'Of course we knew. But now there's something you can do for me. Or rather that he can do for me. But I want *you* to tell him. This has to have his father's weight behind it. And all that means. Then I want to meet him, later today preferably. Before lunch. No, no, I haven't, not yet . . . I probably wouldn't even recognise the bugger. What's he now – twenty-eight, twenty-nine? Last time I saw him he was eight. Our paths didn't cross when he was here before. But you have a number? OK, text it to me after this. And tell him to pick up when I phone. It's like this . . .'

Veldhuizen was indeed back at his desk a full ten minutes earlier than he usually got in.

The Staalkade was the Amsterdam equivalent of a cul-de-sac, a forgotten sliver of quay at a point where two canals almost met, but didn't quite touch, as they joined the Amstel. A block away, people streamed through the alley that linked the two canal bridges, but no one diverted on to this blunt little U-shape unless they had business in one of the six or so buildings on Staalkade, which formed its furthest reach.

Posthumus walked down to the dark, spout-gabled building halfway along, and let himself in. Most of the staff had a key to the outside door. Alex, on the phone, waved and winked as he passed Reception on his way upstairs. No sign of Sulung or Maya yet. He dumped Lotti's plastic coffee, and went to zap out a Nespresso while his computer booted up. He had brought in the espresso machine himself, after his first taste of the foul departmental brew. Two mails in the inbox, both from Alex. The first, a CC to all of them:

Good morning all!

Trust you're back and feeling better, Sulung.

New cases:

We've had quick replies to the faxes. Not great news.

Mrs Visser's family all deceased, no traces for Mr Hageman (there might be a brother, but no record in Amsterdam), and Bart Hooft hadn't even registered at that address. No wills recorded, even Mrs Visser. So, looks like it's house-visits for the last two, a quick pick-up for Mrs V.

Maya, can you take Mrs Visser at the Zonhof (room's been cleared; everything with a Mrs van Dyck, day manager, who can fill you in).

Sulung, can you do Mr Hageman on Madurastraat (Pieter as #2 for house-visit).

Pieter, can you take Bart Hooft (ID yet to be confirmed), attic room on Delistraat (Sulung as #2).

(Both these poss in a day? You can pick up key for Hageman from Eva at social services. I collected the Hooft key from the police yesterday. Also pics of his very odd tattoos, tho I guess that's not much help. Car booked for you all day, anyway.)

Details of all three in New Cases file, yesterday's date, hard-copy files for each on the Pending shelf.

Alex

Typical Alex, thought Posthumus, already locating which police station had the key for the Hooft apartment. She knew it irritated him that they had to phone the general public enquiries number to talk to the police, perform the usual keypad dance of number-options to get through to a live person on a central switchboard, then endure the same muzak (always), for ages sometimes, as someone tracked down just which station (not always the most logically located one) held the key. It didn't usually take long. Ten minutes or so. But they were ten minutes that riled Posthumus, and Alex had sorted it. She'd even collected the key. (Did she know that Posthumus felt uneasy around the police – a hangover from his squatter days, when he'd had the odd clash with the law? He'd been arrested a couple of times: on the frontline at demonstrations, in clashes at the squat, once simply for unruly behaviour. Never charged . . . but still.)

The second email was addressed only to him:

Sorrrry about making you #2 for the messy one! It's around the corner from the attic, so just had to. Makes sense that you and S do both together.

Ax

Lisette was already in her office when Veldhuizen got in. She noticed the chief's Lexus duck down the ramp into the car park. At five to nine she was outside his door. Two knocks.

'Enter!'

There wasn't much to report. Audio was ready for Mansouri and Ahmed Bassir if they used their old phones. There was an observation team in place to set up a tracer immediately if either bought a new SIM card, and to keep tabs on what happened later at Friday prayers. Surveillance was intensified on some of the group's outer circle, like Tarik Alami, who hadn't been arrested.

'Alami's already in the know,' she said. 'He and a new little sidekick, Najib Tahiri, left Amsterdam early this morning, no doubt for Vught.' The high-security prison in the south of the country, where Mansouri, Bassir and Kaddaoui had been held on remand, and where probably, even as Lisette was speaking, they were again seeing the light of day.

'Tahiri knows Bassir from the neighbourhood, it seems, and he started hanging out with the big boys just before the arrest. Aged nineteen, younger than the rest. He was probably brought in by Bassir, looks up to him. Seems harmless, but has an older relative, a cousin of some sort, who came a few weeks ago from Morocco, one Amir Loukili: traditional dress, beard, late twenties. We're keeping an eye on him.'

Veldhuizen made no comment.

Lisette paused. For God's sake, she'd only had one afternoon . . .

He stood up. 'Keep at it.'

He turned his back on her, a step to the window, hands on the sill. 'We are *not* going to fuck it up this time.'

Lisette could see that something was up.

Veldhuizen swung round. 'We need to infiltrate the group. A chis.'

A 'covert human intelligence source'. Typical of him to use the jargon.

'I am putting one in place. That is already sorted. He will report to me. You and I will liaise.'

Lisette felt a cold shaft through her upper gut, like the first time she'd been passed over in appointments for team leader, when logic, experience and personal record had all pointed in her favour. This decision to place and run an agent, setting his bounds, processing the information – all that should be her responsibility. Hers alone.

'That is very irregular, sir. It reads as a lack of trust in me.'

He stared straight at her. Then his shoulders dropped a little, his face relaxed.

'Lisette, you're doing a good job. Both you and the team. This is simply a question of strategy. It is not meant to undermine you; in fact the team should know nothing of it. *Will* know nothing about it, for operational reasons. This is strictly need-to-know. And the team does not need to know.'

Lisette's mouth set hard. She sensed the colour sink from her face, leaving two hot little tidemarks, just below the cheekbones. She pulled her legs further under her chair.

'So you're asking me to lie to my team *as well*. To keep them out of the loop. That makes my work doubly difficult, quite apart from the ethical issues.'

'Dangerous times, daring strategies. You know that.'

'Might I at least know *what* operational reasons?'

'I can't go into that. Not at the moment. This comes from high up. Let's just say we can't risk a leak to the targets. Any slips at all. Even if it's just another memory-stick left on the metro.'

'I'm fully aware there have been leaks in the past, but nothing has *ever* involved my team. Not come anywhere near any one of them. I have complete confidence—' Lisette didn't get the chance to finish.

'Look, I realise this doesn't sit easy with you, but I have to ask you to go with it a little,' said Veldhuizen. 'We are in this game for the same reason, no? And we have the same goal. To stop those little shits taking human lives. So, let's just see how this works out. Give it some time, OK?'

He waited, but it wasn't one of those hard Veldhuizen silences. The taut jaw, the stare.

'Hmm?' He raised both eyebrows.

Lisette nodded. 'Sir.'

Veldhuizen crossed to the door, and held it open for her. There was even almost a smile.

'Good luck.'

Lisette went to the fifth-floor Ladies. It would be quieter. Not many women up on this level. She brushed a speck from under her eye, neatened her hair, straightened up, smoothed her blouse, and stared back at the mirror. 'Give it some time', indeed. She was not going to wait for ever to tell the team. It was a betrayal of trust, keeping something like this from them. She didn't like it. But was he right? The chief and his blah about strategies. Just what *was* ethical any more, in these days of fudged edges and murky grey areas? What was justifiable? The 'necessary transgression' people always talked about? And what if something really *was* going on? If one of the team *was* betraying her, betraying them all? She had stood up for them against Veldhuizen, but despite what she had said about them being so ace in the pep talk she'd given them yesterday, they were a bit of a wonky bunch. Well, maybe not Mick so much. But Ben, she knew, pushed limits with what he got up to in the field, and Rachid really showed his frustration with the job. But surely not. And, anyway, there were other ways of dealing with it. If one of them was suspect, she had the right to know who. A *need* to know.

She wasn't happy with this. Not happy with it *at all*. Yet if she let on to the team about the agent, gave even the slightest hint, and there was a leak, then it would all be on *her* head. Very clever, Veldhuizen. She had allowed herself to be bullied. Manipulated. Or it certainly felt like that. The decision had already been made. OK. She would run with it for a bit, and then review. Meanwhile, it left her with a problem. Running this bunch was tricky enough already; what was she to say if one of them started focusing on the agent? Somehow discourage that? They'd sense something was up. They were trained for that sort of thing, damn it. If one of them found out, even suspected what Veldhuizen was up to – Mick for one was very sharp – the whole thing could just disintegrate. Everything. They'd lose focus. And then what? The bomb? Another lynching of InSec in the media? And her career? Whoa! Lisette closed her eyes and took a deep breath. 'Pull yourself together, girl!' Clarity. Direction. She'd scheduled a team meeting at ten fifteen. She had half an hour.

Back in her office, Lisette tapped in her password to unlock the computer. Incorrect password. She rested her hands on the desk, fingers extended, stared at her nails for one, two, three seconds, and tried once more. An email pinged up immediately. From Security. Ben again: 'Desk Offence'. Probably another Post-it left on his computer screen overnight. She sighed. It was the second time this month. He would be up for a verbal warning. And the last one had only been a drawing. A Smiley. A *Smiley*, for God's sake. The last thing Lisette needed now was a sulky Ben.

She sent an email to the team confirming the meeting time. Another to Ben: her office in ten minutes please. He could be infuriating, that one. But there was something solid under all that streetwise bluff and bluster, a firm sense of right and wrong. He was worth hanging on to. Lisette locked the computer again. She picked up a writing pad, jotted down some points for the meeting. That always helped. Ordered her thoughts, and sometimes led to new ideas. She needed to be tight, focused.

- *Which mosque will they go to for prayers this afternoon?* (Somewhere local with their fathers, reuniting with family after their ordeal, or El Tahweed, where their radical mates hung out – that would be telling.)
- *Ringleader Mansouri planning to get married* (one reason she'd decided to move on it, often a sign of an impending suicide bombing). *Or was. Still happening? Will need new apartment? Sort one?* (Took a bit of work, contacts in a housing association, a Big Brother fit-up, but worth it.)
- *New face: Najib Tahiri* (little Najib, 'as skinny as green asparagus' Ben called him, friend of Ahmed Bassir) *plus older sister Aissa – involved? She wears headscarf, while their mother doesn't.*

Lisette paused. Resources were limited. Not to mention time. She sighed, shrugged, and wrote on.

- *Their relative: Amir Loukili. Why come from Morocco? Intent? Why lodge other side of the neighbourhood, not with/ near Tahiris? Why gone to Belgium day after arrest?*

'Yo, boss!'
Ben, of course, did not knock.

By nine forty-five, Sulung had arrived in the Funeral Team office and he and Posthumus had picked up the apartment keys, checked the gear in the black zip-up holdall (the camera and, just in case, shoe-protectors, rubber gloves and face masks – they looked like the forensic squad on some house-visits), and were driving out east to Madurastraat.

33

'Jeez!' Sulung pushed open the apartment door with difficulty. A collapsed pile of junk-mail magazines, most still in their polythene delivery envelopes, blocked the hall. 'It must have reached the roof!' Four defunct-looking vacuum cleaners, brushes and pipes from a good many more, a stack of old buckets, probably picked off the street, four, no, six supermarket bags stuffed with rubber gloves – sorted: the yellow and the pink. 'Well, at least he *intended* to do some cleaning.' A glimpse through to a kitchen. Cola cans. Hundreds and hundreds of cola cans. Four food-encrusted pots – God knows how old – on the cooker. And on top of them, between them, spilling on to the floor, were folded pieces of used aluminium foil. Disgusting grime everywhere. A door into another room was impenetrable. Decades' worth of newspapers, a pyramid of plastic carrier bags, sagging columns of boxes spewing more paper. The floor inches thick with filthy, trodden scraps and loose pages.

And the stink.

That split-second tantalisation that you were going to smell something sweet . . . then the clutch: the deep, dark, primevally rotten stench that grabbed at the back of your throat, then thrust an arm down into your gut. Posthumus gagged, buried his nose in the crook of his arm and fumbled in the holdall for a mask.

'You'd think they'd have opened some windows,' said Sulung. He was more used to this. Been on the job longer, even though he was a good five years younger than Posthumus. 'Some can lie around for weeks, and hardly smell at all, others reek after a day, and it doesn't go away.' It was as if the odour coated your face, the skin below your nostrils, your tongue, and it stuck there all day – that Posthumus already knew. He'd be getting tangs of this through dinner.

'How can you let life *get* like this?' said Sulung. 'We see it a lot. I don't know.'

'Senility sometimes, or depression, sometimes a psychosis,' said Posthumus from behind the mask. 'It's called the Diogenes Syndrome.' He'd looked into it after the first case he'd come across. Posthumus was the new kid on the block in the Funeral Team, but his years at the Conduct and Integrity Unit had turned him into an assiduous investigator. 'It's a sort of destructive mix. Squalor, hoarding, self-neglect. And withdrawal, to the point of hostility. Social services said he hadn't allowed anyone through the door for years.'

'*You've* been doing your homework,' said Sulung, but without the acid edge Maya's voice would have had. He took a large camera out of the holdall, and started photographing – first the initial page of the Case Report, to identify where they were, then the apartment itself. Every room, flash blitzing. Standard procedure, for the record. The place as they found it. You never knew what family might crawl out of the woodwork further down the line, with all sorts of accusations about what their dear long-lost relative had surely had in the apartment. Posthumus waited to one side till he had finished.

'Start here?' said Sulung, indicating a cleared space on the floor, mattress-shaped. It must have been where Hageman died; the mattress had been taken away. 'And work in opposite directions around the room?'

He placed the slim Case Report folder, containing all the department had on Hageman so far, in the centre of the space left by the mattress.

'Not necessarily.' Posthumus hesitated. 'The thing is to try to put yourself inside his head.'

'No thank you!'

'No, seriously. Could save us time. Alex said there might be a brother, but not in Amsterdam. There's no phone, was no mobile with the body, apparently. That could mean something as old-fashioned as letters. But he would repel any attempt to make contact. Visits, letters, even from a brother.' Posthumus stopped. Especially, maybe, from a brother. Willem again. It never really went away.

'So where does that get us?' Sulung asked.

'Well, he clearly had a thing about paper, so maybe he kept letters. Withdrawal and hoarding.'

Sulung looked sceptical. 'So?'

'So maybe we don't have to tackle this whole garbage pile. Point is, where would he put them?'

'If they exist.'

'If they exist.'

Nothing in the letter-cage at the front door. Nothing with the junk mail, or that had been under the mattress. No boxes that looked in any way different from the rest.

'There does seem to be some sort of a system here,' said Sulung. 'I mean, cleaning stuff in the hall, pink gloves in one bag, yellow in another, metal in the kitchen, paper in this room. But it's not much help if they're in with all the paper – back to square one.'

'Unless,' said Posthumus, 'unless they're *not* paper.'

'What do you mean?'

'This thing grips you, right? The antagonisms, the hoarding, the sorting, the filth. But maybe you *want* to clean? You get a vacuum cleaner, buy rubber gloves. Maybe you *want* to make contact? Maybe that puts the letters not in "paper" but some other category?'

They found them in the kitchen, in the warming-drawer below the oven. All unopened. Not many. Once or twice a year for the past ten years or so. The oldest postmarked Thailand, the last few from Germany.

'Two months ago,' said Posthumus, turning over an envelope. 'Munich. W. J. Hageman. And an address.'

Sulung whooped. 'It *has* to be!' He tore open the envelope

and skimmed the letter. 'Hope you're well, blah blah blah, Maria sends her love . . . *please* drop us a line, blah blah . . . remember when Mama . . . Yes!' He held up the letter in triumph. 'That's it! Family member, must be the brother . . . and sounds like he's friendly enough to take on the funeral.'

Posthumus had been reaching deep into the foetid maw of the oven. He'd produced a darkened shoebox, half filled with banknotes, plus a few open envelopes – maybe savings accounts or insurance.

'And it looks like he can help pay his way, anyway. We'll have to photograph this and count it. A couple of thousand, I'd guess. We can take the docs back to the girls.' It was Alex's task to fill quiet moments on Reception going through finds like this, pulling out anything useful and doing the paperwork. Posthumus photographed the wad of notes in situ, then pushed it into the plastic folder that held the Case Report; the documents and envelopes he put into one of the neatly folded salvaged supermarket carrier bags he had brought along for the purpose.

'That's it, then,' said Sulung. 'If' – he glanced again at the letter – 'if Mr Willem Hageman assumes responsibility, it's all over to him. I reckon we can close up here till we hear back. You OK?'

'It's nothing,' said Posthumus. Then: 'Your case, your call.'

Sulung tossed the apartment keys in the air, and caught them.

'Delistraat?'

The attic room on Delistraat was an easier prospect. There was almost nothing there. A cheap conversion – illegal, Posthumus guessed: a fridge, hotplate and microwave made a kitchen; a single all-purpose sink, curtain around an ad hoc shower. The lavatory was on the landing, from the days when these were servants' rooms. Single bed, desk, no computer, one chair – replaced from where it had probably been when the body was found, kicked over in the middle of the floor, below the exposed central rafter. Posthumus had already spoken to the landlord on the phone. 'Worked as the cleaner at a bar, apparently,' he said, as he took the initial photos. 'Landlord says he worked from two in the morning till six, spent nearly all the rest of the time in here. Poor sod. Long depressions. Clean bedding was part of the deal, but sometimes it would just pile up outside the door. He'd put the old stuff out, then sleep on a bare mattress.'

Same old story, the copper on the phone had said. 'Sad, lonely git ups one day and draws a line under it all.' The police had seen it all before. No forced entry. No suspicious circumstances. Verdict: suicide. No definitive confirmation that his name was indeed Bart Hooft, but police resources were limited. So the buck was passed over to the Funeral Team with the old 'Unknown, probably an illegal' tag.

There had been a phone, pre-paid, but either the address book had always been empty, or he'd wiped it. The only number in the calls record was no longer operative. The landlord didn't know which bar he'd worked in, and had been only too happy to slip under the tax radar with a lodger who didn't want to register at his address. The police had drawn a blank, apart from the name he'd given the landlord. Even in this highly bureaucratised city there was a drift of people, just below the surface, who – for whatever reason of their own – slipped through the construct. They worked cash in hand, lived in sub-lets, spent every day hoping they wouldn't get sick, or have a brush with the law and have to produce an ID, who had no bills, left no mark. Bart Hooft, if that had indeed been his name, had just floated free of that world. This would be a funeral for Posthumus to arrange. He looked about the stark room.

A single poster, advertising a Mark Rothko exhibition in Notre Dame, Indiana. A rack of clothes, enough for about three or four changes, leather jacket, a large box underneath of T-shirts, underwear, socks. Over the desk, a bookshelf. Not much. Early Remco Campert. A book of bleak cartoons by someone called Leunig. Dictionary. Some sort of Indian religious work. Emerson essays. A well-worn copy of *Ecce Homo*. The collected poems of Apollinaire, in French. No fiction. No music.

'Well, he clearly wasn't stupid,' said Posthumus, replacing the Apollinaire. He checked the desk drawers. An envelope with about three hundred euros. Not nearly enough for the funeral. Some pencils, a sharpener, an old fountain pen – but apart from that, nothing personal at all. No knick-knacks, none of those odd little mementos we accumulate, life's flotsam. It was as if Bart Hooft had prepared for this ending. As if he had purposefully wiped the slate of his life clean. That or led a minimalist existence of resolute anonymity.

Posthumus glanced again at the clothes rack. White T-shirts, blue or black jeans. Everything else dun-coloured, black or deep green. Some camouflage stuff, flea-market military. What was there here to take hold of to give the poor guy some sort of a parting shot? On the desk an A4 writing pad. Blank. Beneath it one of those full-sized hard-covered notebooks Posthumus remembered from his school days. Quite a thick one, and much used. He opened it.

'Poetry!' he said. 'Bart Hooft wrote poetry.' Pages and pages of it, neatly copied out, clearly final drafts. 'Might be a lead in this somewhere,' he said. 'We can take this back.' He put it to one side, beside the Case Report.

He reopened the desk drawer. 'And that pen.' He held up the fountain pen. Sulung, who was going through pockets of clothing on the rack, looked across at him quizzically. 'I don't know why. Something about it just niggles me. I've not seen one quite like it before.' Posthumus weighed the pen in his hand. It had an odd, flat top, an old-fashioned lever on the stem to refill it, the black body flecked with gold, an exquisite Bird of Paradise design down one side. 'And it looks valuable,' he said. 'We ought to put it in the safe. Who knows, it might help pay for the funeral.'

But Sulung was busy digging about in the box of socks and underwear. 'Well, well, well,' he said. 'Maybe not quite as airy and intellectual as you thought.' There was a clink of metal as he pulled out a pair of handcuffs, some leather straps. Covering his own hand with a clean T-shirt, he held up a dildo, the shape and size of a human forearm, with a clenched fist. 'A lesson to take heed of: you never know who is going to be poking around in your things when you die.'

'Poor guy,' said Posthumus. 'Things like that don't really seem any of our business.' Then: 'Can I have that a moment?'

'Didn't know you were the type.'

'No, look.' Posthumus turned the arm over. On the underside, in black marker pen, someone had drawn an odd bird shape, set inside a circle within five-point star. 'He had that tattooed on his arm. You know, the photos the police gave Alex . . . all those tattoos.'

'I didn't really look.'

'I'm *sure* it is, though that tattoo had no inscription.' Under the design on the dildo was written: 'Something to remember me by . . .'.

Posthumus flipped open the Case Report file. Four photographs. He slid one out from among the rest.

'Here, look.'

Not the forearm, but the underside of the bicep, near the armpit. The same design, with the exception that on the lowest point of the star was a small red heart surrounding a keyhole.

'Well, I'm not taking *this* back with us,' said Sulung, dropping the dildo back into the underwear box. 'You can photograph it, if you like.' He handed Posthumus the camera.

'Not much point,' said Posthumus. 'We've got the police photos. And it's not really going to get us anywhere, anyway. Tattoo parlours won't keep records of the names of their customers. Let's just leave that where it was.'

Nothing else in the apartment gave any clue as to who Bart Hooft might have been. The men were finished before noon. They went downstairs again.

'We've earned a little extra lunch break,' said Sulung. 'That was an excellent morning's work. And I know just the place.'

An Indonesian snack bar, just a few blocks away. The owner, a stooped woman with grey hair, greeted Sulung like an old friend.

'The only person in town who cooks better than my mother did,' he said, as they waited for their order to come. 'Nice to be in the area, for once. I come all the way across town for this place.'

'Seems an appropriate spot to eat, anyway,' said Posthumus. The surrounding streets were all named after Indonesian islands.

'Ah, the Colonial Quarter,' said Sulung, giving a twist to the usual nickname of Indonesian Quarter.

Posthumus raised an eyebrow. 'That's a bit chippie,' he said.

Sulung shrugged. 'I don't know. I grew up watching my parents having a really hard time here, adapting to a new country, trying to fit in. And we kids caught some flak, too. Small village in the south, the only non-Dutch family.'

A large plate of satay arrived, glistening, the peanut sauce clearly homemade.

'But now, surely . . . it's not like that any more, is it?' said Posthumus.

'Not for us in the bigger cities maybe. I guess now it's the Moroccans who take the shit.'

Sulung took a bite of chicken. 'But my parents at least tried,' he said. 'It's *that* sort of thing that really pisses me off.'

He gestured with his satay stick, his mouth still full. Two women in full veils passed on the pavement outside.

'Makes it harder for everyone,' he said.

It was Posthumus's turn to shrug.

Back at the office, Posthumus handed over the Madurastraat finds to the girl at Reception, as well as Hageman's money and the pen from Bart Hooft's apartment, to be signed for and kept in the safe. No Alex. She studied part-time and had classes on Friday afternoons, so it was a temp behind the desk. Posthumus spent the afternoon trawling the internet to look at fountain pens, avoiding Maya's hostile glances, and reading Bart Hooft's poems.

'Some of these are pretty good,' he said to Sulung. 'Very dark, though. And a bit rough, a good few of them.'

Sulung raised his fist and forearm suggestively. Posthumus frowned, and looked away. He paged past a group of poems entitled '(K)Nights in the Black Tulip'.

'Yet there're others that are really quite touching,' he went on. 'Simple. It's as if there was a whole other side to him. Listen.'

He read:

The Good Friend
I
was always
the single
one
in the room next door
as the one I loved
made love
to the one he loved the more.

Maya snapped a file shut noisily.

'Poignant, don't you think? Given what happened,' said Posthumus.

'Not really my sort of thing,' said Sulung.

'There's nothing I could really use at the funeral,' Posthumus went on, 'but it makes the whole thing sadder. Just *so* sad.'

'We should be like doctors,' said Maya. 'On the Funeral Team, we do not get emotionally involved.'

Ten minutes till noon. Veldhuizen looked about the Mozaïek café. It was perfect for his purposes: in a multicultural arts centre, where a gentrifying patch of Amsterdam West bordered the immigrant neighbourhoods of Bos en Lommer and the Kolenkit Quarter. Too upmarket for any targets or their buddies to hang out, but with enough of a mixed clientele for a middle-aged Dutchman and a twenty-something Syrian not to stand out. A director talking to an actor, perhaps; the Money meeting a musician. Artsy business meetings, such motley socials, went unremarked at the Mozaïek. And it was large, the tables widely spaced. Background music played. And at this time of day just a smattering of customers, all along the window. Perfect. Veldhuizen picked a table at the far end of the room, with a view of the door, and ordered a steak sandwich. That would do for lunch.

The boy walked in just before noon. He crossed directly to Veldhuizen, shook his hand, raised his palm to his heart, and waited to be invited to sit down. You could see his father in him, Veldhuizen thought: in the eyes. But wiry, less thick-set, wearing Western dress. And with a beard that just crossed the divide between fashionable and religious statement. He'd been growing it these past weeks, perhaps. Or he kept it at that chameleon length so that he could pass in two worlds. He was a professional, after all. Of good pedigree. He had quite a bit to live up to.

'So someone is after your blood in Damascus?' said Veldhuizen. He spoke in English.

Fayyad Haddad nodded.

'I don't need to know about that. Nor what you might be doing here for your father.'

'I'm not doing anything here for my father.'

'Then why Amsterdam?'

'Amsterdam has its attractions.'

Veldhuizen thought he detected a smirk, but young Haddad's face gave nothing away.

'Besides,' the young man went on, 'I have some loose ends of my own to tie up.'

'This is not about what you're doing for yourself, this is about what you can do for me,' said Veldhuizen.

Haddad's face remained impassive.

'Same sort of thing you were doing back home,' Veldhuizen went on.

'The targets?'

'Islamist cell. Moroccans mainly.'

'Moroccan Arabic is incomprehensible.'

'They're mostly Berber anyway. And born here, so their standard Arabic isn't up to much. How's your Dutch?'

'Not very good. I learned a bit last time I was here, but this move was somewhat . . . unexpected.'

Veldhuizen smiled. 'You can probably get by in English. And teach them some proper Arabic. They're all scrabbling to learn. Might be a way in. But it means you'll need a good backstory. Impress them with your experience, your daring, a bit of adventure. That and your fervent faith of course.'

There were few people who could outstare Veldhuizen. The

boy's father was one of them, and it seemed the skill ran in the genes.

'But nothing too fancy,' said Veldhuizen. 'Given the language thing, you'll have to stay Syrian. But for fuck's sake change your name. Better still, use the one on your new passport. Base your story on something that really happened, so you're already familiar with the details, don't have to invent too much. Just beef it up a bit, reverse the angle.'

'I know all this.'

'Well, you had better also be quick. I want you to start now, at once. Friday prayers. My guess is they will go to the El Tahweed mosque. Know it? OK. Three of them just got released from custody this morning, will have been back in town an hour or so already. They'll be full of it, easy to spot, but my suggestion would be to approach through someone on the periphery. Work your way in.'

Young Haddad's eyes glazed slightly. Veldhuizen pushed a scrap of paper across the table.

'That is the ID of a Hotmail account. The password is your father's first name written backward. Details of the targets are in a document saved in Draft. I guess I don't have to tell you to destroy the paper once you have memorised the log-in.'

Veldhuizen glanced at him. Haddad had already read the ID, and prodded the scrap back across the table.

'One last thing. This is not . . .' Veldhuizen hesitated. 'This is not a *corporate* move. My organisation has nothing to do with it. This is the repayment of a personal favour. You are responsible only and entirely to me. Any instructions will be in that Draft box, and *I* will contact *you*. You must realise, if anything goes wrong, you are on your own. Completely. I have never heard of Fayyad Haddad, and especially not of Khaled whoever-you-might-be-now.'

'Suleiman.'

'Fine. Suleiman. Any questions?'

'Payment?'

The boy had balls, Veldhuizen gave him that. 'We can talk about that later. Let's say you've already had an advance,' he said, and tapped the side of his jacket where a wallet might be. 'Those nice new documents you've got. They could suddenly not be worth the paper they're written on. And we all know what that means. Understood?'

'Understood.'

'And of course, you would not want to anger your father. I imagine he can be even more unpleasant to deal with than your . . . friends . . . in Damascus.'

'My father will be proud of me. I will make sure of that. I can prove my worth.'

'Well, get to it. You've not got long.'

Veldhuizen watched the young man leave, turning right out of the door, away from the Kolenkit Quarter, towards the El Tahweed mosque, closer to the centre of town. He was looking down at his phone, probably already sussing out the targets on the Hotmail draft. Veldhuizen ordered a coffee, and waited a good ten minutes until after Haddad had gone before leaving himself.

The Mevlana mosque, tucked in a recess behind a sprawling concrete sports centre, brought a touch of conviviality to the drab paved square in the Kolenkit Quarter. Already, in this abnormally warm May, the vines that grew over the pergola covering its portico sprouted delicate pale green leaves. In one corner of the sheltered courtyard, wooden boxes displayed tomatoes, lemons, aubergines, vigorous-looking lettuces, aromatic bunches of mint, coriander, parsley. On the other side, two folding chairs, an upturned crate. Three men sat talking quietly, all in middle age, one in a djellaba and skullcap, the other two in shapeless anoraks, differing shades of beige. Further into the recess, the double doors of the mosque were opened wide, welcoming, though it was early yet, and just ten or so pairs of shoes rested in the entrance-hall rack.

Mohammed Tahiri locked his shop door, and set off for the mosque. Mevlana was a Turkish mosque, but it was just five minutes from the shop and close to home, so when he was busy he went there for Friday prayers all the same. Besides, he had friends there. And he liked the way Turkish mosques kept their doors open, said to the street there was nothing to hide. He wished that more Moroccan congregations would do the same. Perhaps then the Dutch would not feel so threatened by it all.

Mohammed paused while four women, all in hijabs and wearing bright yellow reflective vests, wobbled past on bicycles, their male Dutch instructor calling advice. 'Check over your shoulder. Before turning. *Before* the turn! *Left* shoulder! Another cyclist!'

Mohammed smiled. Well, at least they were trying. Some municipal integration scheme probably. And better than charging about on scooters, like the kids these days. He checked his watch: twelve forty, the first call for *Jumu'ah* would be starting soon. But there'd be time for a chat before prayers. He straightened his tie, and ran his fingers over a short salt and pepper beard. He was wearing a light tweed jacket, grey trousers. Good quality. Mohammed Tahiri had come a long way in thirty years. From timid young man who had come to join his uncle – a guest-worker who stayed – to owner of a successful furniture shop. It was now on the internet, selling Moroccan-style sofas to trendy Dutch people. But he didn't understand anything about that side of things. That had all been done by his son, Najib. Bright lad. For nearly twenty years friends had been able to call Mohammed 'Abu Najib', father of Najib. And they had been good years. It was just in the past few months that the boy had come to cause him concern. He'd become secretive, sulky, hiding away with that computer of his. Perhaps it was time to swing the bridge in the other direction. Perhaps he should send the boy back to Morocco.

Mohammed turned from the Kolenkit Quarter high street to walk down towards the mosque. His life here had not been easy along the way. Factory work, a job on the market, his own stall, and at last the shop. Many setbacks. So much that seemed unfathomable, especially in the beginning, before his Dutch got good. *That* was fine now – even to the point of unravelling the ridiculously complicated city bureaucracy. But it had been even harder for Karima, as a young bride arriving from Morocco in the 1980s. He had insisted that she learn Dutch; many didn't, even now. These days Karima gave lessons to women who had been here longer than her, and couldn't speak a word! Illiterate, some of them, so how were they supposed to learn? All veiled, some even in niqabs, not allowed out of the house except for groceries and lessons, so that was their only social life. Not interested in learning at all. They gave Karima a headache! He had told her when she came over that she should give up the hijab. Did his uncle not go mad at that! But Karima was grateful for it now, he thought. Except that since leaving school, their daughter Aissa had covered her head, criticising her mother, her own mother, for being ashamed of her traditions, of her culture. What that was all about, he could not work out. Aissa was certainly not a traditional young woman. She went out at night, had some Dutch friends. She was even brighter than her younger brother. Good grades at the university. Her graduation had been one of the proudest moments of his life. And now, even more studies. Soon, he hoped, a good marriage, grandchildren.

He reached Ernest Staesplein, and crossed the square to the mosque. Mohammed wondered whether the boy Amir might make a good husband for Aissa. She was twenty-five now. Amir came from a very good branch of the family, the son of a distant cousin, and was just a few years older. She genuinely seemed to like him. When the lad had arrived from Morocco, a few weeks earlier, Mohammed had not been so sure. Amir made Mohammed feel uneasy. He seemed a nervous, troubled young man. And Mohammed didn't like the way he disappeared, for days on end sometimes, without telling anyone. To do business in Brussels for his family, he said. Yet he was quiet and serious, and respectful. Very devout, more than Mohammed had expected. Not in an angry way – that taboo word for Mohammed's generation, 'radical' – like some of the young Muslims around the neighbourhood, but in the more old-fashioned way of men Mohammed had known as a child. 'So,' he had said to Karima, 'perhaps we should just watch and wait and see.'

The mosque. Mohammed's friend Yunnis was sitting outside with some others. Yes, wait and see, Mohammed thought. Besides, he reasoned, for his cousin's sake he ought to keep an eye on Amir. He had assumed Amir would live with them. Family obligation. But the boy already had something set up, it seemed, through his mother's family. An apartment that was empty for a few months. Mohammed thought it odd that he would want to live alone, but at least it was not far from the Kolenkit Quarter, and the lad could come often for meals. And their own place was small, in a little line of 1930s terraced houses, an oddity among the 1950s apartment blocks.

'*As-Salāmu `Alaykumu,*' he greeted the men in the portico. The *adhan*, the first call, was beginning.

'*Alaykum as-salām*, Abu Najib.'

The men rose. The youngest of the three moved the chairs and crate to one side, but the men remained in the portico. For some minutes they exchanged the usual greetings and pleasantries with Mohammed, then: 'Where's your boy, Abu Najib?'

Mohammed could not bring himself to say 'I don't know'.

'He went to the countryside with friends this morning. Should be back soon,' he said. With friends? With some fellow Mohammed had not seen before. Part of Najib's secret internet world. He did not like it. He did not understand it. Karima said these new lads Najib was mixing with had to do with the neighbourhood, that they should move to De Aker, where the apartments were bigger, the people 'more respectable', she said. She'd been going on about it again lately, like a few years back, when the Kolenkit Quarter had been called 'the worst neighbourhood in the Netherlands' in the papers and on TV. (Mohammed had long held out against getting a satellite for the Arabic channels, and had made the family watch Dutch TV – until he realised that not having a satellite was causing Najib to be teased at school.) They had the money to move, of course, but the Kolenkit Quarter was home. They knew the neighbours, had a good butcher, were friendly with the storekeepers, his own shop was just a few minutes' walk from home. And it wasn't the fault of the Kolenkit Quarter. Things were much better, now, anyway; there were all sorts of schemes, the kids themselves helping to clean things up. It wasn't the neighbourhood, it was this internet. He was losing Najib, he could feel it. And he did not know quite what to do.

Najib had always come with his father to *Jumu'ah*. Even these past weeks, when he had been sullen and resentful. And he *was* back in town. Mohammed had seen the car drive past the shop an hour or so earlier, crammed with young men.

He looked up. He had been lost in his thoughts. More men were arriving at the Mevlana mosque. Some wives, too. The little group who had been standing in the portico were going inside. The second call was finishing. He would have to join them.

He knew that, today, Najib would not come.

4

Posthumus took a different route home after work. Like many Amsterdammers, he had one way of going to a place, and a completely different one coming back. This curious cobweb of a city had the trick of changing its shape, depending on your viewpoint – like a kaleidoscope pattern transformed by a tiny tap. The logic behind each path you took seemed impeccable at the time, but it drew you in different directions. He turned right out of the department, walking up to the other end of the Staalkade, right again along the canal, across a little white wooden swing-bridge, and on to the Nieuwmarkt. The Zuiderkerk carillon rang out old folk tunes. A block away from the Nieuwmarkt, as if someone had flicked a switch, subdued canalside elegance gave way to neon lights, smells of fast food, tangs of dope, the jangle and surge of the red-light district. In the midst of it all, as if it had flown in from a fairy tale and plonked itself down unexpectedly in the middle of Nieuwmarkt square, sits De Waag, the medieval city weighhouse with its pixie-capped towers and Rapunzel windows.

Posthumus needed a drink. And he felt like a chat with Anna. His day had rattled him. That first apartment. But more than that, Bart Hooft's poems. Here was someone, his own age, whose life – to all the world, even to himself, perhaps – meant nothing. And yet he could write this really moving stuff. Poems that probably no one else had read. Or would read.

Instead of bearing right towards home on the Rechtboomssloot, Posthumus walked around the left side of De Waag, under the windows of the room where corpses of criminals fresh from the gallows were once cut up for anatomy lessons (another Rembrandt hang-out), to the Zeedijk. When he first came to the neighbourhood – nearly twenty years ago now – the Zeedijk had been the dodgiest street in the sleaziest part of the city, a furtive crawl of junkies and street-dealers at the point where the red-light district met Chinatown. Now it was a popular strip of bars and restaurants, one of the first assault-points of a city council intent on cleaning up the quarter. Up the Zeedijk. Past the big Chinese temple, a wave to the owner of Wing Kee Eating House (still his favourite after all these years). Left, dodging throngs of gawping tourists. He avoided narrower alleys where middle-aged men endlessly filed past the girls in windows. Another bridge. One of the few patches of Amsterdam that was like Venice, buildings coming right to the water, with no street in between. And on to De Dolle Hond. Just a step beyond the red-light district, dispensing beer and good cheer as it had done for maybe four hundred years.

Anna de Vries was already pouring Posthumus his drink as he walked through the door. A superb, citrusy New Zealand Sauvignon Blanc, which she bought in especially for him. Posthumus was not a beer man.

'What's up?'

She had noticed immediately. Posthumus and Anna went back a long way. Back to the days when he'd first arrived in Amsterdam, a village boy from Krommenie, with big dreams and a waft of the provinces. Anna was an Amsterdammer through and through. Her parents had owned this place, her grandparents before that. Maybe even a generation further back, he forgot. De Dolle Hond had been around long before the De Vrieses were on the scene, anyway. Anna had shown him the city. And a lot else besides. They'd been together a while, but that was long ago. Now they were, what? Best friends sounded so playground. Family, really. Neither of them had anyone else; relationships nor relations. Parents dead. She'd been an only child. And he . . . well – no one else.

'Later,' he said. 'I need a drink, first. Need to shed the day.'

De Dolle Hond was empty. Save for Mrs Ting. Day in, day out, Mrs Ting sat working the fruit machine till her fingers were black. For years, she'd been there. She never spoke, shunned all friendly advances. Maybe she didn't know Dutch. Or English – they'd tried. They'd dubbed her Mrs Ting because of the pinging sound the fruit machine gave to announce her occasional winnings. The machine had been an innovation of Anna's father. Anna had opposed it at first; she thought it looked incongruous in the ancient wood-panelled bar, but somehow it had stayed, even after her parents died. And it brought in a trickle of income. Especially with Mrs Ting on the go.

Posthumus took a stool at the bar. His usual one, where the counter met the wall beneath a collection of old medals, pins and badges (way back from who knew when): military stuff, vintage Beatles fan club, one that read Free Kuwait, another ONLY CONNECT, most of them inscrutable. He had peered at them often enough, on busy nights when Anna couldn't talk much. He straightened the little row of cardboard coasters on the bar. Anna closed the newspaper she'd been reading.

'The Amsterdam Cell's been released,' she said. 'But no smoke without fire, if you ask me.'

'Oh, I don't know. Sometimes I think we're getting too jumpy.'

Posthumus glanced at the headline, then raised an eyebrow at the newspaper, a right-wing rag.

'Customer left it behind earlier,' said Anna. '*De Nieuwe Post* didn't arrive today.' Their usual daily. 'That's the third time this week. I've just given their Deliveries a blast. No phone any more, of course. You have to do it via the website, so who knows if anyone really bothers.'

'But it's that sort of thing that worries me,' said Posthumus, tapping a photo of a young man with a beard, wearing a traditional djellaba. 'It feels so excluding. And then the threats to gays, and the way they treat women. No wonder people react badly.'

Mrs Ting had a winning moment. They paused. No reaction. Anna smiled. Anna somehow collected people like Mrs Ting. De Dolle Hond was one of those cosy Amsterdam bars small enough to be run almost single-handedly (Anna managed with a cleaner, and help from a young casual, Simon). A *bruin café*, called 'brown' not just for the wooden floors, furniture and panelling but because aeons of tobacco smoke had stained walls and ceiling. Many bars achieved the effect with varnish or paint, but in De Dolle Hond it was authentic. Move one of the old prints on the strip of wall above the high wainscot, and apparently brown wallpaper revealed itself as startlingly white. Or at least beige.

Perhaps it was because De Dolle Hond was run by a woman that people found refuge here who might not feel at ease alone in other bars in the neighbourhood. But mostly it was Anna's ability to listen. Not that she was a pushover. Anna de Vries dispensed a rough sympathy. If she didn't agree with you she let you know it. Part of that was traditional Amsterdam contrariness. She had a strong streak of 'nobody tells me what to do' Amsterdam defiance running deep through her. But she was astute, read people well, and could guide self-perception with tact. With her teasing eyes, unruly auburn hair and tough warmth, she attracted an odd bag of regulars: raw old

Amsterdammers from the neighbourhood, who had known her since childhood; a few cops, for whom this had been a favoured haunt back in the days when there was still a police station round the corner on the Warmoesstraat; the odd shady character, an underworld small-timer whom the cops would glint-eye across the room; one or two working girls, off duty – Anna was strict about that. But also smart young singles, on their way home from work to the now gentrified patch where Posthumus lived, ten minutes' walk way. They spoke to their friends of De Dolle Hond as 'a real find'. And of course tourists, who were drawn in by the historic look of the place: the walk-in tiled fireplace, the big pieces of Delftware above it (Posthumus was often on at Anna to have them valued), the bric-a-brac of centuries. They would come in for a drink, and stay on till closing, seduced by the conviviality of it all.

'Paul not in yet?' asked Posthumus.

That was one of Anna's innovations, after she took over from her father. Live music at weekends. Paul de Vos played the piano and headed The Fox Trio, but he always came in a couple of hours before the gig, while it was still quiet, for a few beers and a chat.

'He's gone for something to eat . . . So, what's eating *you*?' said Anna. She ignored his pained scowl.

'Oh, it's nothing really. Just a crap day.'

Anna waited.

'Two house-visits, but it was the second one mainly. Guy my age. Hanged himself. Cleaned in a bar, led a nothing life, no friends. Depressed, a loner. Had just six or so books. Nietzsche, Remco Campert – hardly a cheery bunch.'

Mrs Ting had another win.

'But you're going to have to get used to that,' said Anna.

'Yes, but this was a bit different. He wrote poetry. Mostly in Dutch, but some in English, in an old school notebook, by hand – with a beautiful old fountain pen. I've been having a look. I reckon it could be Japanese, lacquer, maybe 1930s; it must have been some sort of memento, inherited, from his grandfather or something.'

'And the poems?'

'Well, that's the point, they're really good. It all seems such a waste.'

'Could you get them published?'

'I don't know. Maybe he wouldn't want that. Seems a bit invasive. And they're certainly not everyone's cup of tea.'

'You talk as if he's still alive. You sure you're not getting too deep into this thing?'

'You're beginning to sound like Maya, at the office. I've got to do something to make this job—'

'A little less dead-end?'

'An*na*!' But he smiled. They'd been over this territory before. His feeling of being sidelined. The problems at the Conduct and Integrity Unit, his determination not to give in, and not only just to stick it out in this new job, but to make something of it. Something meaningful.

'You *are* doing something,' said Anna. 'With these person-alised funerals you're so keen on getting the others to go along with. The music, the readings. Do something like that for him. Read one or two of the poems.'

'I thought of that, but they're not really suitable. Macabre, a bit graphic.'

'And I guess it doesn't matter that nobody's going to be listening?'

'You never know. There were two hundred people at Sulung's last funeral! He'd just done the basics. What we usually do when we can't trace friends or relatives: the bunch of flowers from the city council; arranged for twenty coffees in the anteroom afterwards, in case anyone showed up. And it turned out the guy was an Ajax supporter and generous in the bar after games. Half the local fan club turned out.'

Customers: a couple of tourists about to take a photo when Anna served them. She returned.

'You could always read some other poetry at the funeral. Something from his bookshelf?'

'I thought of that. I'm going to have a look over the weekend. But it'd be nice to have something, I don't know, more personal. Tailor-made. I'd write it myself, but I just feel he deserves something . . . proper. I'm OK for the odd oration, but that's tough enough. I couldn't really run to poetry.'

'You can say that again. Not if your Sinterklaas verses are anything to judge by. How about asking someone, though? Know any writers? What about Alex at work, isn't she studying literature?'

'Philosophy. Anybody come in here, perhaps?'

'No one springs to mind.' Anna thought for a moment. She polished a few glasses. Always a good sign. 'There's Gabrielle's husband,' she said. Gabrielle Lanting, another of their old gang, had transformed her past radical activism into a position as the director of the Green Alliance. She and Anna were still in touch. Her husband had something of a reputation as a poet, gave the odd reading.

'Do you think he might do it?' said Posthumus. 'Constantijn, isn't it?'

'Cornelius. It's worth a try. He could be up for that sort of thing. He sometimes does topical poems for the papers. Sort of public-mouthpiece stuff; he did one when that little girl was found abandoned at Central Station.'

'That's a recommendation in itself – he'd have to knock something out in a day or two. But there might be some money in it for him, if there's any sort of budget left with all the cutbacks. I think the department director approves of my funeral idea, even if Maya doesn't. He said something the other day about it being something that was "very Amsterdam". You know, a bit odd, but human scale. He said, "We love people here, even dead ones." I could ask him direct.'

'I could have a word with Gabrielle if you like. Do it that way. Sound Cornelius out first, before you do anything through the office.' Anna looked up. Two more customers, and behind them Paul, bearing a faint aroma of chips and mayonnaise. He came over to Posthumus.

'Howdy, partner!'

'Paul. A drink?'

'Thanks, PP.' Anna called him that. Curiously enough, Alex did too. But it riled him that Paul had picked it up. He would have preferred the usual 'Pieter'. Piet, at most. He did not order himself a refill, but chatted on until his glass was empty, waited a few polite moments, then got up to go.

'I'm off,' he said to Anna.

'See you later? Oh God, hang on a minute. Almost forgot.' She came back over. 'There was a message for you. On the café voicemail, must have been this morning some time.'

'For *me*? *Here*?'

'Well, you're not in the book, I guess. She asked if you still drank here. Limburg accent. She left a number, hang on a sec.' Anna rummaged among the bills, business cards and other bits and pieces beside the till, and fished out a scrap of paper.

Posthumus read it. 'I don't know anybody from Limburg. Merel Dekkers?' It was a mobile number.

'Confession. I googled her,' said Anna, playful but a touch embarrassed. 'It's been a slow afternoon. She's *very* pretty. Thirty-one. Lives in Amsterdam, a journalist with *De Nieuwe Post*.'

'Merel *Dekkers*?' Posthumus shrugged, frowned, pocketed the paper, pecked Anna three times on the cheeks, and left.

By the time he reached the bridge leading back to Wing

Kee, he had taken out his phone. He thumbed in the number. She answered immediately, but was clearly in the middle of another conversation.

'Enough. Enough! Don't laugh!' She was laughing herself. 'Sorry. Merel Dekkers.' He could hear the soft Limburg burr.

'Posthumus. You left a message for me at De Dolle Hond.'

A beat.

'Uncle Pieter.'

Posthumus froze. He came to a dead halt in the middle of the bridge. People pushed past him. It was a while before he spoke: 'We need to talk.'

SUNDAY
15 MAY 2011

5

Sunday afternoons at De Dolle Hond had a tranquil, homely air. The red-light revellers were back home nursing hangovers, tourists went on their museum rounds, and the drinkers who came after work had other things to do with their weekends. Sunday afternoons were for steadfast regulars, friendly neighbours, people Anna had known for years. She bought in homemade apple pie from De Bakkerswinkel around the corner, put a better quality coffee in the machine, and De Dolle Hond became her *huiskamer*.

Posthumus was always there, in the same way that Anna, on Monday, her day off, always came to his apartment for dinner. It had been that way for years. So it made sense to Posthumus that this should be the time and place to meet Merel. Somewhere at once home and public. Somewhere he felt comfortable; somewhere he could flee. He chose a table at the window and waited. Anna, without his having to ask, left him alone and busied herself at the far end of the bar counter, chatting with Paul de Vos, who was sitting on the little band platform at the back of the café. There was no music on Sundays, but Paul was becoming something of a fixture. He was spread star-shaped from his piano stool, lanky legs apart, both elbows propped behind him on the lid of the keyboard. He hadn't shaved, and was wearing what he'd had on the night before.

Posthumus sipped his coffee. Merel *Dekkers*? She must

have got married. And why suddenly this contact? The last time he had heard 'Uncle Pieter' was in the weeks after his brother's funeral. Before Willem's wife Heleen had put up the barriers, taken the two little girls away to Maastricht. Yet it was 'Uncle Pieter' who had been banished. Shut out from ever seeing any of them again.

He recognised her the moment she walked through the door. Not that there was much there of the pretty little blonde girl of twenty years ago. Rather, she had grown into a feminine Willem. Very nearly the age he was when he was killed. Willem the beauty. Willem the golden boy. For a moment, Posthumus knew that he would not be able to speak. He was glad that Merel looked first to the back of the café, before turning to the table at the window. Anna had slipped away from the bar into the kitchen.

Posthumus stood up. They both hesitated. It seemed wrong to shake hands, even more so to hug or peck cheeks. In the end they touched each other lightly on the shoulder. Merel took a seat.

'Coffee?'

'Thank you.'

Anna reappeared just long enough to make it. Posthumus returned to the table. He had been rehearsing his opening lines, but they had all flown.

'You look like him,' he said. 'But I imagine people tell you that.'

'And I remember. I was already eleven.'

The exchange prolonged rather than broke the silence. Posthumus went for small talk.

'So, you're in Amsterdam now.'

'Mother doesn't like that. She was upset when I went to Rotterdam and joined Dad's old paper. Even more so when I came here to work for *De Nieuwe Post*.'

'She knows you've been in touch?'

'I told her that I'd tracked you down. She said nothing, then, "I can't stop you."' Merel looked at him enquiringly.

'She's still in Maastricht?' said Posthumus.

Merel nodded. 'Teaching.'

'And *De Nieuwe Post*?'

Merel took the offered escape route. She spoke quickly. A little too quickly. 'A wild world out there. You wouldn't believe the pressure. With the internet and falling circulation and everything. I missed a story last week. You'd think I'd killed the queen! My editor yelling about last chances, and I'd better get something big quick, and first, and sensational. A miracle or tsssk.' Merel drew a finger across her throat.

'You're on home news, aren't you? I think I've seen a byline from time to time.'

'Yes, and topical features. I'm doing something at the moment on Muslim women in Amsterdam, their attitudes and opinions, you know, because of the Amsterdam Cell.'

'It's just with "Dekkers" I didn't make the link. You're married?' They were moving back on to dangerous territory.

'Mum remarried after two years. She made both Bella and me take our new father's name. He adopted us. Now it just seems natural to me. *My* name.'

Posthumus let that pass.

'And Bella?'

'Teaching, also. One daughter in Father's footsteps, the other in Mother's.'

Another silence.

'She wouldn't talk about it, you know. Ever. After the funeral, she seemed . . . I don't know . . . to hate you, and blank him out completely. Then we moved to Maastricht, and when Wim came along – he's also called Willem – it was "You have a new father now." That was it. Bella and I, we asked about you, in the beginning at least, but after a while . . .' Merel paused. 'She blames you, you know. Mum, I mean. For Dad – my first Dad.'

'She has every right to.'

'Howdy, partner!' Paul de Vos was looming over the table, with a smirky smile on his lips. '*You* must have hidden talents, PP! Aren't you going to introduce me to your charming lady friend?'

'My niece, Merel Dekkers. Paul de Vos.'

'Niece? I had no idea . . . *very* pleased to meet you, I'm sure . . .'

'Paul! Can you come and give me a hand, please?' Anna to the rescue, from the far end of the bar. The intrusion drew uncle and niece together a little.

'Yuk!' said Merel.

'Got it in one.'

'And you don't like being called PP.'

'I certainly don't like *him* calling me PP.'

Merel laughed. The soft chuckling laugh he'd heard over the phone. Posthumus smiled in response. There was something about being family – even such odd, fractured family as this – that gave a gentle undercurrent of intimacy to the conversation. *How* she reminded him of Willem. It wasn't just the looks, it was something deeper than that. Her mother must find it unbearable.

'So what do you mean, she has every right to blame you? It was just an accident, wasn't it? Crazy driver. That's what everyone said.'

Merel clearly also had her father's talents as a reporter. Not just the sharp eye, but the hard core. The doggedness. Posthumus did not talk about this to anyone. Not even, any more, to Anna. Yet not a day went by that it did not push its way in. An echo; a sudden sour tang of guilt.

'You have to understand this about me and your dad,' he said. 'We were very different. Him, the model son. Married early, two beautiful daughters, sky-rocketing career. Me, the dropout. Didn't finish my sociology degree, spent months travelling abroad, couldn't hold down a proper job, lived in a squat in Amsterdam, didn't grow up. Yet we were incredibly close. Not just siblings. We loved each other.' He felt his voice go all wrong. 'We were soulmates, in a strange sort of yin and yang way.'

Posthumus faltered. 'Now I'm sounding like an old hippy . . . Look, I'm sorry. Your phone call, seeing you after such a long time . . . Can . . . can we just leave it? At least for now?'

'And stifle my journalist's curiosity?' said Merel. But there was a softness in her tone. 'Really, Uncle Pieter. You don't know me.'

That tipped him.

Merel waited a while, then reached over and gave his arm a single squeeze. 'I didn't know men still *carried* handkerchiefs,' she said.

Her gentle mocking reminded him of Alex. Posthumus couldn't help a smile. He blew his nose hard, and put the handkerchief back in his pocket.

'It's me who should apologise,' said Merel. 'I'm sorry.' She hesitated. 'I'm not on a quest, or anything like that. It's just . . . I remembered you. The fun times Bella and I had with you. I couldn't come to live in Amsterdam and *not* try to find out more. I just wanted to understand, you know, what it was all about . . .'

'Hello. Merel, isn't it?'

Anna, her antennae perfectly attuned, had sensed that this was the time to come over to the table.

'Remember me?'

'Anna?' said Merel. 'Uncle Pieter's girlfriend? Or you were, anyway. It's why I took a stab at phoning this place. I thought you might still be together.'

'A long time not,' said Anna. 'And I reckon you should drop the "uncle" thing. PP's already self-conscious about going grey. Another coffee?'

'No, no . . . I must be going. I've got a lecture at four.'

'A lecture?'

'Well, debate really, at the library. For work. On young women and the veil.' Merel looked at Posthumus. 'You'll be needing one yourself soon. You *are* going grey.' She held his eye a moment. 'PP, then? May I? And some other time?' she said.

Anna smiled.

'That . . . that would be nice,' said Posthumus.

Merel got up, leaned over, and gave his cheek a cautious kiss. 'But I really do have to fly,' she said. She rested a hand on Anna's forearm. 'Nice to meet you again. I'll be seeing you.' And she was out of the door and walking up towards the Damrak.

Posthumus stood up. Anna gave his shoulders a quick hug.

'Sorry to break in on the happy family!' Paul de Vos's voice boomed in his ear. 'I'm just going out for something to eat.' He winked at Posthumus, and put his hand on Anna's bum as he passed, giving the flesh a gentle squeeze.

Posthumus gazed horrified after the departing musician. He turned to Anna. 'Anna, you didn't! You *didn't*? Not *him*!'

6

Damrak and Station Square surged with Sunday sightseers.
Yet another warm, limpid blue day in this uncharacteristically
glorious May. Glass-topped waterbuses rounded the hull of
Renzo Piano's ship-like Nemo building, thrust into the waters
of the IJ. A student party, precarious in a small tin boat, blasted
music and popped beers. Seagulls dive-bombed half a pizza
that bobbed on the water. In the gaudy floating pagoda of the
Sea Palace, Chinese families gathered at large round tables for
afternoon dim sum.

'No crispy sesame toast or prawn dumplings for me,' muttered
Ben to himself, as he climbed the steps to the OBA, Amsterdam's
Public Library across the way. 'I'd better bloody well be able to
claim overtime for this. And how's about chilling a bit on "desk
offences" and stray Post-its while they're at it.' He stepped out
of the sunshine into the shade of the OBA, and went indoors.
'Designer-dandy' he called the place, with its hip furniture and
fancy bookshelves. And the banks of flat-screen computers that
in saver mode flashed up random words in bold black capitals:
OH! PLUMBER, BOOK, TIGHTS, TIME-BOMB. Weird,
thought Ben. It'll be JIHAD next. Free internet access. Hundreds
of terminals. That's what brought the kids here. Those whose
parents couldn't afford computers at home. Mansouri and his
gang, too, from time to time. Not for any dodgy business – dingy
telephone centres out west were the place for that – but to hang
out, network, keep an eye on little brothers at the games stations.

The OBA was busy. All ages. And a big, jumbly scoop from Amsterdam's race bag. There were eight floors of it, with zigzagging escalators up the centre. Countless study-corners, meeting-nooks, conversation-alcoves – lonely clusters of designer seating screened by strategically placed bookcases. Perfect for a quiet garrotting, Ben joked to his friends, or the old hypodermic-tipped pen in the back. Ben used the OBA to meet with his go-men, as he called his sources. And to keep a bit of an eye on things himself. Unofficial. Hands-on. He liked that.

Inside, Ben went up to the first level – an open U-shaped balcony, with ample view of the main entrance and escalators. A line of computers ran all the way around it; those on the far side were in a shadow created by a dimly lit rest area. Fewer people along that far stretch. Hardly any at all. A middle-aged woman in a tracksuit at the very furthest screen. Her daughter, probably, with her. On the corner a young Moroccan guy with one of the cropped Mohawk haircuts that had become hip the past few months. Ben sat one stool away from him, positioning himself for a good view of the lobby. He brought up Facebook.

'Yo, *mattie*. What's up?' he said softly, as if to the screen.

'Squit,' said the Mohawk. 'That Amir dude you ask about, you know, the new dude what come over from Morocco, he's still in Brussels. Was hanging about a lot before he went, man. And sniffin' the Tahiri sister, know what I mean? He's a sort of cousin or whatever. She's here today, man. Talkin' about hijab at some discussion thing.'

'And our friends?' Ben tapped a few words on the keyboard.

'Them was pissed about the arrest! Bad, man. No happy-happy welcome-home party. Just *vexed*. Mansouri was at prayers Friday, with Bassir. Yellin', man. I mean *seriously* vexed.'

'Others there?'

Still staring at his own screen, the Mohawk, almost imperceptibly, shook his head. 'Uh-uh. Except the guy what drove to pick them lot up from Vught, and the little Tahiri brother Najib. And there's a new face tagging along. Syrian. Speaks Arabic. Shit-all Dutch, man. Call himself Khaled.'

'Friend of?'

'Dunno. Hung out with Najib, spoutin' English. Kept asking what Mansouri was sayin'. Then lots of "brother this" and "brother that", know what I mean? Full of noise on his own adventures.'

'That's cool, *mattie*, thanks.' Ben got up to go. 'Keep an eye on the newbie.'

'Hey, man! I'm *piek-squit*,' said the Mohawk.

Ben looked confused. For the first time the two made eye contact.

'Skint. Broke. No money,' said the Mohawk.

'Yeah, yeah, sure,' said Ben. 'And I am so, *so* careless with my things.' He walked away from the computer. Under the keyboard was a small sealed envelope.

Posthumus opened his fridge door and chose a bottle of wine. He couldn't believe Anna had slept with that slimebag. Just a one-off, she'd said. A Saturday night. Why not? she'd said. 'Besides, you don't know the half of it!' He didn't like the glint in her eye. The cork popped. A large glass. And he took the bottle with him. It had been quite some afternoon.

He walked the full stretch of his long apartment – the top floor of a warehouse in the seventeenth century – to the sitting area at the front, and opened the window overlooking the canal. Large, arched, reaching all the way to the floor, the window had once been the door through which goods were hoisted. Posthumus had removed the low safety rail the builders put

across it during the conversion. There were never any children in the house. He took a cushion from the sofa, placed it
on the floor in a triangle of light made by the afternoon sun,
and sat, back against the edge of the wall, legs extended across
the opening, inches from the drop.

Families. He had never forgiven himself for Willem's death;
had felt that Heleen had every right to blame him, to cut the
girls off from their uncle's reckless influence. The girls he
had made fatherless. But seeing Merel this afternoon. Seeing
Willem . . . Perhaps he had cut himself off from them, too?
Willem's death had shaken him to the core. Soon afterwards,
he left the squat, got a job with the council and finished his
studies part-time. He bought the apartment when his mother
died and left him a little money. Once he'd got the job, settled
down, had something to show for himself – couldn't he then
have made more of an attempt to patch things up? It had
surprised him, that feeling of a family tie this afternoon. Little
moments of closeness that caught him unawares. Sure, he had
Anna. They were an ad hoc family, the two of them. A strong
one. He wasn't a 'sad, lonely git' like that young copper called
the poor sod hanging in the attic room on Delistraat.

Posthumus's mind turned to Bart Hooft. How could your
brother, your son, die like that – or even like the old man in the
filthy apartment – and no one know? Sure, it was Posthumus's
administrative duty to track down a family – from the official
point of view, largely in the hope that someone would pay for
the funeral – but for him it was something stronger than that.
A *need*. He had spent much of the weekend reading the poems.
Nothing there gave any clues. No names, no clear indications
of a town. The poems in that '(K)Nights in the Black Tulip'
section, the roughest ones, seemed to refer to a place. Some
sort of bar or club, maybe? He'd check it out. But that pen?
There was something about that pen. Posthumus swung up

from the floor with a single, easy movement and walked over to his workspace, tucked behind the spiral staircase that led up to the bedroom. He opened a black, cloth-covered box on the desk.

The box dated back to his days on the Conduct and Integrity Unit. It was, he supposed, the grown-up equivalent of the boxes of treasures he and Willem had kept under their beds as schoolboys. But this one contained an assortment of photographs, copies of documents, handwritten notes, together with a curious collection of objects: a cardboard beer-mat, a toy Ferrari, a cocktail-party invitation. Fetishes, almost. Reminders of things that had bothered him in corruption investigations. Cases that might well be signed-off, stamped, sealed – even with people successfully prosecuted – but which he felt he somehow had not got to the bottom of. Often, of an evening, Posthumus would open the box, and with the air of somebody enjoying a crossword, would take out the items related to a case and puzzle over them. And puzzle. Once, just once, this had led to a retrial. Nothing had gone into the box for nearly a year. Until this weekend. On top of the pile was a printout of a photo of a Japanese lacquered fountain pen.

Posthumus stared at the photo for a moment, then snatched it up and glanced across at the kitchen clock: five twenty-five, a reasonably social hour for a Sunday. He opened his front door and ran downstairs to his neighbour one floor below. 'Gusta, why didn't I think of her?' he said out loud, as he knocked on the door. Gusta spent her life at arts and antiques fairs.

'Gusta! Hello! Sorry to disturb you.'

'You look excited . . . come in.' The apartment was crammed with twenties' and thirties' bric-a-brac. It smelled of a mixture of talcum powder and cigarette smoke.

'Just something I'm working on at the moment. I was wondering if you could tell me anything about this.' Posthumus

75

showed her the photograph. 'Where it might have come from. It looks special.'

Gusta raised both eyebrows, took the cigarette she'd been smoking from its holder, and stubbed it out in an angular tortoiseshell ashtray.

'That's easy. It's a Namiki.'

'That name had come up. I've been doing some internet trawling, but can you tell me more? *Is* it special?'

'It's that all right. The company's still going, it dates back to the beginning of last century, I think. They started doing these beautiful lacquer pens in the twenties, which is how I know them, and some wonderful ones with dragons in the sixties. Made to order, many of them. But this isn't really my field. I couldn't give you an evaluation. But I do know – I've coveted one long enough – that if it's real you're talking thousands.'

'It's not so much the value I'm interested in, but rather if it is special enough to locate it; someone who collects or deals in Amsterdam?'

'You could ask at Akkerman on Kalverstraat, but this looks to me as if it is out of their league. I don't know anyone else. Not here, anyway. There was an old guy who collected just this sort of pen. Lovely old man. We used to chat a lot. He had a stall at De Looier – you know, the antiques market in the Jordaan. I was thinking of trying my hand at the business, had a weekend job in those very distant days when I was a student, looking after the stall next door to his. But he died years ago, back in the eighties.'

'Did anyone take it over? Any family?'

'From old Mr Hooft? No, I don't think so.'

'*Hooft?*'

'There was a son. Some sort of academic, who emigrated in the seventies. Didn't even come back for his father's funeral. He'd be getting on a bit himself by now.'

'Emigrated? Where to?'

'Now that I cannot remember. Australia, maybe, or it might have been Canada.'

Posthumus beamed. Hooft. It *had* to be. Not that this narrowed it down much. Still, it could have been worse. It could have been "Smit" or "Van Dam". But there had to be some sort of emigration record somewhere. It was a start.

'Gusta, you're a star! Thank you.' Posthumus pecked her on the cheek, and ran out, shutting the door behind him.

Augusta Besselink looked startled, and stood still for a moment, as she heard her neighbour rush back upstairs. Then she shook her head, selected a cigarette from a silver case, placed it in her holder, and lit up.

Ben glanced at his phone. Just after five thirty. He slid the tray with his mug and the plate covered with sausage-roll flakes on to a conveyor-belt that carried it into the washing-up area. He bought himself another coffee and walked out on to the terrace. The OBA was a skyscraper in this low-rise town. From the end of the café terrace on the top floor you felt you were flying. As if you could soar out over edgy new architecture in one direction, old spires and dinky gables in another. It was exhilarating. Ben walked across to the railing, and stood face to the wind, looking out over the rooftops of the red-light district. He drank a few sips, put the mug on a table behind him, and took out his phone again. He tapped in:

wossup? drink?

An immediate answer.

@ Diep in 20 mins?

Ben pinged back an OK, and turned to pick up his mug, but stopped dead. Standing in the doorway leading on to the terrace was Rachid. They noticed each other at the same time.

For a moment Rachid hesitated, as if he would go back inside. Then he walked over.

'Dude!' said Ben. 'Surprise, surprise.'

'Just returning DVDs,' said Rachid. 'Then I hung around for that debate on headscarves. That Tahiri girl was there, you know, the sister, Aissa. She was being interviewed by some journalist afterwards. On the podium she talked about the hijab as a statement of defiance, against the right, against parents who had lost the plot. Otherwise nothing really new. Same old arguments from everyone else. And you?'

'I've been doing some research.' Ben winked. There was a pause. 'Come here a lot? I've not seen you before.'

'They've got a good film collection. Usually my wife brings things back, but she's taken our daughters to visit their aunt in Rotterdam, so I came in. It's amazing, isn't it? I used to hang out at the old library on Prinsengracht when I was a kid, but it was nothing like this.'

The two men were still standing.

'Can I join you?' said Rachid.

'I was just going,' said Ben. They both glanced at his nearly full mug. 'But, yeah, OK, I can finish this off.'

'Busy weekend?' Rachid asked.

'Something like that.' They sat down. 'Our man . . .' Ben looked around. There was no one really within earshot. 'Our man Mansouri I'm told is *well* rattled. Sounding off. Interesting, no? Could just do something that makes it easier to nail him.'

Rachid looked uneasy. 'Well, we can talk about that on Monday.'

'Yeah, sure. And I could just be notching up some

good-conduct points with the boss while I'm at it. The name "Khaled" mean anything to you? Syrian.'

Rachid shook his head.

'Thought not. Look out for it. One to watch, if you ask me. News to brighten the boss's Monday morning.'

Ben looked across at his colleague's untouched pizza slice.

'Hey, eat up! You don't like her, do you?'

'Lisette? She's very competent.'

'It's Veldhuizen I don't go for. Hard bastard. In it for himself. Ruthless and a big ego, *bad* combination. And fancies himself as a cool dude, too.'

'You mean the Lexus, instead of your standard-issue Volvo?'

Ben laughed. 'And the shaved head . . . but what is it with you, then? Why the attitude last week?'

Rachid had on that set, expressionless look he so often had at the office.

'Nothing,' he said. Then: 'Just bored with what I'm doing, that's all. It's pointless. I should be on analysis.'

'Ingrid is good. Never friggin' says anything, but when she does, it's *sharp.*'

'We need a Moroccan analyst. At least someone who knows the culture better. And not just from books and journals. She makes mistakes.'

'Like what?'

'Like when she said the spontaneous visits between targets, meeting in each other's houses, was "suspicious conspiratorial behaviour". That went into the report. But young Moroccan guys do that. You don't phone first. You just go round to someone's house. See what's up. Like the whole thing with Mansouri growing a beard and wearing a djellaba. It can simply mean he's religious, not that he's radicalised. But guess what gets into the report.'

'Why don't you speak up, then?'

79

'I do. Well, I used to. It just doesn't seem to get through to the rest of you.'

'Hey, come on.'

'Well, you asked. I'm telling you.'

'But what about all that other stuff, then? The bomb chemicals and such? You can see there's something going on.'

'Yeah. And the targets were released.'

'Because the DA is an incompetent prick.'

'Because that report was full of holes. I tell you, we need an analyst who knows the community more.'

'And of course, there's only one real Moroccan in the running . . .'

'I'm Dutch.'

'You know what I mean.'

'And you know what *I* mean.'

'Hey, man, you're a rare case. If you guys only integrated more . . .'

'Look at the football teams. Look at TV. And music, comedy – AliB, Najib Amhali. Look at new Dutch writing. And you say we're not integrated?'

'And look at the coffee shops. *Well* integrated, I'd say. Into the criminal world. Business in Amsterdam, nice little family dope plantation back home. And that's where everybody will be in a month or two, no? The big summer migration. Back "home". 'Cos that's how you guys see it, isn't it? You can't have it both ways.'

'What's wrong with feeling you're both? You can be two things, like you can love two different kids. I remember once being up in this tiny village in the Atlases, really relaxed and happy, and then seeing a guy wearing an Ajax T-shirt, and suddenly feeling all homesick for Holland. Even my parents, when they go back for the summer, really miss Amsterdam after a while. They long to come back.'

'Still, along with the rest of the gang, half the targets are probably going to disappear to Morocco in the next few weeks. So we had better get moving on this case, because either something is going to happen soon, or we'll have the whole summer to put our feet up. That's *my* analysis.'

Rachid was quiet. Then he said softly, 'That's just what I mean. Ramadan is in August this year. People don't like going back to Morocco when Ramadan is in the summer because it's so hot and you can't drink during the day. So chances are most of the targets will stay here this year. Till after Ramadan, at least.'

Ben's phone jangled into life.

A text message.

Oi! Am @ Diep. Where u?

Ben pocketed the phone, stood up, winked and made a gun-shape at Rachid with one hand.

'Saved by the bell. Gotta go,' he said. He tapped two fingers to his temple in a momentary salute, and walked quickly back into the OBA.

TWO WEEKS LATER

MONDAY 30 MAY 2011

7

'Can you get it?' Posthumus was in the kitchen when the doorbell rang, in the middle of making a Hollandaise sauce. Risky to do it so early, he knew, but he wanted to spend time with his guests, and there was still the risotto further down the line. Besides, he had a trick of storing the sauce in a wide-necked thermos that kept it at just the right temperature. He'd got the jar from Rob Mulder down at the city morgue, but not even Anna knew that.

Anna pressed the buzzer to open the street door. She was still slightly sour at the invasion of their regular Monday night dinner together. Monday was precious time. Family night in, she called it, as her father had before her, when they gathered for dinner in the apartment above De Dolle Hond. 'Third floor!' she called down the stairwell. 'And jiggle the lock down there, it sometimes doesn't close properly.' Occasionally, she got in young Simon, who usually covered mornings, to work Tuesdays, so that she had a two-day break. But on these single nights off she cherished not having to make conversation with anyone. This was different, she supposed. It made sense they came tonight. It was she who was more friendly with Gabrielle, and PP wanted to do something special as a thank-you to Cornelius for coming up with a poem for the funeral of that lonely poet who had killed himself.

They were at the door. Pecks on cheeks. Flowers.

'With you in a moment!' called Posthumus.

★ ★ ★

Najib moved noisily around the sitting room. Picking things up, putting them down with too much force. Zapping through three, four, five TV channels, then chucking the remote on to the sofa. Mohammed avoided his son's eye, ignored the flicking channels, and read the Dutch newspaper. Karima was in the kitchen, his daughter Aissa was preparing the table for dinner. Cousin Amir was late.

'You *will* stay for dinner with Amir,' Mohammed had instructed Najib. 'It's a while since we've all eaten together.'

'If he wants to go off to Brussels all the time, that's his business,' Najib had answered. 'I've made arrangements tonight.' He stalked and thumped around the room. 'What's so great about Amir, anyway? You just want him to marry Aissa.'

From the dining table, Aissa caught her brother's eye. She raised her eyebrows slightly. Najib swung round to look out of the street window. He was fiercely protective of his older sister, and seemed to have taken against this relative from Morocco.

'I like him,' said Aissa. 'He makes me laugh. He talks to me like I've got a brain in my head. Not many of *your* friends do that.'

'Khaled does.'

'Only because he doesn't speak much Dutch, and my English is better than yours. Arabic, too, for that matter.'

Najib did not reply.

'Amir seems a very sensitive and serious young man,' said Mohammed. He was addressing his son, but looking at his daughter. He had not met this Khaled, or any of Najib's new friends, when it came to that. 'Besides, who Aissa marries is for her to decide. You know what your mum and I feel about this. We'll give our guidance . . .'

'Firm guidance,' called Karima from the kitchen.

'Firm guidance,' said Mohammed, 'but in the end it is up to

you.' He turned to Najib. 'What are these "arrangements" that are so urgent tonight, anyway?'

'Nothing. Just out. Friends.'

'Well, it can wait until after dinner, then.'

Najib shrugged his shoulders, and gave a dismissive pffff.

But he stayed. He was getting sullen and cheeky, but he still obeyed his father. For how long? Mohammed wondered. He cast a quick glance at Najib from behind his paper. 'Arrangements'. Well, that was something at least. Better than spending all the time in his bedroom. It had been getting like it was five years ago, when Najib was teased at school. He was in his bedroom all day, crying. He never told his father anything. Karima sometimes, or he'd talk to Aissa – that's how Mohammed had learned about the TV, finally relented and got a satellite. Then a computer for the boy. His own – few of his school friends had that. Not back then, anyway. The first of three. How anything so expensive could be useless and out of date so quickly perplexed Mohammed. But he loved his son, and wanted to see him happy, successful, two feet planted firmly on the ground.

Slowly, things had got better. Najib had set up that website, selling the sofas. It did good business, and Mohammed was proud of his son even if he himself didn't know how it all worked. He looked forward to Najib coming into the business when internet sales were generating enough money, taking what his father had sweated to establish off in a new direction. But these past months, it all seemed to be happening again. The bedroom. The silences. The distance. It began, Mohammed thought, around the time Najib had that little scuffle with the police – he'd been turned away from entering a nightclub or something. Nothing serious, no charges. Just the boy's hotheadedness, and it had come at a bad time; one of those days when little things build up, things that happen from time to time suddenly seeming to occur all at once, and be directed at personally thwarting and frustrating you. Najib had been turned down for a computer job he wanted, without even an interview. 'One look at the name was enough!' he'd said. Then that same afternoon on the tram an old Dutch woman had glowered at him, and moved her handbag to the other side as he sat down. Who knows how many times that had happened to Mohammed himself when he first came over. You got used to it. But the lad had exploded. 'She wants me to be a thief, I'll *be* a thief!' he'd said. 'I felt like mugging the old cow just to show her!'

And since then no other real job. Nothing he liked anyway. He wanted something to do with the internet, and there Mohammed couldn't help. His son seemed bored working at the shop, bored even, once he had set up the website, with selling the sofas. These days Najib didn't even come downstairs to watch television. All in the bedroom. On that computer. And these new friends that Mohammed never met. That was all the internet. The boy never listened to his advice any more. Or that given by uncles, or the imam, even. It was only the internet. But it seemed to Mohammed that the internet did not give advice, instead it gave you the answers you were looking for. Mohammed did not understand his son any more, and he did not like the internet.

Najib slumped suddenly on to the sofa. Mohammed looked up. Through the sitting-room window he could see Amir, in a white cotton djellaba, turning from the street on to the short path that led to their front door. Mohammed edged past Aissa at the dining table, and walked through to the tiny hallway to let the boy in himself.

'Drink?' said Anna. 'PP has come up with a new prosecco cocktail.'

'I'd prefer jenever,' said Cornelius. 'Young, if you have it, with ice.'

Clearly the usual, Anna thought, her professional eye marking the hard little pink veins on his cheeks. He was a good ten years older than Gabi, Anna knew that. Mid-fifties at least, she reckoned, and hung up about it. Vain. He was wearing a burgundy bow tie. Anna had always found him a touch irritating. Gabrielle opted for the cocktail. Anna went to pour the drinks, and to find a vase for the flowers. Posthumus walked across from the kitchen.

'Piet, it's been ages,' said Gabrielle. 'Still the natty dresser, I see.' She turned to her husband. 'Prissy Piet we used to call him.' But she softened the jibe with: 'Nice shirt. Raw silk?'

Posthumus nodded. 'I shouldn't be cooking in it, I suppose.'

They moved to the front of the apartment to sit looking out over the canal.

'I hear the Posthumus cuisine is as legendary as the couture,' said Cornelius, as Anna handed him his glass. 'What sweet delights are in store for us tonight?'

'Everything is so early this year,' said Posthumus. 'So, first asparagus, then a strawberry risotto, and then duckling . . . Sorry, just a moment. Sauce. The oven,' he said, and hurried back towards the kitchen.

'*Strawberry* risotto?' said Gabrielle sotto voce to Anna. 'He is joking, right?'

'Nope,' said Anna. 'And it's not dessert, either.' She looked across to Gabi's husband, rather hoping to see him thrown, but the man looked impressed.

'Interesting,' he said, 'but let's hope it is not a case of "Things sweet to taste that prove upon digestion sour". Shakespeare. *Richard the Second*.' Cornelius chuckled to himself, and embarked on a story about a visit to Piedmont.

Posthumus came back from the kitchen, drying his hands on a tea towel. He picked up his glass.

'To interrupt for a moment,' he said, 'before we get under way. A toast. To Cornelius. With thanks for a fine poem at Bart Hooft's funeral.'

Cornelius beamed, nodded an acknowledgement, and began:

> We all knew him,
> > the invisible man.
> Six books, a bed, a rack of clothes
> > behind a dirty attic window.
> Stepping from a chair,
> > this is air
> And this is not—

'Perhaps not just now, dear?' Gabrielle broke in.

Cornelius shot her a glance, bowed his head and opened both palms.

'Absolutely,' he said. 'But it's *merci* to you, my dear Pieter, for securing me a fee in these straitened times.' He drained his glass.

Anna suspected that it did not sit easy with him that his wife was the major money earner in the family. It certainly wasn't a poet's income that bought an apartment in Zuid, and sent little Lukas to private lessons with a top violinist.

'And to Anna,' said Posthumus. 'It was her idea to have a custom-written poem.'

'Oh, he probably took one off the shelf,' said Gabrielle.

'I absolutely did *not*,' said Cornelius. 'Even though I had only a couple of days to do it. I took it most seriously. Piet made me copies of the man's poems. Read 'em all. English ones also. Built up quite a picture of the fellow. And I must say they were rather good, even the somewhat insalubrious ones.'

He winked across the room at Posthumus.

'And I very much enjoyed the experience. Perhaps,' he said, holding up his empty glass, 'to many another funeral ode?'

Posthumus fetched the jenever bottle. He paused before refilling Cornelius's glass – for so long that the poet gave him a quizzical look.

'You know, you could be on to something there,' said Posthumus. 'A poem for every funeral . . .'

'That was even more delicious than I have eaten back home, Um Najib,' said Amir to Karima.

'My wife's chicken tagine with apricots is known throughout the Kolenkit!' said Mohammed. There had been enough for seven or eight people, rather than just the five of them, but now the dish lay between them with only the politest morsel remaining.

Karima rose, and went to fetch the water jug and basin. Aissa took the tagine back to the kitchen.

Mohammed sighed, and surveyed the two young men seated on each side of him: Najib to his left, Amir, the guest, to his right. A future son-in-law? He and Aissa seemed to like each other, even if Najib was so rude to the lad, challenging him scornfully about his faith. Just where was his son going, these days? Mohammed wondered. For himself, it was true, he knew, that he coasted along with the basics, the five pillars: *shahadah*, fasting during Ramadan, prayer five times a day, giving to the poor. He had once made the Hajj. But Amir was a devout young man, with the gentle, old-fashioned faith of back home. Not the hard, angry belief of some of the boys out here – the sort of religion that, though Mohammed kept trying to deny this to himself, he felt was entangling Najib. Mohammed had hoped that Amir could keep an eye on the boy, be allowed into places in his son's mind and heart where he himself was no longer permitted to enter. Now he was not so sure. Mohammed looked up at Karima holding the water jug beside him as he dried his hands. He would make one last try.

'So,' he said to Najib, 'this study group you're setting up with your new friends, how about inviting your cousin along?'

Aissa returned with a fresh pot of mint tea, and a plate of pastries.

Amir was eager to join, he said. He knew his Qur'an, had attended a number of madrasahs, and not only in Morocco, had much he could contribute.

'If you won't let *me* come along, you could at least invite Amir to go,' said Aissa.

Amir smiled at her.

'He's never here, anyway,' said Najib finally, as if his cousin were not in the room.

'I told you,' said Amir, 'Brussels is for work, business deals for my mother's family, people they have asked me to see.'

'And this will be going on for long?' said Karima.

'I've got to go one last time, Um Najib, on Wednesday. I'll be back next week. For Friday prayers, latest, and then that's it. Here for good.'

'I'm glad to hear it,' said Karima.

Najib gave his cousin a look of contempt. Karima caught her daughter's eye, and smiled.

Cocktails gave way to a rich Alsace Riesling, which in turn led to a gutsy Pomerol. The Hollandaise sauce was perfect, the risotto pronounced 'much tastier than you might have thought', and the pepper-lemon duckling was a triumph. By the time chocolate mousse and a bottle of fine Banyuls were on the table, Cornelius was as good as installed as official poet to the municipal funeral department. Paid, of course.

'Seriously,' said Posthumus. 'I'd really like to do this. For the anonymous ones, especially. If we trace a family, it's their responsibility; though sometimes they just don't want to know, and the funeral ends up in our hands, anyway. But it's the completely anonymous ones – and there are more than you'd think – that I really like to do something for.'

'He calls them his "clients",' said Anna, 'which is going a bit far, if you ask me.'

But Posthumus was warming to his topic. 'You could even come along with us on house-visits. It is amazing what you can tell from the books, the music, the décor. The picture you can build up of someone.'

Cornelius's mouth was full, but he waved a hand to indicate that this, perhaps, would not be essential to his muse.

'The problem is,' Posthumus went on, 'that they're usually the ones with no money. The aloners, I mean. But I'll talk with the director tomorrow. Surely we can squeeze something out of a budget somewhere.'

'I wouldn't hold your breath,' said Anna. She got up to make them some coffee. 'Not after the Bart Hooft blow-up, anyway,' she went on.

There were times she despaired of her friend. The funeral Cornelius had contributed his poem to had been delayed by nearly two weeks, as PP searched fruitlessly through records trying to track down someone who might just possibly have been family, who might perhaps have emigrated. The delay led to another showdown with Maya at the office; more evenings of PP limping in, downcast, to De Dolle Hond for a drink after work. Anna had never met Maya, but she felt a twinge of sympathy for her. There came a point where you simply had to draw the line, to let go, admit defeat, acknowledge that things didn't always tie up neatly together. The Funeral Team had a job to get on with, and PP's fossicking must drive them mad. Honestly!

Sometimes that man . . . he'd be moved off this job, too, she could see it. Just like before.

'You're a civil servant, PP,' she said as she cleared the dessert plates and took them off to the kitchen. 'Not a detective.'

Mohammed broke the silence.

'Well, when you return from Brussels, you must eat more often with us. Your parents are both well, I hope?'

'Very well, thank you, Abu Najib. They both send warm wishes. I spoke to them this afternoon.'

'And all is well back home?'

'It seems so. Everyone is talking about the king and reforms.'

Until then, Najib had been sullen, silent, constantly flicking backward glances over his shoulder to the street window, even though the curtains were drawn. Now it was as if a flame had been lit under him.

'He is destroying Islam, he is not worthy to be called Commander of the Faithful!' Najib burst out. 'And you're all the same!'

'King Mohammed?' Amir looked shocked. Mohammed, too, was taken aback, as his son launched into a tirade, not against reforms, but attacking young men who came over from Morocco in general, and against the king himself.

'An infidel, a *kafir*!' Najib was shouting, building himself up into a fury. 'And you know what you are? Another little piece of the king's *shit*, believing all his lies. Reform *this*, reform *that*.' He leaned over the table and pushed Amir hard in the chest.

'Enough!' Mohammed jumped up. 'You will not talk like that in this house!'

Najib was quiet, and glared at his father. Mohammed did not often lose his temper. The others looked on nonplussed. Najib's outburst had been so sudden. He sat back, seething.

'My little brother is a bit of a hothead,' said Aissa, smiling apologetically to Amir, defusing the tension slightly, as
Karima refilled empty teacups.

'An apology!' Mohammed demanded of his son. But Najib
sat tight-lipped.

The doorbell rang.

Najib was up like a shot, and out into the hall.

Mohammed waited a moment, then leaned to his right to
see who Najib was talking to. Whoever it was had not come in,
and was standing in a shadow on the doorstep. Mohammed
glanced enquiringly at Amir, who would have a better view of
the front door, but the boy had eyes only for Aissa, still apolo-
gising on behalf of her brother. Mohammed strained to hear
what Najib was saying. He was speaking in English. 'I know, I
know, I'm coming . . .' Something about 'father' and 'dinner'
and 'family'. Something about Brussels. Something about the
study group. This must be one of them, Mohammed thought,
probably the Khaled fellow Najib was always on about, and
now he would see for himself. Meet the man. He got up to go
to the door, but before he reached the hallway, Najib was back
in the room.

'Why didn't you invite your friend in?' asked Mohammed.

'He wouldn't come, because Mother was unveiled,' said
Najib. Sullen again, with an accusing scowl at Karima.
'Besides, I've made him late. I said we'd meet earlier, and it's
already past nine o'clock. But I'm going to join the others,
anyway.'

Amir rose, as if to leave. Najib stared challengingly at his
father.

'It will soon be time for *salat*,' Mohammed said. 'You should
both stay. I think after this evening we need a little calm before
God.'

Najib said nothing, but stormed upstairs.

'I'll stay for the prayer, Abu Najib,' said Amir to Mohammed, 'but I'll go after that.'

Ten minutes later, Najib was back. Mohammed was astonished to see that he had changed jeans and T-shirt for a djellaba. He had not seen his son wearing traditional dress in Amsterdam, other than at weddings and festivals.

'I'm *going*,' Najib said to his father, then to Amir: '*You* and me are not done yet . . .'

The door slammed behind him.

'No, no, I'll walk,' said Anna, 'it's only a few minutes.'

Gabi and Cornelius had offered her a lift to De Dolle Hond in the taxi they had called to take them back to Zuid. To their smart little quarter in this city of villages, hermetic neighbourhoods where almost everything you needed was in walking distance. But it was early yet. There was still a wash of colour through the sky. It was a beautiful evening. Anna picked up her handbag from the spot where she always left it, on the first step of the spiral staircase that led up to PP's bedroom. A carhorn beeped outside. Cornelius crossed to the window to see if it was for them.

'Jesus!' he said, grabbing the wall unsteadily. 'What happened to the railing!'

'Took you a while to notice,' Posthumus laughed.

There was a little flurry of farewells at the door. Anna left at the same time. Posthumus walked to the window, saluted the departing cab, and gave a single wave to Anna as she crossed the bridge below. She turned, and blew him back a kiss. Forgiven. For whatever it was he had done.

Posthumus cleared up, stacked the dishwasher, then washed and dried whatever remained. By the time all was once again spick and span, the kitchen clock was edging towards ten thirty, but he was still on a dinner-party buzz. Posthumus selected a whisky tumbler, threw in a few blocks of ice, and poured himself a generous Cointreau. He crossed to his workspace, took the black cloth-covered ponder-box from his desk, and sat on the sofa by the window, where he turned on a reading light. As the dishwasher chugged and whooshed through its cycle, Posthumus settled down to a good half-hour's puzzling.

Amir remained with the family for the *Maghrib* prayer. Then he spoke a while with Aissa, as Karima busied herself in the kitchen and Mohammed pretended to watch television. At ten thirty, Amir left. He crossed the flat stretch of wasteland between Mohammed's house and the high street. Tall weeds. Dusty grass. At the far end stood the Surinam church, its sides alternate columns of brick and glass, lit up tonight from inside like a giant ribcage, with one stark bone jutting into the sky. No sign of a bus. No matter. He would walk. It was twenty minutes at most. It was a warm evening, the sky not completely drained of colour. Buses made him feel claustrophobic.

Amir turned left towards the city. Traffic growled from the underpass as he crossed the ring road. He walked on, past the market square – dark, empty, sucked of activity. A converted 1960s office block rose behind it, with a single, blue neon sign flashing HOTEL uninvitingly. Amir turned right on to Hoofdweg. There was quite a bit of traffic and just a few people walking. Four women, veiled, leaving the Sultan's Palace restaurant. A group of young men hanging about on the corner, tough-looking, disconsolate, their heads shaved down the sides, with a tight cropped stripe on the crown, like a Mohawk Indian. Amir began to cross the street, but leapt back as a scooter tore in the wrong direction up the cycle path, coming so close he felt it brush his djellaba. The driver cackled a laugh; the boy on the back turned and swore at him in Berber. Amir took the strap of the shoulder bag he carried and placed it over his head, so that it hung around one side of his neck and crossed diagonally over his chest.

On the other side of Hoofdweg he passed a large girl, iPhone tucked tightly against her ear under her hijab, talking hands-free. He left the road, on to a footpath with a canal on either side. So much water in this city! Amir still could not get used to it. The path skirted the Erasmuspark. The route seemed shorter this way, but Amir had not taken the path at night before. He knew the park was wide and flat and open, but now it seemed impenetrably dark, the bushes thicker. Amir did not like the dark. It made him feel he was being followed. He felt that tonight. He shook a shiver from between his shoulder blades and walked on. He was training himself to master these fears. And the path was wide, with lamps that threw arcs of greenish light, almost touching. There were some people about. Dutch, mainly, walking dogs. More young guys, hanging around where the path took a sharp right at the corner of the park. 'Amir!' Somebody called his name. But not him. Another Amir.

Back on to the busy road. Five more minutes. Amir passed the familiar shops. The Vacuum King, the Turkish tailor, the crowded coffee house, television blaring, the Iranian pottery shop. He came to a metal swing-bridge over the broad Westelijk Marktkanaal. Nearly home. Down one side of the canal there was a small park. Across on the other was the edge of the Kop van Jut, an odd promontory of land shaped like the tip of Africa, on which, in one of six almost identical apartment blocks, Amir lived. He crossed the bridge. The footpath home led beside the canal, past the tall, metal-grey rear wall of Marcanti College and the back of one of the apartment blocks. Small, square bathroom windows, mostly dark. Willows, already heavily in leaf, grew side by side on the strip of grass along the water. Gnarled, bent, like arthritic old men stooped over the edge. One of the pathway lamps was broken. Amir quickened his pace. A night-time jogger was coming up behind. Amir stepped towards the grass verge to let him pass, turning to nod a greeting.

'But you—' he said.

The blackness and the pain hit him at the same time. His body juddered as the electric shock passed through it, crumpled, and slipped over the bank into the canal. A tram thundering over the metal bridge drowned any sound it might have made.

THURSDAY
9 JUNE 2011

8

'*Good* morning. Johnnie Witteveen here. Amsterdam-Amstelland Police. Got one for you. Canal job.' Perky voice. Sounded like he was selling soap powder. Posthumus recognised it. A cocky little copper who relished these calls, he'd had him on the line before. Posthumus reached for a blank Case Report form. He was in the middle of winding up a tricky bank account. Martijn van Dam, an ex-civil servant who had died alone in a poky apartment on the Vinkenstraat. Complicated financial affairs. It was the fourth interruption that morning. Posthumus made a small pencil mark and shifted the bank statements to the left-hand corner of his desk, the space he reserved for tasks that had been interrupted.

'Go ahead,' he said. Curt. That was the way to deal with the chirpy little tosser. The man riled him. Why did he think of him as 'little'? He sounded that way. A terrier.

'You probably read about it last week,' the terrier said. 'Body in the Prinsengracht. Been dancing with an underwater bicycle. No ID. No claimants. No one reported missing. Wearing one of those djellaba things. What was left of it, anyway. He's been classified as an anonymous illegal. Maybe we've been saved from a bombing somewhere.'

Posthumus was methodically filling in the boxes on the Case Report. Rein in the terrier. Keep a tight leash.

'Male, I take it,' he said.

'The beard led us to believe this, yes. And the dick.'

Posthumus wondered whether he was supposed to laugh. He tightened the leash.

'Age?'

'Late twenties.'

'Date of discovery of body?'

'Last Tuesday. Thirty-first of May.'

'Date of death?'

'Estimated between 10 p.m. and 2 a.m., night of thirtieth May. Drowning.' The terrier was now hopping obediently from box to box, responding to discipline. 'No clear sign of violence, though the body was badly cut up, probably by a boat propeller. Foul play not suspected.' A moment's relapse. 'Probably another of your drunken foreigners taking a piss into the canal, and falling in. How many have we had this year?'

Posthumus ignored the question.

'And no address, I take it,' he said.

'Actually, yes. There was a bag. The strap was all twisted around the shoulder and neck. At first, we thought it might have been a strangulation, but the lungs were filled with water, pathology said, so he drowned; he was alive when he hit the water, maybe knocked himself out on the way down, or couldn't swim, or passed out and fell. Anyway, as I was saying, the bag was all cut up and empty, but there was this side pocket. Bit of cash. Keys. Train ticket to Brussels. Some little passport shots, they got wet, but it's him all right.'

'And the address?' said Posthumus.

'Hang in there, we're getting to that. There was a diary or notebook or something, pages all stuck together and in Arabic anyway. But an address in normal writing inside the cover. Marcantilaan 97. On the Kop van Jut . . . know it? It's out west, near the wholesale market. Anyway, we checked it out, tried the keys and bingo!'

'Marcantilaan 97,' said Posthumus.

'Yup. But no luck in the apartment. Empty pretty much, nothing of help to us anyway. He just camped there, it seems. And no ID; that must've been in the bag.'

'And his name not on the lease?'

'We may be busy, but we do our job.' The terrier's back was up. 'Sub-let. Been so for years. You know the story. Original lessee moves out, charges lump-sum rent to someone else in cash, way over what he's paying the housing association, keeps electricity and the like in his name, but still makes a fat profit. And as long as the envelope is slipped under his door each month, he doesn't give a monkey's who's in there. We tried. Passed from one to the other. List as long as your arm. Full of all-purpose Moroccan names, gets lost in dot dot dot. You know what they're like.'

Posthumus was silent. What he *did* know was how impossible it was to find affordable housing in Amsterdam.

'And we've got a pretty picture for you, too. Of a birthmark or something, on the torso. You can't see it clearly, 'cos the body's all cut up. Didn't help us any, but with you lot, you never know . . . Anyway, it's with the keys. Prinsengracht depot. Other effects at the morgue with the body.'

If he had been a real terrier, his tail would be wagging, thought Posthumus. He was certain the photograph wouldn't have been passed on if it weren't so gory. The cocky little bastard had done it before – on Posthumus's first case, a body that had spent all night roasting in a sauna. He really didn't like this cop. But at least they knew which depot to collect the keys from. That made a change.

Posthumous ended the call, slipped the Case Report into a plastic folder, put the details on computer, and alerted Alex. No need for faxes to the registry or the Probate Office for this one. He took a cardboard file from the stationery cupboard – yellow, each year had a different colour – labelled it Marcantilaan 97, then phoned the undertakers and arranged for the body to be collected from the morgue and sent to Uitvaartcentrum Zuid. He liked the set-up there, and they had a discreet ritual washing room. Posthumus reasoned this would be a Muslim ceremony. It would be a burial, anyway. Anonymous cases always were, in a shallow grave, easily exhumed if family suddenly showed up. He made a note about the transfer on the Case Report, dropped the report into the yellow file, and put the file in the general intray.

Sulung was out of the office, doing admin rounds – he always seemed to take twice as long as Maya or even Posthumus did when work took him away from his desk. Sometimes Posthumus wondered whether Sulung didn't have another job on the side. Maya was on the telephone, by the sounds of things to the niece she had traced for the old lady who had died a few days earlier at the VU hospital.

'We didn't find any insurance, and there is less than two thousand euros in her bank account,' she was saying. 'You should bear in mind that a basic funeral costs between five and seven thousand euros.'

Posthumus sighed. It was the easiest thing in the world to get yourself funeral insurance. Cheap, too. He reached to the left-hand corner of his desk for the van Dam bank account. As he did so, an email pinged in from Alex.

Canalman seems one for you, no?

That raised a smile. Alex's levity charmed him. Unlike the terrier's. Posthumus read on.

I've just spoken to Sulung, he'll be back after lunch (or so he says). So you could do the visit this afternoon with

Sulung, or tomorrow morning with Maya. Take your
pick.
  Ax

Posthumus glanced across at Maya. She was still grappling
with the niece.

'If you haven't seen your aunt for twenty years, I can understand that, but if you accept the inheritance then you also take
on all debts and expenses, and that includes the funeral.'

Posthumus tapped Alex a reply.

That's a choice?? S and today fine, as soon as he appears.

He paused a moment, then added:

Lunch in an hour? That hip new sandwich bar around the
corner?
  If we're lucky we may get a canal table. This nice weather
all ends tomorrow, apparently. Might as well make the most
of it.
  PP

'In that case the municipality will take responsibility,' Maya
was saying. The niece was clearly holding back. 'No, it is
perfectly respectable. The municipal package is this. You have
an hour at the undertakers the day before the funeral, in a
chapel of rest where you can say your goodbyes to the deceased
– an open coffin, if the body is presentable – then a half-hour
ceremony next day at the cemetery, with three pieces of music,
one bouquet of flowers from us, and twenty cups of coffee.
People may say something at the ceremony, if they wish, but
any longer than half an hour and any more than twenty coffees
will incur costs, which must be reckoned up beforehand.'

Alex's OK pinged back right away. Posthumus reached once more for the bank statement. The phone again.

'Good morning. This is Hans Bekker.'

Posthumus's mind raced. That was always a problem. Everyone who phoned assumed that you knew exactly who they were, thought they were the only one whose relative had died, the only one you'd spoken to all week. Of course they did.

'You left a message for me yesterday?' said the voice.

That was it! The Bart Hooft landlord. Hooft had been buried two weeks or so now, but something about that case troubled Posthumus. The need to tell Hooft's parents, to give them the poems so that the man had not simply faded anonymously from the world – yes, there was that, but there was something else, too. Posthumus didn't know what, exactly. Not yet. But he couldn't let it go. It was an instinct he'd developed in the Conduct and Integrity Unit. He looked across the room. Maya was still on the phone. Good. He spoke softly.

'Look, I realise this seems odd, but I had a question, about Bart Hooft, you know the man who . . .'

'Yes?'

'How good was his Dutch?'

'What do you mean?'

'Was he foreign?'

'No. Not really.'

'What do you mean "not really"?'

'Well, he had this odd accent. I couldn't place it. I hardly spoke to him, you know, but still. Not a foreign accent. Just, I don't know, odd. Old-fashioned.'

'That's interesting, thank you.'

'What's this about? Is there something wrong?'

'No, no, not at all. This isn't anything official . . . just something that perplexed me. You've been very helpful. Thank you.'

Posthumus put down the phone. So Bart Hooft could well have been his real name. And he was most likely Dutch, but lived like an illegal. *Why?* How come no traces at all? And odd, old-fashioned Dutch? Like the accent of someone who had grown up abroad, with Dutch-speaking parents, perhaps? Must be. *Must* be.

Maya had finished her call. Posthumus returned to the bank statement. Twenty minutes later, he drew a line under the van Dam case, faxed the bank finally to close the account (ridiculous, these days, that it still had to be a fax), and took the file across to the Closed Cases shelf. There he hesitated a moment, removed the Bart Hooft file, and, with a glance towards Maya, walked purposefully out of the office and downstairs to Alex.

'I need to go out for a moment. I'm still on for lunch, but can I meet you there instead?' he said. 'You know the place? Deli's, I think it's called. Grab a table if I'm a bit late.'

'Sure. What's up?'

'Something that's niggling me. Just want to check it out.'

Posthumus gave a wave with the Hooft file, and stepped out on to the Staalkade. He turned to follow the route he usually took home, through the red-light district. Ten minutes later, he pushed at a door bearing a decorative Open sign.

The little tattoo parlour was empty save for the owner – an old hippy, scrawny, balding, but with what hair he had left drawn back into a long, grey ponytail. An almost equally long Mandarin beard dangled from his chin. He nodded to Posthumus. Although Posthumus had never been in to the parlour, he passed it almost daily, and in warm weather the owner often sat outside, on a wooden chair on the stoop. Posthumus looked about him. The walls, the counter, even the ceiling were plastered with prints of tattoo designs. The tattooist, wearing a singlet, every inch of his skin an advertisement for his art, seemed to have taken on the hues of his surroundings as a chameleon might assume the colours of a leafy twig. He seemed to realise that Posthumus hadn't come in for a tattoo, and sat silently, waiting for him to speak.

Posthumus opened Bart Hooft's file, took out the police photos of his tattoos, and spread them out on the counter. An odd collection: a bright yellow duck with a black mask over its head; at the base of Bart's spine, a circle similar to the yin/yang symbol, but with three elements instead of two; below it the outline of a triangle, its inverted apex disappearing into the cleft between Bart's buttocks; an intricate woven chain, encircling both his ankles; a barcode on the back of his neck; the bird and star design on his arm.

'I wonder if you could tell me anything about these?' said Posthumus.

The tattooist glanced at the photos, and looked up at Posthumus, his face registering faint surprise.

'BDSM,' he said.

'Sorry?'

'Bondage, discipline, sadism, masochism. Or maybe it's dominance and submission. Something like that. They're symbols, like.'

'That figures, I suppose,' said Posthumus, recalling some of the poems. He'd checked out the 'Black Tulip' some of them referred to. It was a sort of sex club, a cellar-bar down one of those corridor-sized alleys a few blocks away. 'But a *duck*?'

'Playful,' said the tattooist. 'Dunno quite what it's about, but I've done a couple of those myself before now. Ankle chains, fairly obvious. The triangle's probably supposed to mean he's gay. Yin/yang thing, that's the BDSM secret sign. Between themselves, like. So's they can spot each other.'

'What does it mean?'

'That would be telling, wouldn't it?'

'And the star with the bird in it?'

'Dunno, that don't fit. But the red heart with a keyhole, there, also inside the star, that's a slave heart, that is. Means someone owns him.'

'*Owns* him?'

'A master. Not for real, of course. Consenting adults and all that. That's what the barcode's all about. Means he's on the Slave Register. It's a website.'

Posthumus looked disbelieving.

'It's true! Believe me. Get to learn a lot about life in my trade, you do.' The tattooist gave a wink. 'The scene is mainly online these days, and parties. Still a few bars about, though,' he went on.

'So I could trace this man through a website?'

'You'd have to register, I guess. And he'd have to respond to your . . . request.'

'That wouldn't work in this case,' said Posthumus. 'Is there anywhere else I can find out more about these? About who this might be?'

'Bit desperate, aren't you?'

The man chuckled. Posthumus gave him a sour look and flipped the file closed to show its official City of Amsterdam cover. It was the tattooist's turn to look askance.

'Well, that bird and star thing, that's probably something to do with a master,' he said. 'I've been asked before to integrate a slave heart with some other design, some emblem of a master. But that's shoddy work, that is. Done on the quick. Not put together well.'

'None of these yours then?'

'Nope. Not that I remember, anyway. As I said, I get asked to do all sorts of things in here.'

Posthumus suspected it was more the odour of dope that hung about the place than the bewildering variety of tattoo requests that baffled his sense of recall.

'Someone else might know? In another shop?' he said.

'Possibly. If he went to the same place each time. You could ask about,' the tattoo man said.

'How many tattoo parlours are there in Amsterdam?'

'I dunno. Twenty. Maybe thirty. But then again, maybe it wasn't even done here.'

Posthumus saw that this was all he was going to get. He gathered the photos together again, and replaced them in the file.

'Thank you for your help,' he said, as he headed out into the sunlight, and to lunch with Alex. He reasoned that a traipse around every tattoo joint in town would probably prove fruitless. He'd do it if he had to, but best perhaps to try another tack. He wouldn't let this go just yet. There was something about that bird and star image that seemed hazily familiar, rang a very faint bell at the back of his brain.

Thursday morning. Already. Time flew. Lisette was in the meeting room a good ten minutes early for the regular Team C report-back, fresh from another encounter with Veldhuizen. If 'fresh' was the word. Frazzled, more like. He hadn't let up. It felt to Lisette like an interrogation. What was going on? Were they missing something? Two of the cell had simply disappeared. Disappeared for Christ's sake! (Lisette had to admit the team had somehow lost track of El Mardi and Kaddaoui. They had gone to Brussels and evaporated. She didn't let on her unease that the Tahiri cousin, Amir Loukili, might have done the same thing.) The chief hadn't yelled. He'd been cold, quiet. Vehement. Results! He wanted results. And *now*. Did it take a bomb to go off before they woke up to what was in front of their eyes? What of this rivalry between Mansouri and Bassir? Were they on top of that? That could spark something. The chis reported an attack was imminent. She was on to that, right? (Ah yes, the Syrian. Lisette knew very well who *he* was.) She had again pressured for the team to be told about the agent, but the chief would have none of it.

It was silent in the meeting room. The dull silence of heavy soundproofing. Lisette flicked back a strand of hair, picked up a plastic pen between the forefingers of one hand, and with a rapid to-and-fro movement whirled it back and forth like a propeller, beating out a staccato tattoo on the table. The more she had to deal with Onno Veldhuizen, the more intensely she disliked him. He was so convinced he was right. Even more than the rest of them. Nothing shook him. And he was full of himself, anyone could see that. He had big ambitions at InSec, and now that his department, Constitutional Order, was going to be amalgamated with part of the Foreign Intelligence section, the chief could well see his job swallowed up. That, or climb on the back of whoever headed the new section to an even higher position. Nailing the Amsterdam Cell was the step up he needed, and a university type like her was not going to scupper his plans.

But there was more to it than that. Lisette stopped rattling the pen. There was some strange personal antagonism between her boss and the DA that she couldn't quite fathom. Something was going on beyond her reach, beyond her control, and once again Lisette had the feeling that blame was being knocked along down the line, and that she would be the last domino in the row to fall. Unless of course the whole game was blown before it finished. She laid the pen across her notes. The wall clock clicked on one minute: ten twenty-five. Mick and the analyst Ingrid, who Lisette had asked to join them, and who had worked on the team before her promotion, came in together. Mick was early. As always. Rachid came in alone, bang on time. Ben a little late, with the usual 'Yo, gang!'

Lisette did not mention her collision with the chief.

'Ops tells me the Mansouri apartment is up and running,' she began. 'Thanks, Mick, for sorting that so quickly.' It had fallen into their laps, that one: ringleader Hassan Mansouri getting married so soon after the release, looking for an apartment. A few calls from Mick to a housing association and behold! Choice accommodation at a reasonable rent, with the Mansouris at the top of the list. An apartment the team dubbed the Big Brother House, for obvious reasons.

'Rachid, anything?'

Rachid had been listening to the hours and hours of tapes, making transcripts and translating anything from conversations in Berber that he thought relevant.

'Well, there was a bit of a row between Mansouri and Bassir about Bassir bringing someone to the house. Not clear who, just that Bassir wanted this friend along, and Mansouri didn't like it.'

Rachid flicked through some transcript notes.

'Other than that, not a lot,' he went on, 'except Najib and Bassir talked about an imam they both dislike, and Khaled Suleiman, the new arrival, that Syrian who speaks English with them . . .'

Rachid looked up to check the others knew who he meant. Mick nodded.

'He's been teaching them Arabic,' continued Rachid, 'and has convinced them all to hold private prayer meetings and a discussion group. At the house.'

'That tallies,' Ben chimed in. 'They're not going to the mosque any more.'

'This is significant,' said Ingrid. The analyst's rare pronouncements always had the effect of stopping the team in its tracks for a moment. She went on: 'If they are rejecting the teachings of the imam, it is a sure sign of radicalisation.'

'I agree that we should be keeping more of an eye on

Suleiman,' said Rachid. 'Mansouri and the others seem pretty impressed by him, except for Bassir, maybe.' Now that was even rarer: Rachid in harmony with something Ingrid said.

But Lisette looked away from him. She couldn't let this happen. She had to deflect attention, at least until the chief gave the go-ahead to come clean about the agent he had planted. This was *exactly* what she thought would happen, the objection she had raised with Veldhuizen. They didn't have the time and resources to waste on a pointless diversion. Let alone what the sense of betrayal would do to morale when it all came out.

'I take your point, Rachid, about this Suleiman, but for the time being I think we should keep our focus on Mansouri as ringleader,' she said.

'Based largely on the astonishing revelation that he is a distant relative of one of the Madrid bombers,' said Rachid, with a dismissive look at Ingrid, whose trawling through old Spanish intelligence reports had brought the connection to the surface.

'That, and the fact that he was the first to start wearing traditional dress, and has just got married,' said Lisette.

'Which could simply mean that he is devout, and that he wanted a wife,' said Rachid.

'But together it all fits the profile of a potential suicide bomber,' said Lisette. 'And he does draw the others around him, has done so especially over the past few weeks.'

'Because he has his own apartment now, and the others all live with their parents,' said Rachid. 'It's somewhere to go.'

'The man is *heavy* on the religion,' said Ben. 'His own new-style magic-show, the old homespun's not good enough for him. He was on to skinny Najib a while back about the young guys coming over from Morocco not being true believers, and according to the prophet it was *this*, and according to the prophet it was *that*, and the prophet said who knows what, and these guys from Morocco were just infiltrators and spies sent to undermine them.'

'And it was Mansouri who did all that online purchasing, whose computer had accessed all those dodgy websites,' said Mick, as usual clinching the argument. Lisette gave him a subtle nod of gratitude. If it wasn't for Mick, keeping Team C on track would be so much harder.

Rachid didn't answer. His face took on the bored, set expression it so often wore. Lisette edged the meeting onward, past the ever-present pitfalls – Rachid's negativity, Ben's irritating flippancy – into plans, strategies and action.

Two floors up, Onno Veldhuizen reached for his phone. He had heightened the truth a little about young Haddad reporting that 'an attack was imminent', but the Lammers woman needed a rocket up her arse. Too clever by half, she thought herself. Things needed to move faster. Needed a bit of a push. And he had just the idea of how that could happen, and of the man who would do it. He punched in a number in The Hague. There was barely half a ringtone before it was answered.

'Communications and Strategy. Mark Koning.'

'You old tosser.'

'Onno! James Bond himself.'

'How's life as the country's most imaginative "political aide"?' Veldhuizen's voice gave the job title an ironic turn.

'What is it you want?'

'The Amsterdam Cell.'

'Yes?'

'*You* know they are guilty, *I* know they are guilty, we all know they are guilty.'

'We do.'

'But our hands are tied. We thought we had them, but poof!

Free as birds. Because the fences *we* have to jump over are too high.'

'My associates certainly believe our current laws are inadequate to deal with terrorism.'

'And a group of conspirators caught on the eve of an act of terror, stopped in the nick of time, might spur things on a bit? Make the climate favourable for a review of the law?'

'It would. In fact, off the record, it's something my associates have rather been hoping might happen.'

'Good. And being in on the game would certainly be a nice little boost to *your* career. I'm experiencing pressure from similar quarters. Problem *is* . . .' Veldhuizen paused. 'The problem is that these men sometimes need a bit of a spur themselves.'

Silence.

Veldhuizen continued. 'A gentle push. Nothing too violent. Nothing that would actually *cause* any danger, just something that would bring them out of the undergrowth, make them panic a little, become a bit careless, make them slip. But that would nudge them into action – so we could pounce. Just in time.'

'You had in mind?'

'Well, a newspaper report. Something that slipped out a little titbit of harmless, trivial information that let them know someone was on to them. Snapping at their heels. That if they didn't get moving quick, the big dog would bite.'

'And you have an idea of what sort of little titbit might do that?'

'What are you doing for lunch?'

'That was delicious,' said Alex, leaning back in her chair. 'Really different.' She was wearing a 1950s print dress, with large crimson flowers, her hair swept up and knotted in a matching scarf. She looked as if she had been plucked from an exotic forest.

'It wasn't so long ago that lunch in Amsterdam meant bread and cheese or bread and ham, and a glass of buttermilk,' said Posthumus. 'And that was it. Or spread with some sort of mayonnaise-laden so-called salad if you were feeling adventurous. Foreigners couldn't believe it. Grown-ups drinking buttermilk, especially. Can you imagine being invited out to a business lunch, and expecting three courses and wine, and getting bread rolls and *buttermilk*?'

'My poor father,' said Alex. '*Mangiare da ospedale* he called it, "hospital food", and it pained his Sicilian soul. At home, he always cooked something for us himself, *and* we got a little watered-down wine. That shocked my friends.'

They had managed to get the last table on the narrow terrace – at knee-knocking distance from passing bicycles, squeezed up against an ivy-covered wall and next-door's front steps. But it was at least outdoors, on a car-free street, shaded by the trees along the canal.

'But this was good,' Posthumus agreed, folding his paper napkin into a tiny, neat square and placing it back on the table. 'Even if the service was slow. I mean, just how long does it *take* to make a sandwich? Even one with roasted beetroot, watercress and homemade hummus.'

'That's Amsterdam for you, laid-back . . .'

'And inefficient. I was in this restaurant in Brussels once, one of those old-fashioned places where the waiters flambé meat and make sauces at the table, and within a couple of minutes our waiter had made a sauce, brought the bill to one table, said goodbye and found the coats for the guests at another, *and* remembered the extra glass of wine I'd ordered. In Amsterdam that would have taken five times as long. And they'd have forgotten the wine. I think it should be a rule that every waiter in this city be taken to that restaurant and hung on a hook on the wall to watch for a week, to see how it's done.'

Alex laughed. 'Too much of that "we're all equals" attitude here, you think?'

'Service is not servility,' said Posthumus. 'It's simply a question of taking pride in your work. French waiters do. Italians. The Belgians. It's an honourable job, worth doing properly. But' – he raised his hands in defeat – 'don't get me started. We don't seem to notice bad service here. Foreigners are always complaining, though. Anna gets an earful from time to time. And, I admit, it's become a hobbyhorse of mine.'

'Pride in your work means a lot to you, doesn't it?'

Before he could answer, Posthumus's mobile rang. He reached into his pocket to switch it off, but saw the name on the screen.

'Oh, I'm sorry,' he said. 'It's rude of me, but do you mind if I take this?'

Alex signalled a 'go ahead'.

'Merel,' said Posthumus. 'How are you?'

The voice at the other end of the line sounded excited.

'Uncle Pieter . . . PP. Look, I'm so so so sorry. I can't make tonight. I've just had this call – Mark Koning, big spin doctor guy in The Hague with all *sorts* of connections and insider info, who I've been pestering for ages, and he's never returned a call, then suddenly he phones, completely out of the blue and says he read the first in my series on women, you know, women and Islam and life in Amsterdam, and says I'm ideal for this hot info, don't know what it is yet, I guess you'd call it an exclusive. Anyway he wants to meet, and I have to go across to The Hague at five, then I'll have to do the story right away. I'm sorry, I'm sorry. But I'm babbling . . .'

'Don't worry, it's really no problem. Work comes first.'

'It's just that this will save my neck with the editor. It's exactly the sort of "results, results" he's been going on at me about, shows him I really do have contacts and special access.

I can't let this slip away. And I've got the next of the women pieces to do tonight as well. I can't do it now because it's all based on this really wonderful Aissa woman I met, you know the day I met you and went on to a lecture at the library? Well, I interviewed her then, and she's very clued-up and insightful, and we're having a coffee later today, and I can't write the piece until I've spoken to her, and besides I think we're sort of becoming friends. I don't know, it's all very delicate, tentative. I don't know any Moroccans. Do you? We all live in our own little ghettoes, don't you think? But, hey, I'm babbling again. Look, can I give you a ring in a couple of days, when it's clearer where this Mark Koning thing is going, and we can sort out another time? I'm *so* sorry about tonight.'

Posthumus said a quiet goodbye, and replaced his phone in his pocket. Was she pulling back? It had taken him some courage to set that up. He was uncertain of this new feeling of a family bond, of whether he wanted it, of what could so easily snap it again. And the awkward turn of their first meeting hadn't made calling again any easier. Merel hadn't mentioned that when he finally did ring her, nor had she mentioned her father. But still. The whole situation had dredged up stuff about Willem that always lurked below the surface, something he was constantly aware of but managed to get by without facing full-on. Now all that was being hauled up into the light of day, bent and broken like that poor boy in the canal. Part of him wanted to run, part of him wanted to reach out to Merel, to comfort them both.

'The long-lost niece?' said Alex. 'The one you met a couple of weeks ago?' She was looking at Posthumus carefully.

'Yes. Yes, nearly a month ago now. It's difficult. There's a long, complicated history. We were going to meet up again tonight.'

'But she cancelled?'

Posthumus nodded.

'For a good reason?'

'Yes, I suppose so. This was going to be the first time, since she made contact. I didn't get back in touch at first, was waiting for her to call again . . .'

'But she didn't? Perhaps she thought it was your turn. She had made the first move, after all.'

'That's what Anna said. Anyway, I phoned her last week, and we were supposed to have dinner together tonight.'

'And now not.'

'No.'

'Oi! You two!' It was Sulung, walking around the corner from the Staalkade. 'Skiving, or what? I'm ready to go.'

Posthumus leapt up, looking at his watch. He was very rarely late.

'I hadn't noticed! I'll get the bill. No, no – my treat.'

Alex was reaching for her purse.

'But could you put this in your bag?'

Posthumus slipped her the Bart Hooft file. Alex gave him a look of mock reproof, and did what he asked.

'I stopped at Uitvaartcentrum Zuid on my way back,' said Sulung to Alex, as he reached the table, 'picked up that backlog of personal effects that I forgot to collect last week.' The brown envelopes containing whatever corpses may have had on them when they died. 'All sealed and signed for. Nothing much, just the usual. Bank passes, rings, pendants, the odd mobile. It's all on your desk. Oh, and the new one, too. The canal guy. Came in as I was leaving.'

Posthumus was still inside, waiting to pay. Sulung fidgeted impatiently. He didn't make conversation, but glanced at his watch a few times, and across the canal to the City Hall.

'I'll go fetch the car,' he said at last. 'Tell him I'll meet him on the corner.'

★ ★ ★

The apartment on Kop van Jut was on the ground floor, near the footpath that led up to the street. The door opened at a touch. Looked as if it had been forced.

'Careless,' said Sulung. The police usually closed up immediately if they had to force entry. 'Besides, they had the key.'

The men exchanged a glance.

Posthumus dropped his voice to a whisper. 'Someone in there, you think?' he said.

They could hear nothing. Usually, as a matter of course, they would ring the doorbell before entering, just in case there was a neighbour, family member, or flatmate inside, someone who for some reason had not shown up on records. Sulung reached for the bell, but Posthumus put a restraining hand on his wrist.

'Shall we call the police?'

'For what? If there was anyone there, they've gone,' said Sulung. 'Besides, we're big boys. Come on.'

He pushed the door open quietly, and Posthumus followed him inside. No one there. Small studio apartment, door opening directly into the living room, bedroom alcove to one side. It was, as the irritating cop had said, pretty much empty. Just the basics. TV still there. A few Arabic texts pinned up on one wall, the snake of a laptop cord lying across the table. If the place had been burgled, that was all the thief had bothered to take. Or the guy had had it with him when he drowned.

Posthumus took the camera out of the bag. Nothing much to photograph, but procedures had to be followed. He handed the camera to Sulung.

'Could you do this? I really have to take a leak. Should have gone at lunch.'

The bathroom was back beside the front door. The blue flash was already blitzing off the bare white walls behind him as he let himself in. Posthumus aimed at the bowl, closed his eyes and sighed.

Later, when he looked back on that moment, it seemed to Posthumus that he had heard the plastic runners on the shower curtain rattle. He couldn't be sure. One thing he was certain of was the pain. Just below the right shoulder blade. Then the sensation that his limbs were no longer his own, as his whole body went into spasm and collapsed, his head hitting the edge of the lavatory bowl. He thought he caught a glimpse of a pair of black and gold trainers as he went down. Or maybe that bit was something Sulung said.

Afterwards, Sulung's face, furrowed with concern, was the first thing Posthumus remembered seeing.

'Feel all right, mate?' the face was saying. 'Seems we disturbed a burglar after all.'

'You got yourself tasered,' the young doctor at the hospital told him. 'And managed to get knocked out in the process. The taser zapped you with fifty thousand volts, that's what made you collapse, hitting your head on the toilet did the rest. But there shouldn't be any long-term effects, your heart and blood pressure seem OK. You keep quite fit, don't you?'

Posthumus nodded. All those laps he swam each week at the Zuiderbad had done their bit. He winced slightly. Nodding sent a throb through his brain. But still, *tasered*?

'It's becoming the weapon of choice in parts of the criminal fraternity,' the doctor went on, as if he had asked the question aloud. 'Knocks you down for a bit, but no real harm done.'

It certainly didn't feel that way. Did this man know what he was talking about? He wasn't even Merel's age.

'Just two little marks below the shoulder blade, where the darts went in, like a snakebite,' the doctor continued. 'You can hardly see them, and they'll disappear in a day or two. But you hit your head, too, so we need to check for concussion. Feeling dizzy? Nauseated?'

Posthumus wasn't. And he could remember going to the apartment with Sulung, handing him the camera, going to the bathroom. He could repeat what Sulung had told him as they drove to the hospital. About hearing a yell from the bathroom, and seeing a skinny young man in a djellaba running out of the door and up the footpath.

'Short-term memory seems OK,' the doctor said. 'I reckon you can go home, if there's someone to keep an eye on you.'

'That's it?' said Posthumus. It seemed all very brisk.

'Well, we could keep you in here for observation, but you're not badly concussed. If there's any dizziness later, if you're having difficulty concentrating, or start losing your memory, then come back in. Go to bed early, and it's a good idea if someone can wake you up from time to time, just to make sure you can regain consciousness. You'll be fine.'

Posthumus said he did not feel fine, but the doctor was gone.

'That was quick,' he said to Sulung. He rubbed the side of his forehead where a small bump was forming. An odd wave of disfocus seemed to pass through his brain. Perhaps it was dizziness. Should they call the doctor again?

'Come on, mate, I'll get you home,' Sulung answered. 'Bit of a shock, and a bump on the head. You'll be all right.'

Bit of a shock? He would never forget that pain.

'I think De Dolle Hond would be a better idea,' said Posthumus. 'My friend Anna can take care of me. But what about the apartment?' They shouldn't leave that unlocked. Nothing examined yet.

'I'll sort that,' said Sulung. 'There wasn't much there, just religious texts. It won't hurt for once if I do it alone, provided you're OK to sign off on it. And I'll report the attack to the

police. Hope they find the little bastard. So where is this Dolle
Hond, anyway?'

Posthumus went immediately upstairs to rest, telling Anna to
call an ambulance if she could not rouse him. At six o'clock,
he came down again. As he opened the connecting door to the
café, he stopped. Alex was at the bar, her hair no longer knotted up in a scarf, but a loose tumble of black curls.

'PP! Are you all right?' She was across the room in seconds,
gave him a hug, and steered him towards the nearest chair.
'Something to drink?'

'Some fresh orange juice would be nice. Good to see you.
I'm OK, thanks, a bit dazed that's all. Not an invalid yet!' It
felt good to have her arm around him, all the same.

Anna came over with the orange juice.

'I think a good glass of the Sauvignon would do you
wonders,' she told him, then to Alex: 'Honestly, he's impossible when he's sick. But if he's refusing wine, then there must
be something wrong.'

Posthumus looked up at the two women. He felt warm.
Oddly elated.

'What were you two guys *thinking*, going in when the door
had been forced?' said Alex, sitting down at the table. 'Sulung
has been back there, anyway, with the police. Nothing taken,
they say. The laptop wasn't there when the police went round
originally. And nothing useful from our point of view, Sulung
says. And no other witnesses. No strange people reported
running away. Sulung said the police didn't seem very hope-
ful about finding whoever did it. Very sorry for you, and all
that. But a non-burglary from an anonymous dead person . . .
he said they gave the impression they had better things to do.'

'Like fining people for cycling without lights.' Anna couldn't
resist. She had been done a few days before. Outraged. In the

city where cyclists ruled, not having a functioning light on
your bike was as time-honoured a tradition as slagging off the
Rotterdam football team. She went back to the bar.

'You're staying here tonight?' Alex asked.

'Probably. The doctor says I should be woken up from time
to time,' said Posthumus. 'Anna has a spare room,' he added.
'And I think I might take tomorrow off. Rest a bit. It's Friday,
after all.'

'Actually, I was rather hoping you would come in,' said
Alex.

Posthumus looked at her. She'd put on a neat little black
jacket over the dress she'd been wearing at lunch, with a
fluff of a feather collar. Black stockings that really showed
off her legs.

'You see, I've found something,' Alex went on.

'Found something?'

'In Canalman's notebook. The one the police got his
address from. The notebook's all completely stuck together,
like papier mâché, though it's dried out a bit more since they
had it, I guess. I didn't notice at first, but it's one of those with
a little folder built into the inside cover. I managed to slit it
open, and there were business cards inside.'

'His?'

'No. No names or anything. They're more like ads. Just
three. One for a restaurant, in Brussels I think, it's hard to
read, and it's stuck to the other one, which is for a computer repair shop, also in Brussels. And there's a little laminated
one, announcing a website for a sofa company.'

'And you thought that because his laptop wasn't in the
apartment . . .'

'Exactly. Perhaps he didn't have it on him, either. Perhaps
he had taken it in for repair.'

'And so we could contact the shop, and ask if they have a

computer someone hasn't collected . . .' Posthumus thought a moment. 'They wouldn't necessarily have his name,' he said.

'But they would have the computer. There might be something on that.'

'It could take ages. There's sure to be more than one computer waiting for a late pick-up; we'd have to wait for the others to be eliminated, then convince them to send us the remaining one. That or travel to Brussels, and then there'd probably be a password, so you couldn't access anything.'

'The computer shop might help with that.'

'It would all take ages. Maya will blow a fuse.'

'She already has.' Alex looked sheepish. 'I already ran the idea past her and Sulung this afternoon. Sulung was quite curious, but Maya! Talk about *apoplexy*. I thought we were going to have another corpse on our hands.'

'So *that's* why you want me to come in tomorrow.'

'Maya's threatening to take over the case.'

'Then I'm definitely coming in!'

'It gets worse. You can't really read the address or telephone number on the card, but I googled the company name. There are three branches in Brussels.'

'Ah. So everything we've just said, times three. And maybe he did collect it after all, and it's at the bottom of a canal somewhere. It could all be a wild goose chase.' Posthumus caught the glint in Alex's eye. 'But worth it. You know I can't resist something like this. We can't just let it go.'

Alex grinned. A red glass earring flashed from beneath her curls. Posthumus sipped the last of his drink.

'But there could just be something closer to home,' he said, after a while. 'That sofa website, was it dot nl?'

'Yes. I remember it. Casablancasofas dot nl.'

'So maybe he was buying a sofa. The apartment was pretty bare.'

'And they'd have some record?'

'Could be.'

Alex took out her iPhone. Within seconds she was on the website.

'That's interesting,' she said. 'It's not just online. Seems to be part of a furniture shop on Bos en Lommerweg. That's near the apartment, isn't it?' Another few seconds. 'Pretty much walking distance.'

'So maybe he wasn't shopping online.'

'Went in to the shop, you mean?'

'Maybe that's where he picked up the card. Maybe the website shows a bigger selection.'

'And if he was buying something, the shop could have his name.'

'Possibly. Nothing's been delivered yet. It's a long shot, but it's worth a try. Before tackling Brussels . . . and Maya.'

'There's a number,' said Alex, looking back at her iPhone. 'You'll phone tomorrow? Ask if they had an order for, what was it?'

'Marcantilaan 97. Yes, first thing.'

'Brilliant!' Alex jumped up, and gave Posthumus a high five. 'I'll be in the office in the morning. University in the afternoon, but you'll do it in the morning? I want to find out! I can see why you get into this sort of thing. But, look, I've got to go, I'm going to be late.'

'Lectures this evening, too?' asked Posthumus.

'No, dinner.'

'Hot date?'

Alex gave him a wink. 'I certainly hope so.'

She kissed the air rapidly three times, turned and waved to Anna, who was pouring a beer, and was gone.

Posthumus stood up, and made his way over to the bar. He was still feeling a little odd. Detached. Almost as if he were stoned. The patterns on the Delft vases, the moustachioed heads carved into the shelf-supports along the top of the wooden wainscoting, stood out with an extraordinary clarity. Like he was seeing them for the first time.

'Feeling all right?' asked Anna. 'You look a little crestfallen.'

'Think I'll sit here for a bit,' said Posthumus.

He took up his usual stool, against the wall.

'What was all that about?' asked Anna. 'Alex looked very animated.'

'A possible lead in the canal case,' said Posthumus.

'Listen to you! "Leads", "cases". Sherlock Holmes strikes again.'

'I think I'd be more Hercules Poirot,' said Posthumus with a laugh. 'Perhaps I should have tisane instead of another juice.'

De Dolle Hond was filling fast. The usual Thursday-night crowd of Amsterdammers out on the town before the week-end tourist takeover. Anna brought Posthumus his orange juice, but did not stop to talk. He looked about him, enjoying the sensation of the familiar suddenly seeming sharp, bright, new. Things he was sure he had not noticed before. A print of the Oude Kerk near the fireplace, the fact that the expression of the face on a Toby jug exactly matched the one carved in the shelf bracket below it; the way the collection of old medals and badges pinned on the board by the bar glinted. I Love Ringo! Free Kuwait. ONLY CONNECT. Flashing like neon. Posthumus stood up.

'I think I'll go and lie down for a bit,' he said to Anna.

She came over.

'You OK?'

'Just a little light-headed.'

'I'll come up and check on you in a minute.'

'If you could.' Posthumus looked again at the medals. He bent forward, and examined a few intently. That was it! A faint bell that had been ringing at the back of his head clanged more loudly. *Military.*

'Where did you get these?' he asked, cradling a couple of the medals, still dangling on their ribbons, in his palm.

'How on earth should I know? Most of those have been around all my life. Customers used to pin things up there all the time. Are you *sure* you're OK?'

Posthumus nodded. He scrutinised the medals again, selected one, unpinned it, and turned to go back upstairs. The number of times he had sat below that board of badges and medals, incuriously taking it in. No *wonder* the image had seemed familiar. He slipped the little medallion he had chosen into his pocket. It was made of dull metal, and depicted an eagle inside a star.

Not quite the same, but near enough to be going on with. It was like the design that had been drawn on that distasteful dildo. That Bart Hooft had tattooed on his arm.

FRIDAY
10 JUNE 2011

9

Posthumus did not die during the night. He did not even slip into a coma. But in the morning he rather wished he had. He felt as if his head were filled with gravel, and coarsely ground sand stuffed the eye sockets. His limbs were limp, and it seemed that a suction pipe fitted just below the ribcage had drained every part of his body of any sort of vibrancy. This was nothing to do with concussion. It was the result of his insistence (now much regretted) that Anna obey doctor's orders to the letter, and wake him every two hours during the night. Anna, who all her life had been able to drop off to sleep as her head hit the pillow, had shaken the inveterate insomniac into consciousness, leaving him to lie sleepless for an hour or so and then, just as he was slipping back into sweet oblivion, reappeared like a malicious harpy to snatch sleep from him all over again.

The coffee tasted sour and gritty. It was the usual week-day stuff, not the special Sunday-afternoon brew. Posthumus stood at the bar. No time to sit. He was late. It was raining. He was wearing the same clothes as the day before. The bump on his forehead hurt. He should have phoned in sick, but there was no way that he was going to give Maya a gap to come in and stomp all over this. He wanted to do it properly. Besides, something had occurred to him in that suspended half-asleep state in which he had spent most of the night. He said a brusque goodbye to Anna, took an umbrella from the stash of abandoned ones in an old coal scuttle just inside the door, and set out for the Staalkade. He was on the bridge leading across to the Wing Kee Eating House before he noticed that two ribs of the umbrella were broken, bent like fractured bird's wings, directing a stream of water down the back of the light, linen jacket that had seemed appropriate the day before. The temperature had dropped a good eight or nine degrees since then.

Posthumus made his way to the Nieuwmarkt, and across the square where a few desultory stallkeepers were setting up for the little daily food market. His leather soles slipped on the zigzag paving. Scraps of paper flitted about the square, grew damper and heavier, gave up the struggle, flopped on to the stones and got plastered there by the battering rain. Posthumus dredged into his brain, trying to reconstruct what had seemed so clear as he'd lain awake hours earlier. Something about the canal case and that terrier cop. He remembered. 'Probably one of your drunken foreigners taking a piss into the canal, and falling in,' the cop had said. Couldn't be. Surely not. If the guy was Muslim, surely he wouldn't drink? Even more so if he was in traditional dress, from a Muslim country. But then Posthumus had drunk Moroccan wine. And there was Turkish *raki*. So, maybe. But pissing in the canal? Wouldn't that be a no go? The Moroccan guys at the Zuiderbad even showered in their underwear. But there were other explanations. Like the terrier had said. Maybe he tripped, maybe he was unwell, couldn't swim. The cops and the coroner had done their jobs. No foul play. Yet something, for Posthumus, did not quite fit. Did not ring true. The same as with Bart Hooft. Something wasn't in the right place, and when that happened, it was Posthumus who became the terrier. He could not let go.

'PP!' Alex called over to him from Reception the moment he was through the door.

'Speak to you in a minute,' he said. 'I'm soaked.'

'I've got to talk to you now, before you go upstairs. I've messed up.' She was pale.

'What's the matter?'

'When you were late, I thought you'd decided to stay home after all. You're *never* late.' She was almost accusing. 'I know that it's not my job, I should have left this to you, but I thought I'd check on that furniture shop. Before phoning round those computer stores. It was either that or take it all up to Maya right away. I thought that maybe if I'd already done some-thing, if it was already happening she wouldn't just quash it. But now you've got to move quick. *Please.* The canal guy . . . he's the cousin or something of the man who owns the shop. "Like a son to me," the man said.'

'You told him?'

'No, no, I couldn't. I just mentioned the address, Marcantilaan 97, and asked if they had a delivery due there, and he said no of course not, it was the address of his relative. Then he got all panicked and asked what this was about, was something the matter with papers. He'd heard me say "city council", but didn't catch the department, and was going on about Amir being a good boy, could not have done anything wrong, that he had been in Brussels, would be back today lunchtime at the latest. I just didn't have the heart. Not over the phone. Besides, we're not even sure . . .'

'And?'

'And I told him not to worry, but that we needed to speak to him, and that we'd be there right away.' Alex stood up, one hand twisting and tugging at the silk scarf she was wearing as a belt. 'Sorry. I didn't know what to do. I've just got off the phone now. Sulung's not here. I thought of telling Maya I felt sick, and then going there myself. Or of confessing to her. Or to phone you. But thank God you've come in. The poor man's just waiting there, thinking who knows what? I'm sorry, I shouldn't have done this. I've made it all worse.'

'OK, all right,' said Posthumus. It wasn't easy breaking the news of a death over the telephone, he knew. He'd had to do it before, didn't like it himself. He preferred to send a letter, if he could. But he'd not had to do it face to face before, and he liked that idea even less. 'Perhaps I should phone him,' he said.

'But the man's waiting there for a visit, and all stressed out. And it might all be a mix-up. We don't really know if it is his relative. Would you go? Now? Please? For my sake? There are those photos that were in the bag, and the other stuff, the notebook. He might recognise them. Then at least it's certain there's no mix-up. He sounded so nice over the phone.'

Posthumus sighed. This was even worse. An identification interview. But then he had been trained for moments like this – though what did a week-long counselling course ever teach you? He held out his hand for the car keys.

'Thank you. You're a lovely man.' Alex leaned over the Reception desk, hugged his neck and kissed his cheek. She handed him the brown envelope that had come from the undertakers.

The SatNav took him past the Royal Palace and the Westerkerk, around the edge of the Jordaan, beyond his normal patch of the city; across the Kostverlorenvaart and out through the immigrant neighbourhoods of De Baarsjes and Bos en Lommer. Satellite dishes everywhere. Arabic on shop signs, Turkish names on storefronts, a shisha smoking lounge. Posthumus had last smoked a hubbly bubbly pipe when he was in his twenties, but that had been a dope thing. He guessed this was something else. Or maybe not. The rain clattered on the Smart car roof, scudded off its snubby bonnet. He had switched on the heating in the car, hung his jacket over the back of the passenger seat. He hoped it was drying out. He felt sticky, tired, worn thin. The gravel in his skull had become cotton wool, his own fuel reserves clunked on Empty. He didn't feel up to this. If it hadn't been Alex who had asked . . .

Dully he obeyed the voice from the dashboard, skirting the Erasmuspark, and turning into Hoofdweg, towards the angular, edged skyline over Bos en Lommerplein. The gables of the city centre seemed far behind him. Here Amsterdam was high-rise. His eye caught a grey 1960s office block with a single HOTEL sign at the top. Who would want to stay here? Posthumus shrugged, stopped at the red light at the junction with Bos en Lommerweg. He looked across at the market square. Nearly all the women were in headscarves – loosely draped, tightly bound, black, white, multicoloured. Did they all really want to dress like that? Even those who said they did, wasn't that something forced on them by husbands, fathers, brothers? Objects of male possession. Posthumus felt uneasy. Women had always been comfortable equals in his milieu. For a moment he had the impression he was not in Amsterdam.

Left on to Bos en Lommerweg, and then across, where ring-road traffic thundered into an underpass below him, into the Kolenkit Quarter. That must be the 'Coalscuttle' church, across the way from a stretch of wasteland. It looked more like the skeleton of a dead animal, Posthumus thought, a ribcage and one stark leg bone sticking up in the air. He slowed the car. The disembodied voice told him he was nearing his destination.

Casablanca Sofas took up a double shopfront between a greengrocer and a boutique selling elaborate Moroccan bridal gowns. Posthumus pushed open the door. A neatly dressed Moroccan man about his own age, with a short-clipped beard, was waiting just inside the door.

'You are from the girl I spoke to earlier? From the council?' The man held out his hand. 'Mohammed Tahiri. I am from Amir's family. What has he done? I can't believe it. I have papers, I can vouch for him.'

The man's Dutch was good. Posthumus had been expecting a struggle. He introduced himself. Didn't mention his department.

'Are there any other relatives in Amsterdam? Close relatives?'

'In Morocco, yes. Not in Amsterdam. Just me, my wife, son and daughter. He is a cousin, from a distant branch of the family.'

'Is there anywhere we can talk?' Posthumus looked around. There was no separate office, only a desk in the far corner. There was no one else in the shop. Tahiri locked the door, flipped the sign to Closed, and walked towards the desk.

'Here, here, please sit,' he said, indicating one of the customer chairs, placed to face the desk, with their backs to the shop.

Mohammed was glad the man from the council – what was his name? Postma-something – could not see his face as he walked back towards his desk. His stomach knotted. He felt sick, and short of breath. Mohammed knew. From the man's look, from his questions, from his whole bearing, Mohammed knew: Amir was dead. The man did not have to say. But it came. Photographs. Small, damaged photographs. But, yes, Amir. Mohammed felt light, very calm. Empty. The words passed him by. Like a fragrance. Dates, times, details. Canal. Drowning. Common accident. Drunkenness. Swimming. Mohammed responded, heard his answers coming as if some other person was giving them. Yes, formal identification. Body. Police. Undertakers.

Mohammed leaned his elbows on the desk and cupped his face in his hands.

'He was young, so young. And *my* responsibility in Amsterdam. I have failed my family.'

Posthumus waited a while, then went on. 'As I was saying, you will probably have to make a formal identification.' He felt frayed. Not up to this at all. 'I will notify the police that we now know who . . .' He stopped himself saying 'the body' just in time. '. . . who Amir is. They will probably contact you. If the family wants to repatriate him, the funeral director can help with that.' He jotted down names and numbers on a pad on the desk. 'Look, I've written everything down. The funeral company, the police details. And here is my card. Technically, now that we have established family who will look after funeral arrangements, this is no longer anything to do with us, but please give me a ring if anything is not clear, or later if you have any questions.' He thought a moment, then added: 'And look, it's nearly the weekend. I'll write my mobile number on the back.' He handed his card back to Mohammed. 'My condolences.'

'This besmirches his name!' said Mohammed. 'He was a devout boy, a good boy, a careful boy. I hoped he would marry my daughter, give guidance to my son. He was not the sort of boy to fall in a canal. He did not drink alcohol. Monday you said? Monday last week? He was with us that night. We had dinner. He stayed for the evening prayer. He was not drunk!'

There was a rattle at the door. Mohammed looked up. Najib, putting his face to the glass and looking in. Then suddenly he was gone.

'My son,' said Mohammed, with a gesture to the front of the shop. 'I'll go and see.'

He walked across the shop and opened the door, looking up and down the street.

'I don't understand,' he said as he returned. 'He's just disappeared.'

Posthumus had already risen to go. It was almost lunch-time, and he had not even had breakfast.

'I don't understand,' said Mohammed. 'Something is wrong.'

'Once again, Mr Tahiri, my condolences.' He needed to get out.

Posthumus walked towards the Smart car, looking up and down Bos en Lommerweg. Something was wrong, all right. When Mohammed Tahiri had looked up to the door from his desk, Posthumus had turned in his seat. He had caught a glimpse of a skinny youth wearing a traditional Moroccan djellaba. He could not be sure, but as the lad disappeared from view Posthumus thought that – just above the low sill of the plate-glass window – he had seen the flash of black and gold trainers.

The rain had stopped. Posthumus drove back along the Bos en Lommerweg, away from the Kolenkit Quarter. He missed the turn on to Hoofdweg. He was tired, sunk in thought. Not to mention ravenous. He hadn't bothered with the SatNav. But he could take a right a little further on, then go through the Jordaan. He was about to change lanes for the turn, when he saw a parking spot, and across the road a large white building, with lines of windows shaped like Arabic tile patterns. Theatrecafé Mozaïek. Coffee, food and a break. Posthumus parked the car, crossed the street and went in.

To his left, widely spaced tables, some girls talking loudly by the window, a middle-aged man in the far corner with a young man in a djellaba. Posthumus felt a sharp stab in the gut. He turned to look full on. The Dutchman was staring at him aggressively, the young man was speaking on his telephone, face down, chin cocked towards the wall. Posthumus looked at the youth's feet. Plain black shoes. No need to be paranoid. Up ahead, around the corner of the bar was a cosier nook. Secluded, quieter, soft armchairs and sofas. Posthumus sank into a seat, and picked up a menu.

Fayyad Haddad, known to most around him as Khaled, ended the call, opened the back of his phone and slipped out the battery and SIM card.

'I know, I know,' he said. His English, like that of the man opposite him at the Theatrecafé Mozaïek, was accented, but correct. 'Standard procedure. I was about to do it when the thing rang. I can't be off for too long. Looks suspicious. And I don't like meeting here, now that they know me. It's too close. I could be seen.'

'There are some things that can't happen by email,' said Veldhuizen. He glanced at the crumpled supermarket bag on the floor between the table and the wall. 'And *you* would attract less attention if you'd come here in Western dress.'

'Even worse if they saw me like that. I'm supposed to beam myself in here from home? Next time somewhere further away, please, and not a café.'

Veldhuizen was silent. Cheeky little shit, telling him his job.

'And what's going on, anyway?' said Haddad. 'That was Najib Tahiri, screaming like a cat because the police were at his cousin's apartment photographing the place, two of them, and now at his father's shop. No uniforms. Something to do with you lot?'

'Who the fuck's his cousin?'

Haddad did not answer immediately.

'Amir Loukili, know the name?' He held Veldhuizen's eye.

Veldhuizen shrugged.

'He tasered one of them!' Haddad grinned. 'Then fled.

Quite the little hothead is Najib, and he likes his new toy. He says his cousin was away. Our little man seems to have been taking the opportunity to have a good snoop, and almost got himself busted. But a useful man, our Najib, has initiative. Needs controlling, but he's open to new ideas. He's very attentive to my little talks. Even wants me to marry his sister.'

'You!'

'Oh, I'm in there.' Haddad grinned again. 'I've always been good at mixing business with pleasure. I'm steering clear of the parents for the moment, but playing along happily. She is, shall we say, responsive. Clever woman. Mind of her own. Certainly not one to let her brother or anyone else arrange a marriage for her, I'd guess. Still, we can let Najib have his little fantasies. Wouldn't be a bad match, though. I can also be quite . . . *forceful*.'

Veldhuizen was unamused. 'Business,' he said. 'This Najib might appreciate my little gift.' He nodded again to the supermarket bag.

'Some rounds as well?'

'Sufficient. I want movement. Fast. That's why I wanted to see you in person, to *emphasise* . . .' Veldhuizen's eyes fixed on the young man. 'To emphasise this fact, and the consequences of inaction.' He managed to outstare Haddad. 'There's a piece in today's *Nieuwe Post* . . .'

'Merel Dekkers.'

'You read it? With *your* bad Dutch?'

'Najib was ranting about it. Got Alami and Mansouri all worked up. Bassir tried to calm them down, said they shouldn't take it seriously. There was another piece by the same woman, all about Najib's sister. He was going on about family honour and betrayal, and to top it this Dekkers woman comes up with a finger-pointing story on the "Amsterdam Cell". That makes her enemy number one as far as Najib is concerned.'

'And the others?'

'Haven't heard. Mansouri will be pissed, I know. It seems this Dekkers pretty much says he's about to blow up Central Station or a politician or something. He and his family from Spain. No names, but it's clear it's him.'

'And?'

'That could swing him to do something, but Mansouri is not your man. Bassir is the one to watch.'

'My people say Mansouri is the ringleader.'

'He's religious, yes, but that's all – though this could push him further. I tell you, Bassir is your man. Najib's a friend of his, and he told me that once—'

Veldhuizen gave a dismissive flick of the hand. 'I don't care who does what, but something must happen. And soon,' he said. 'Use that newspaper piece. Get them going. I'll give you this week. And I want good warning up front.'

'I have an idea,' said Haddad. 'And I know what to do with this.' He bent over and put the supermarket bag into his backpack. 'Now I've got to go. Friday prayers in a minute, at Mansouri's house, and I'm star of the show.'

He got up, slipped the battery and SIM card back into his phone, and without waiting to be dismissed walked out of the café.

Posthumus had followed a spinach and feta omelette with an excellent New York-style cheesecake. He knocked back the remains of a third cup of coffee, got up to pay at the bar, and left. The café was beginning to fill for lunch. The Dutchman and the Arabic-looking youth had gone. The food had helped, but now his brain buzzed with caffeine, while still somehow remaining grained, fuzzy. The bridge over the Kostverlorenvaart was up. A long wait, while three boats passed.

There was a temp on Reception by the time he got back to Staalkade, Alex having already left for her university classes. Maya and Sulung were not in the office. There was an angry note from Maya on his desk. She had booked the car from midmorning, would he kindly adhere to procedures, blah blah. Off on a house-visit. He felt sorry for Sulung, but hoped the house-visit was a killer. One of those that took all day. There were only two emails in his inbox. One from the department director. Posthumus opened it immediately, and whooped. He wrote a quick reply, then hit New Message:

Cornelius

Good news! The powers that be have unknotted the budget handkerchief and dropped out a few coins. Not a lot, and not often – for a trial period, and only the real anonymous ones: no name, no family (almost had one for you today). Later, perhaps poems for others as well. Will forward details, and you'll need to contact Accounts to sort a contract.

Best

Pieter Posthumus

The email from Alex was full of more apologies, also regarding the car and Maya, and asking him to let her know how it went. With her mobile number, in case he did not know it. Later, thought Posthumus. He didn't have the energy just now. He fetched the yellow file marked Marcantilaan 97, amended the cover to include the name Amir Loukili, made the relevant adjustments to the Case Report and in the computer, then placed the file on the Closed Cases shelf. He faxed the police with his findings, glad that he did not have to speak to anyone. What was it about the police that always made him feel guilty about something? That sent a twinge of nervousness through him even when he went in to a station to pick up house keys? Sure, there were the clashes in the eighties and nineties when the police raided the squat, and being arrested hadn't been pleasant. But nothing heavy. Why was the now respectable, middle-aged Pieter Posthumus afraid of the law? Some deep sense of not fitting in, perhaps?

Posthumus sighed, and tapped the papers and pens (knocked askew by Maya) on his desk back into neatness. He made a single call, to Rob Mulder at the city morgue. Made a few notes, then began work on the bank accounts backlog. By three o'clock he'd had enough. This was hardly the most riveting aspect of his work, even at the best of times. He told the temp at Reception that he'd had a bad night, was not feeling well, and was going home.

It was only as he was crossing the bridge to the City Hall and the flea market that Posthumus realised he was returning along the route he took *into* work in the mornings. On the way home, he usually carried on clockwise from the Staalkade, to make a circle back to Krom Boomssloot through the Nieuwmarkt. Now, he'd walked anti-clockwise instinctively. Maybe because he had started the day in reverse, coming in from De Dolle Hond.

'*Schat!* You look a mess!' Lotti was doing her last coffee round before packing up for the day. 'Just look at you! Stubble, crumbled clothes. Not like you at all, *schat*. Have you been on the piss, or what? Here, coffee for you, on the house.'

Posthumus's heart sank. He couldn't refuse. Lotti trundled her cart closer.

'My God and little fishes! Is that a bump on your head? Been in a fight?'

'It's a long story,' said Posthumus. 'I got it at work.'

'Heavens preserve us! Zombies!'

Posthumus managed a laugh. 'Something like that,' he said.

'You need the protection of a good woman, that's what you need. Coming up, Marie!'

Lotti swayed off to deliver a coffee. Posthumus took cautious sips of plasticky brew, and looked around him. Tools, bicycle parts, scrappy metal obscurities this end of the market, spread on the ground. One or two proper stalls. Vinyl LPs, the stamp man. Posthumus felt in his shirt pocket, placed the coffee unfinished on Lotti's cart, and walked across to the stall. The stamp man also sold coins, badges and medals. In his pocket, Posthumus still had the medallion he had taken from the board at De Dolle Hond.

'I wonder if you can help me?' he asked.

'As long as you're not a time-waster,' the stamp man said. He looked Posthumus up and down, glanced at his head. 'Or a thief.'

'It's about a military medal,' said Posthumus. 'Or at least, I *think* it might be military. A badge of some sort maybe. A bit similar to this, but . . . do you have a pen?'

From memory, Posthumus sketched the design of Bart Hooft's tattoo on the scrap of paper the stamp man had half-heartedly proffered. The man examined the medal. He seemed suddenly more alert.

'Want to sell this?' he said.

'No. It belongs to a friend. But I'd be interested to know if this other one means anything to you.'

'From the same friend? Also a medal?'

'I . . . I think so,' said Posthumus. 'I haven't seen that one yet.'

The man eyed him suspiciously. He picked up the scrap of paper, his lips curving downwards. 'Couldn't say for sure. I'd have to see it,' he said.

Posthumus put out his hand to retrieve the medal. 'I'd be really interested to know,' said Posthumus. 'Anywhere I could find out? My friend might well want to part with them, but wants to check first.'

The stamp man shrugged. 'You come past most days, don't you?' he said.

Posthumus nodded.

The man reluctantly dropped the medal into Posthumus's open palm, folded the scrap of paper, and put it in his own pocket. 'I'll have a look through some catalogues at home,' he said.

'Don't you like my coffee, then?' Lotti's voice sounded just behind Posthumus's shoulder.

'No, no, just doing some business,' he said, draining the cup she was holding out to him, managing not to grimace.

Posthumus walked quickly through the market and up the stairs past the Rembrandt House, edging his way through a tour group dawdling aimlessly on the pavement, waiting to go in. One more thing, while his mind was on Bart. It wouldn't take long, and he was sure there was an internet café just a bit further up. He didn't want to do this on his own computer, and certainly not at work.

The attendant was absorbed in a computer game of his own. Good, thought Posthumus, but still selected a screen at an angle to the attendant's line of vision. He googled Slave Register. Lots about Africa, the Caribbean, the American South, but there it was: the Slave Register, adult site for registration of slaves and submissives, each assigned a Slave Registration Number. Posthumus fished in his pocket for the scrap of paper on which he had noted the barcode number from the tattoo on the back of Bart's neck. He glanced around him sheepishly, clicked on the website, and was relieved to see he didn't have to register himself for access. He accepted the website's terms and conditions, clicked Continue as a Guest and entered Bart's number in the search box. Immediately, the message flashed back. Profile Deleted. Posthumus sighed. It was as he had thought. Bart Hooft had wiped his slate clean.

Back on the Krom Boomssloot, Posthumus opened the narrow street door, picked up his post and newspaper, and slowly climbed the stairs. Outside Gusta's apartment, he used one toe to smooth out the doormat, which was half curled up against the wall and had been irritating him all week. He could smell tobacco smoke through the door. He was letting himself into his own apartment when his mobile rang. He didn't recognise the number, was about to ignore it, but sighed and pushed Receive.

'Yes?'

'Mr Posthumus. It is Mohammed Tahiri. Please, I need your help.'

Posthumus closed his eyes.

'Mr Posthumus, I have been to the undertakers. It is indeed Amir, his father is going to repatriate him. And I have spoken to the police.'

There was a pause.

'I am glad to hear that,' said Posthumus. 'But I am not sure how I can now be of help.'

'Something is *wrong*, Mr Posthumus. It is not normal. This is not like Amir. I said to the police that Amir was not the sort of boy to fall in a canal, but the officer would not listen.'

'If the police think nothing is wrong, then perhaps they are right. This is their business, surely?'

'Sometimes, Mr Posthumus, it does not help to have a name like Mohammed Tahiri.'

Posthumus walked over to his front window.

'You seem a good man, Mr Posthumus, and you know something of these things. Will you help me? I want to know what happened.'

Posthumus looked out over the canal. His resistance was down. Besides, he had already made a decision for himself, earlier that morning.

'Will you?'

'Perhaps we should meet again.'

'Thank you. *Thank* you. There are some things I want to tell you.'

'Would tomorrow morning suit you, about ten?' said Posthumus.

'At the shop? My house, rather. I'll send you the address. I will be waiting. And thank you again, Mr Posthumus.'

'Please, call me Pieter.'

His jacket was still damp. Posthumus slipped it off, and hung it over the back of a chair. A hot shower. First, a quick text to Alex.

Body in canal indeed = shop cousin, but odd developments.
     Too tired now. OK phone over w/e?

A text with Mohammed Tahiri's home address beeped in. Posthumus was putting the phone down on the table when it rang. Irritated, he glanced at the screen. Merel.

'Oh, PP, I need some fatherly advice.'

Ouch.

'I've made a mess of things. Those two articles I told you about yesterday, on the Amsterdam Cell?'

'I haven't seen them yet, I've only just got my paper now.'

'One of them's created a bit of a stir. I've been getting odd phone calls on my landline since. You know the sort of thing. Rings, number withheld, someone hangs up. But it's not that so much. I guess I can get that sorted out if it carries on. What somehow bothers me more is that I think I've really offended Aissa, you know, the woman I told you about, and I was hoping we could be friends? She's just cancelled on me, was really upset. Her brother is really hassling her about the interview, and I feel I'm to blame. I didn't tell her about the other piece, and apparently he's accusing her of betrayal, by associating with me. And on top of it all she's just heard a relative of hers has died. Drowned. It's awful!'

'Drowned? Was he called Amir? Is her name Aissa Tahiri?'

'How did you know? What is all this?'

Merel suddenly sounded panicked.

'Don't worry. Just something to do with work. And not now. At the moment *nothing* is going to stand in between me and a hot shower. I've also had a pretty torrid day.'

'Sorry! Here's me just launching in to my troubles, I didn't even ask. What's happened?'

Posthumus's shoulders slumped. Perhaps he had sighed, he wasn't sure. There was a silence.

'That's if you don't mind me asking,' said Merel, a stranger once again.

'No, no,' said Posthumus. 'But let's save it all for one go. I'd really like to meet up . . . and to be of any help I can. Maybe later tonight?'

'I have a date, but I could try to change it.'

'Tomorrow, then. In the morning?'

'That would be lovely. Thanks, PP.' Her voice warmer, engaging. Even over the phone there was a quality of Willem about her. Or maybe he was simply tired. Imagining things.

'You live out west, don't you?' he said.

'Just off the Kinkerstraat.'

'I'm going to be out that way, and I've found a great café, does an excellent cheesecake, Café Mozaïek. Do you know it? It's a bit further than you, at the start of the Bos en Lommerweg, but you have a bike?'

'Yes, to all those.'

'Good. Till tomorrow then. About eleven?'

'Catcha then, PP!'

A sharp breath. Willem used to say that. Posthumus began to speak. But she was gone.

That shower.

'As Heisenberg himself put it,' said the professor, 'what we observe is not nature itself, but nature exposed to our method of questioning.'

He looked up at the students in the raked tiers of the lecture hall. Not a spark. Most staring into laptop screens, a few even sending text messages on their telephones.

'One way of putting it,' the professor went on, 'is that the Uncertainty Principle is a form of *observer effect*. It's like checking the pressure in a car tyre.'

He smiled and looked about again. Still nothing.

'It is difficult to do that, you see, without letting out a little of the air. So in checking the pressure, we change it.'

Alex's phone beeped. She winced. She was certain she had turned it off. But she could not resist a glance at the screen. PP. Discreetly she opened the message, then texted back:

Intrigued. Yes phone me. Ax

She switched off the telephone, looked up, and caught the professor's disapproving eye.

'I am sorry to get you in last thing on a Friday,' said Lisette, 'but you've all seen the article in *De Nieuwe Post*. The chief believes this is going to spur the targets into action, and I must say I think he has a point.' She hadn't taken a meeting room. Team C was in her office. Ingrid, the analyst, too. 'That's why I asked you, Rachid and Ingrid in particular, to leave off everything and jump to today's midday prayers, and to anything that's been picked up this morning.' She nodded to them both. 'I know there's a backlog, and this is disruptive, but thank you.'

'Mountains of stuff,' said Rachid. His voice still had the hard edge of complaint Lisette had tried to smooth earlier that morning. 'All the calls, everything in the Big Brother House. I'm the thin point it all has to come through. It's too much.'

'Mick has been helping,' said Ingrid quietly.

'And I think you and the chief are right,' said Mick, with a glance to Lisette. 'Things are on the boil. Khaled, the Syrian, was very fiery in what I guess passes as a Friday sermon at the house. Said the journalist who wrote it should be taught a lesson, that it was time to act. But more than that. Calling for jihad.' He sifted through the papers in front of him, and read aloud: 'They think we are guilty, whether we do something or not. So let's show them! We'll do something.'

'Nothing more concrete?' said Lisette. 'That could just be hot talk. Anyone else say anything?'

'Mansouri strangely silent. El Mardi chipping in. He's been at the house a lot, by the way, since he got back from Brussels. Joining in quite vehemently. Bassir also coming up with strong stuff about sharia law and an Islamic state, but nothing to grab on to. It's the Syrian who's the most outspoken. Says he has an idea, actually calls it "a plan of action". That could be something, he says he needs to speak to people first. But something is going on there.'

'I told you he and the Tahiri boy needed watching,' said Rachid.

'The boy wasn't there today.'

'Something's up at Casa Tahiri, my go-man says,' said Ben. 'Shop closed, sister a blizzard on a Vespa coming home from uni at lunchtime, don't know about Najib. And the Syrian's up to something, too. Spotted after midnight last weekend, slipping out in Western dress. But the go-man is on to that.'

'The upset at the Tahiris could be because of the other article in *De Nieuwe Post*,' said Mick. 'Part of a series on young women and the veil. The Tahiri girl was the main focus. Same spread, so you could easily make the association that she was somehow involved with the Cell. Both stories were by the same journalist.' He checked his notes again. 'Merel Dekkers.'

'I should very much like to know where she got her information from,' said Lisette. She kept her voice light, neutral, but her gaze took in each of the team in turn. She had just done something she'd never done before, hoped never to have to do again. She'd discreetly asked Coco, who headed up Team B, to look into the Dekkers woman. Under wraps. She hated this. The Syrian, and now this. It felt like a double betrayal, but Veldhuizen's implications of a leak from her own team had got to her.

'The Spanish connection is old information,' Lisette went on. 'It was in the report to the DA, so the knowledge was out there, though far from public. That Mansouri is considered the ringleader brings things closer to home. Could be deduction, but it could also raise the question of a leak. And that he is up to something new is news even to us. It would seem.'

There was an awkward silence.

'We can look into her possible sources,' said Mick. 'It could well be from something the Tahiri woman knows, even something she is party to, that she's passed on.' He looked at Ingrid, who nodded. 'Or maybe the journalist is putting two and two together, from what she's found out. And as Ingrid pointed out yesterday, not just with Mansouri but with all of them, we have *all* the signs: the radical talk, the traditional dress, the religious fervour, meeting in private and not at the mosque, all this with sharia and jihad and "doing something".'

'You are so completely missing the point!' said Rachid. His earlier irritation was turning to anger. 'These guys are young. They're troubled, looking for something. Like we all did at one time. Rebelling. Making a life, finding a way, defining who they are. Or trying to! Here everyone says you're Moroccan, in Morocco they all call you a Dutchie. Their fathers can't help – their lives are so different – and they don't want to talk about things, the older generation. To them "radical" is a taboo word. And you lot turn your backs.'

Lisette sensed a personal history. She began to intervene, but Rachid went straight on, speaking over her, anger now on the boil. A lid, long jammed tight, blew off.

'You just don't get it, do you? There's no one to tell them, no one to help! All they're doing is trying to find an identity, and they get it from religion. And we sit watching it all go wrong! We should be out there doing something, putting them on the right track, giving them the space to find things out, but offering some *direction*. Not just dumping them down with the way ahead blocked, but putting someone in there who can *help*. It's not the police we should be alerting, but someone who can step in, prevent it all, change their course.'

'At InSec, Rachid,' said Mick, 'we are observers, not participants.'

For a moment Lisette thought Rachid was going to hit him.

'I think that whatever personal differences and points of view we might have, we all agree that over the next few days we have to be on our toes,' she said quickly. 'Absolutely vigilant and on the ball.'

She glanced at her watch.

'But it's nearly five. So for now, why don't we go downstairs for a drink? We can talk a little more there.'

On Fridays, snacks and a few bottles were put out in the canteen for a pre-weekend wind-down.

'I don't drink,' said Rachid. But he walked with them to the lift, all the same.

Participants, indeed, thought Lisette, as they descended to Café Minus in silence. The time had come to draw the line with Onno Veldhuizen.

SATURDAY
11 JUNE 2011

10

Posthumus did not readily give up a Saturday morning. It was a sacred part of the week. He kept the morning free of obligations and appointments, allowing those first hours of the weekend to fall naturally into whatever shape he might feel inclined to let them take at the time. There were the regular components: the farmers' market on Noordermarkt, a long breakfast, things that needed doing around the apartment. But he held the control and rhythm of it all, as his and his alone. Not today. He was up earlier than he would have liked. Breakfast taken standing up. And the visit to the market would have to be rushed. No mid-morning snack of fresh oysters at the fish stall, no chat with the goat's-cheese man. Purely functional. And for what? Posthumus was not at all sure he wanted to be involved with this Mohammed character. But the man had a point. Posthumus was glad he was not the only one to find the young Moroccan's death strange. And somewhere, lurking at the back of it all, was whoever it was who had tasered him. That was no burglar, he was growing convinced.

Posthumus looked out at the weather. It was one of those dull, grey, shadowless days, where nothing seems to breathe. A low sky. But dry at least. Nevertheless, something water-proof, just in case. He took a light leather flying jacket off the rack, and went downstairs to his bike. He wanted to get to the bottom of this. There was no need to mention the attack in the apartment to this Mohammed just yet, but somehow the attack and the death in the canal were linked. Two parts of the same story, two pieces of the picture he was building. He needed the one in between. No, there would be no harm in finding out a little more about Amir Loukili. And he wanted a good look at the Tahiri boy.

Gusta from downstairs was unlocking her bicycle – an extraordinary creation, with a mound of artificial flowers entwined around the handlebars and plastic vines threaded through the spokes. It was fastened to the bridge railing near his own.

'Any news on that Namiki pen you were so excited about?' she called over to him, as he was shutting the street door.

'Haven't really had a chance to follow it up.'

'Busy? Must be. You're out early for a Saturday.'

'A quick shop, then I've got an appointment out west,' he said as he approached, 'in the Kolenkit Quarter.'

'You're cycling out *there*? Isn't it dangerous?'

Posthumus smiled. 'Well, not in my experience so far.'

'Certainly doesn't look like it. Is that a bump? What happened?'

'A long story,' said Posthumus, and – not wanting to be caught in one of the interminable conversations in which a chance remark to Gusta could enmesh one – added hastily, 'And you? Where are you off to?'

'Art Deco fair, in De Rode Hoed. Doors open in a few minutes, and I want to be in with the first.'

She gave him a flutter of a wave, and with a perfectly straight back, one hand extended Bette Davis-style with cigarette and holder, her skirt and the various pieces of chiffon that draped her form rippling as she rode, she cycled off along the canal. At the next bridge, two tourists turned to take a photograph.

Posthumus watched her go. That was one of the delights of Amsterdam: the way (for the time being at least) that rent control and liberal housing policies threw all manner of people together. In his own building, for instance, you got a genteel old hippy like Gusta, Dr Jansen on the ground floor, the succession of students in the basement apartment. Next door, the computer nerd who had made good, and now ran a little empire from his attic; the young sculptor a few doors down, the melancholy transvestite across the canal. And because everyone walked or cycled, you encountered each other, came across lives that, in the sort of city where you disappeared out of your front door into a car, you might know nothing about.

He unlocked his bicycle, a heavy, black machine of a design barely altered since the 1930s: no gears, back-pedal brakes, a plastic milk crate fastened to the front carrier where once a basket would have been. More Miss Marple than Tour de France, it was barely distinguishable from a thousand others around town, but, like his fellow Amsterdammers, Posthumus could pick out his bike from the myriad, subliminally aware of every dent and scratch, the angle of the bell, the hue of the saddle. He set off in Gusta's wake, with an irate ring at the two tourists, who were now standing side by side in the middle of the road, staring up at gables.

The Chinese social club along the canal was already opening its doors, the first old couples arriving for a morning of mahjong. Yes, we're an odd mix, thought Posthumus. All tumbled together, nodding politely to each other in the street, tolerant of each other's differences and oddities, but not *neighbourly*. Not in the smiley American bring-round-some-apple-pie sense. Living together but apart, holding the distance, not treading on any toes. Growing up as a Catholic in the sixties and seventies, it had been the same. All one, but with subtle, unspoken divisions. There was the Catholic newsagent and the Protestant newsagent, the Catholic school and the Protestant school. And you knew where to shop, where to send your children. *Zuilen*, people called it then, pillars, separate columns on which social order rested. Was that happening all over again? *Zuilen*. Apart but equal. From activist meetings in his youth Posthumus remembered 'separate development' – the old South African euphemism for apartheid. Was he cycling towards an Islamic *zuil* out west? Or was it simply a ghetto?

The farmers' market lay on his way. There was just enough time to pick up what he needed: smoked garlic from the herb man; his favourite olive oil from the Italians; a swoop by his regular produce stall for early broad beans and fat, purple seasonal aubergines, all piled into the plastic crate on his bicycle. Then on to the Kolenkit Quarter.

He found the Tahiris' house easily. It was across the vacant lot he'd seen when he drove out the first time, part of a little terrace of two-storey 1930s cottages at odds with the surrounding high-rise blocks. A path led to the door. He could lock his bike in view of the place. For a moment Posthumus contemplated leaving his groceries in the crate, decided against it, and was awkwardly clutching shopping bags when Mohammed answered the door.

'Ah, my wife is also doing the shopping,' said Mohammed, as he shook hands with Posthumus. 'Please. Welcome. Come in.'

Posthumus followed the flick of Mohammed's glance and quickly slipped off his shoes, placing them beside his groceries in the hall.

Mohammed had not wanted Karima to be around for this conversation. It would distress her. He had asked Najib to look after the shop. The boy had kicked up a fuss. Nothing new in that, these days, but in the end Aissa had got him to listen to reason. Aissa was perhaps the most upset by Amir's death, but Mohammed felt she knew the young man best of all of them, that she might help. Besides, she was a strong and sensible girl. He had watched Pieter Posthumus come up the path, and felt his initial instinct confirmed, that this was a good man. A little odd, perhaps, arriving at the door carrying shopping, but good, and Mohammed liked it that he knew to remove his shoes.

Posthumus followed his host, and looked about him. It was a small living room, yet a large crystal chandelier hung from the ceiling. Two sofas – opulent, with tasselled bolsters, the sort on sale in the shop – but otherwise subdued, sober.

'Please, some tea?' said Mohammed, indicating that he should sit down.

A young woman came from the kitchen with a teapot, small glass cups and a plate of glistening bite-sized pastries. She was wearing a red headscarf. This must be her, Posthumus thought, the one Merel had written about.

'My daughter, Aissa,' said Mohammed.

Posthumus hesitated; he had read that in this culture, men should not touch women who were not family. But Aissa put out her hand.

'Don't worry, I'm not that hung up on *every* aspect of tradition,' she said. 'Despite appearances,' she added, touching her headscarf and smiling. She reminded Posthumus of Alex.

Aissa poured the tea, and sat beside her father. On the second sofa, Posthumus sat slightly forward in his seat, and smoothed straight a splayed tassel on one of the bolsters.

'I must say at the outset,' he began, 'that, like you, I personally find something odd about the way Amir drowned. But this visit is not official. As far as my department is concerned, the case is closed.'

'And the police, too.'

'Yes. But you would like to know more about what happened, and so would I. Maybe I can help in putting together the pieces of what took place that night. To give you what the Americans call "closure".'

'That is all I am asking. It would mean very much to me, to us all.'

Posthumus paused. Mohammed did not beg, did not grab his hand imploringly. He simply looked down. He seemed broken. Posthumus nodded.

'It would help me to know more about Amir. What was he doing in Amsterdam, for instance? Where might he have been going that night?'

'Nowhere, nowhere!' said Mohammed. 'Prinsengracht, the police said! *Why?* He had nothing on the Prinsengracht. It cannot be!'

Aissa put a hand on her father's arm.

'He had been here nearly two months,' she said. 'He was looking into business possibilities for his mother's family. They manufacture clothing, especially traditional stuff. Djellabas, wedding dresses.'

Mohammed had composed himself a little.

'I thought my son Najib could help him in that direction. He has made me an excellent website for the shop, he's a real genius with computers. But they didn't click. They had religious differences. And I was also hoping – Aissa knows this – that some attraction might develop between her and Amir. He was a quiet, serious, hard-working boy. He would have made a good husband.'

Posthumus glanced at Aissa, and detected an almost imperceptible shake of the head.

'Do you know any of his business contacts here?' he asked.

'No, he did not speak much about that. He spent most of his time in Brussels. That was also for his mother's family.'

'Brussels? Yes, he had a ticket for Brussels in . . . Sorry.'

'It is no matter. We must speak about these things.'

'He had a ticket for Brussels with him. And a few other things. I don't have them with me, I'm afraid my department is a little behind with our administration. These are usually sent to you within a week or so. There was nothing valuable, but it could be that he has a computer in Brussels, too. Do you know who he was seeing there?'

'I would have to ask his father about all this,' said Mohammed. 'It is a distant part of the family, you understand. We did not see much of them, even when we went back to Morocco. The last time I saw Amir before he came to Amsterdam was when he was five, maybe six.'

'And the night he died, you say he was having dinner here?'

'With no alcohol! We none of us drink.'

'You mentioned when I saw you yesterday that he stayed for the evening prayer?'

'He said one should pray as if one *saw* God.' Mohammed smiled, and shook his head slowly. 'Yes, he prayed with us,' he said.

'So what time would he have left?'

'At ten thirty,' said Aissa. 'I remember. I was glad it wasn't too late because I had early lectures the next day.'

'Did he say he was going anywhere?'

'No, home,' said Mohammed. 'Home, for sure. It is close by.'

'And he could not have got lost?'

'There's a direct bus,' said Aissa. 'Two. The 80 and 82. You have to wait a while sometimes, but it's almost door-to-door. He'd done it before. He wouldn't have got lost.'

She offered Posthumus a second pastry. He didn't hesitate. They were delicious.

'That night, the whole family was here?' asked Posthumus.

'Yes.'

'But Amir left alone? No one went with him, saw where he went?'

'No one. We stayed on here,' said Mohammed. 'My son Najib had already left, he was meeting friends. One of them came to call him.'

'At ten thirty at night?'

'No, he left before that. He didn't stay for prayers.' Mohammed sighed. 'You have children?'

Posthumus shook his head.

'They bring joy, and they bring worry. With Najib at the moment it is worry. We don't always see eye to eye as far as religion goes. About many things. Not these days anyway. And these friends he goes to meet, I don't know them. I was hoping Amir could help, but that night Najib was scorning Amir's faith, too.'

'Nothing new in that,' said Aissa. 'My brother can fly off the handle when it comes to Islam,' she explained to Posthumus. 'He has grown some strong ideas of late, and he gets hung up on small things. He launched into an old school friend the other day because the guy has a tattoo, and tattoos are *haram*. And at the moment he has it in for the King of Morocco. Says he is only a partial Muslim, and that goes for anyone who supports him, like Amir.'

'This all comes from the internet,' said Mohammed. 'From the internet and from these new friends. On the one hand he makes me a beautiful website, on the other he finds these ideas. As I say, joy and worry, worry and joy.'

'I don't know which came first, the ideas or the friends,' said Aissa, largely for her father's benefit, 'but he feels they understand him. *Know where he's at.'* She used the English phrase. Posthumus could see she frequently played the role of intermediary.

'The company a young man keeps determines his destiny,' said Mohammed. It sounded as if he was quoting a proverb.

'I have met some of them,' said Aissa. 'And they are quite as serious and respectable as Amir is . . . was.'

'Perhaps I could talk with Najib some time?' said Posthumus.

'He is in the shop this morning,' said Mohammed.

'I could walk with you there later, if you liked, introduce you,' said Aissa. 'My father has to go to the undertakers.'

'I am taking some clothing for Amir,' Mohammed explained. 'He should not travel to his family the way he is now.'

Posthumus accepted a third pastry. He asked more about Amir, his character, his family, his plans. Carefully, he put the question as to whether Amir might have been depressed. Mohammed looked at him squarely.

'Suicide is *haram,'* he said. 'When he came, at first I thought he was troubled, nervous. But Amir was devout. He would not do that. We believe every soul is created by God, and is owned by Him. We do not own our soul or the body in which it lives. To damage your body is a sin, to attempt to kill it would bring damnation. He would not do that.'

'Martyrdom is different,' said Aissa. She clearly saw the question that was forming, unspoken, in Posthumus's mind.

Posthumus returned to safer ground. Gradually, the conversation ebbed into the awkward generalities that indicated it was nearing an end. He rose to go. Mohammed shook his hand, keeping hold of it, firmly.

'From my heart, from my family, thank you,' he said.

In the hall Mohammed busied himself with the package he was taking to the undertakers. Posthumus left, together with Aissa, to speak to Najib. They walked along the edge of the vacant lot, towards the Bos en Lommerweg, Posthumus pushing his bicycle.

'You didn't want to marry Amir,' said Posthumus after a while.

Aissa looked at him closely. 'Perceptive of you. No. He was clever. Lovely to talk to, a very sweet guy, and I could see he liked me, but – how would my father put it? – for me, it did not "click".'

'And that was no problem?'

'No! No. We're not all like you read in the papers.'

Posthumus gave a shrug of apology.

'My parents would never make me marry someone I didn't want to. They know I have a mind of my own.' Aissa seemed to be reading Posthumus quite as much as he was trying to read her.

'Outside home, I can be quite outspoken, you know. It's just that with my parents, I try to avoid confrontation if I can. Unlike Najib.'

Some kids were kicking around a ball between the weeds on the lot. A small, fat boy on a toy electric quad-bike cut in front of Posthumus, and shot off into the scrub.

'Who are these friends of his?' asked Posthumus.

It was a long while before Aissa answered.

'I don't know all of them. It's more a study circle than a group of guys hanging out on a street corner. Reading the Qur'an, discussions, that sort of stuff. The thing is that one or two of them were arrested recently. Part of what the papers called the Amsterdam Cell.'

Posthumus let out a soft whistle.

'No, no . . . Najib is not involved in anything like that,' said Aissa.

'You can be sure of that?'

Posthumus looked sceptical. Again, Aissa was silent. When she spoke, her voice was firm.

'Yes, I can. I'm sure. Not Najib. You see, for him it's only partly to do with Islam, being with these friends. It's more the feeling that no one understands him, or his problems, his needs, and that at last he's found someone who does. That's something precious to him, something he feels he has to hold on to for himself. To my father that looks secretive.'

'And to you?' asked Posthumus.

'No. I can see where he's coming from.'

'*You* feel misunderstood.'

'Discriminated against, you mean?' said Aissa.

'That's what you're getting at, isn't it?' said Posthumus. He was surprised at how forthright he was being. There was something about Aissa, a confidence, a quiet intelligence, that demanded frankness. He could see why Merel liked her.

'At times, of course, but that's not what I'm talking about,' she said. 'I'm not as devout as Najib, but my religion is important to me, part of me. That's what some people don't seem to get.'

Posthumus prickled. There was something in her tone of 'people like you'.

'Hence the hijab,' he said.

'That, I admit, began as a sort of adolescent rebellion,' she said. 'My mother goes unveiled. So, perhaps I'm a bit confrontational after all.' Aissa flashed him a smile. 'Later I thought it through a little, and now I see it more as a statement of identity,' she went on.

'Even if wearing it alienates people?'

'That's just the point. It shouldn't, and I don't want it to. And yes, yes, I *know* what you're going to say about women, and subservience and all the rest . . .' Aissa held up her hands in mock surrender. 'That's just not true in my case, but we'd need longer than a walk around the corner to my father's shop to go into all that. Have a look at yesterday's *Nieuwe Post*, if you want to know what I think. I was interviewed. The journalist got it almost right for once.'

Posthumus was about to mention Merel, but Aissa went straight on.

'Najib is always going on about the West wanting to make us citizens without religion,' she said. 'I don't think that's true, but I do want to stand up for myself, to make it visible that my religion is part of who I am. My parents are content with just keeping to the basics of Islam, almost as a cultural thing. To me it's something more.'

'But not quite as much as to Najib.'

'Exactly.'

They were across the street from the shop, waiting to cross.

'Well, surprise surprise,' said Aissa. 'He can twist her round his little finger!'

Posthumus looked at her quizzically.

'Najib. He's not there – that's my mother with those customers. He must have phoned her with some story, got her to come in and take his place. Just like him! I really had to twist his arm this morning, lay a guilt trip on him about family duty. But he is very wilful, my little brother. As you see, he's got his own way.'

A woman about Posthumus's age was holding out upholstery fabric to the only other two people in the shop. The traffic lights changed.

'Look,' said Aissa, holding back from crossing. 'Maybe it's better if you don't go in. My father didn't want her to know he was doing this. Not for the moment, anyway.'

'I should be going, in any case,' said Posthumus. 'I'm

meeting someone.' He hesitated. The lights changed back to red. 'I recognised your name,' he went on. 'I read the article in *De Nieuwe Post*.'

Aissa turned and looked at him full on. 'Well, you already knew a little about how I think, then.'

'I think I should tell you that the person I am going to meet is Merel Dekkers. She's my niece.'

Aissa said nothing.

'I wanted you to know that. I didn't want you to think I was hiding the fact, for some reason.'

Still nothing.

'Merel is worried that she has offended you. She heard that Najib was angry about your interview . . . and the other article. She really valued speaking with you, I know. She had been hoping to see more of you.'

The lights were green again. Aissa turned to cross the street.

'Goodbye, Mr Posthumus. And thank you for helping my father.'

She did not shake his hand.

'Tell her to ring me,' she said, over her shoulder as she walked away.

Merel was waiting at the Mozaïek Café when Posthumus walked in.

'Nice jacket,' she said as he came up to her. 'Italian?'

'You've got a good eye.'

'And you have a very odd head!' said Merel, as they pecked cheeks. 'What happened? And what are you doing up this end of town anyway?'

Posthumus mentioned the incident in Amir's apartment, explained about Mohammed's concern with Amir's death, and his own belief that the two were linked. Then he related his conversation with Aissa.

'You know that Najib has links with the Amsterdam Cell?' he asked.

Merel nodded.

'"Just good friends", apparently. Aissa mentioned it,' she said. 'She said there's nothing in it, and I think I believe her. You?'

'I don't know. Jury's out. I don't think *she's* lying, but I wonder about Najib,' he said. 'Anyway, she said to phone her. I'm afraid I bungled it a bit, saying I was coming to meet you, but I wanted to be up front if I'm going to try to find out more about how Amir died.'

'And you are?'

'Looks like I'm in it already.' Posthumus rubbed the bump on his head. 'And you, too, it would appear. Aissa seems a fine young woman. It was just a "tell her to ring me" as she walked away, but I got the feeling she liked you, really did want to talk. And if you want my "fatherly advice" . . . it would be to go for it. It would be worth it, for both of you. If there's one thing I'm beginning to realise in this whole affair, it's how enclosed our little worlds are in this city. And what an effort it takes to break through.'

He absorbed the sight of his niece, across the table. So very like her father. That look of attentiveness. A look that warmed you, that made you feel that for the moment no one else in the world mattered to her but you, and what you had to say. Willem had been able to do that.

'It's lovely to see you,' he said. 'I really didn't want you to disappear, now that you're back again.'

'It's odd, isn't it,' said Merel. 'The family thing.'

Posthumus heard himself draw sharp breath.

'Don't worry,' said Merel, with a smile. 'I'm not going to ask about Dad.' She paused. 'I do want to know, though. Some time. But I've lived with it for twenty years. It can wait. And, hey, I'm enjoying getting to know you as an adult. I'm not going to push it. I'm sorry about cancelling the other night . . . Oh, a coffee please.' A waitress had arrived at the table.

'You must try the cheesecake,' said Posthumus quickly. 'It's proper. Baked. I shouldn't, I've been hogging pastries all morning.'

Two coffees, and a slice of New York cheesecake.

There was a silence after they had placed their order. Posthumus broke it.

'No problem about the other night. It's good to see you anyway,' he said. 'And now, how about I tap that journalist's instinct of yours? To set me off down a track of thinking I've maybe missed.'

Merel laughed. 'So, where do we start?' she said.

'With Amir, I think,' said Posthumus. 'Seeing as I've yet to catch anything but a fleeting glimpse of Najib. Where did Amir go after dinner? He was found in the Prinsengracht. What was he doing in town? How did he get there? Aissa said he wouldn't have got lost on the way home, there's a bus door to door.'

'Where does it end up?'

'Good point. There are two, actually, 80 and 82. We could check outside at a bus stop.'

'No need.' Merel took out a smartphone.

'I'm not quite there yet on the technology, am I?' said Posthumus, clearing aside some leaflets on the table as their order arrived.

'Both end at Marnixstraat,' said Merel after a moment. 'So, just a short walk from the Prinsengracht.'

'Along one of the canals in the Jordaan. But it's so busy around there. How come no one saw him fall in?'

'Could have been late at night. On the way back again from somewhere.'

'That's the other thing. I spoke to a friend at the morgue. The official police report puts the time of death as between 10 p.m. and two in the morning. They're always officially very cautious with these estimates; it's hard to tell with a body in the water. But Rob has seen a lot of this sort of thing, and he's prepared to go out on a limb. He said he thought the body had been in the water a while, that he'd put the death towards the beginning of that scale.'

'So . . . soon after Amir left the Tahiris. Where would he have gone?'

'Mohammed was adamant he was going straight home. Said he was a bit of a loner, didn't seem to have any friends. And I must say, from all they said, I got the impression that he really was a quiet, devout, withdrawn sort of guy.'

'That he told them the truth, you mean, about going home? No shady business. Then maybe he did go straight back. Fell in a canal closer to base. You're right about this cheesecake, by the way.'

'Then how did he end up in the Prinsengracht? We're back to square one.'

'What night was this?'

'Monday before last.'

'Monday? They clean the canals.'

'What do you mean?'

'Thousands of litres of water are pumped through the whole network, from a pump station out east. Starting from midnight, the water is on the move. I did a story on it once, with a group of school kids, dropping plastic pennants in floating bottles all over town one afternoon, and seeing where they ended up next day. The pennant had an image – a butterfly or a hat or something – and a phone number on it that people were asked to ring if they found one. We wanted to track the currents.'

'And?'

'Not a success. The general movement of the water is out to the IJ. Most of the bottles disappeared. But a few people did get back to us, from all over the place. It turns out that though the general movement is from east to west, all sorts of factors – boats, canal-angles, things underwater – can redirect the currents. There's no knowing. It was all a bit of a mess. The story was pulled.'

'Then square one again. He could have fallen in anywhere.'

'So we might as well begin at his place, it's as good as any. Is there a canal nearby?'

'Right there. He lived on the Kop van Jut.'

'And how long would it take, from Mohammed's to his place?'

'Depends how long he had to wait for a bus. On a bike it would be about ten or fifteen minutes, I guess.'

'So if your friend Rob is right, he might have fallen in the canal near home,' said Merel. 'Know what? I think we should take a ride over and check out the Kop van Jut.'

Her bike was in the square behind the Mozaïek Café. They cut through side streets, ran up against the canal that edged the Erasmuspark.

'Perhaps he came along here?' said Posthumus. 'Maybe he walked?'

'He might have. It was a beautiful night that Monday, I remember. I was drinking on a terrace with friends till nearly midnight. But walking through the park, at night?'

'It would be lit, you can see all those lamp posts. And there are two canals, by the looks of things.'

One was right beside the footpath, very exposed, the other bordered by a thicket of trees and bushes. They crossed a bridge and pushed their bicycles down the ramp into the park.

'No reason for him to go in there,' said Merel, peering into the greenery beside the inner canal.

'Unless someone called him,' said Posthumus.

'Are you thinking what I'm thinking?'

'That Najib has something to do with it? Mohammed said they didn't get on, and there was some sort of fallout over Islam. But that's hardly a reason to push someone in the canal.'

'Maybe it wasn't just about Islam,' said Merel. 'You say Mohammed was making wedding noises, and that Amir at least seemed keen, even if Aissa wasn't. Maybe Najib didn't fancy Amir having designs on his sister.'

'You mean it could have been a fight that got out of hand?'

'Maybe. And there is something fishy about Najib. You have to ask yourself what he was doing in Amir's apartment a week later.'

'If that was Najib.'

They walked into the little wood.

'I don't think anyone would come in here at night, off the path, even if someone did call him,' said Merel. 'And especially if it was someone he had just had an argument with.'

'Something to bear in mind, though.'

They walked on. At the point where the path rejoined the road, up a concrete stairway, they pushed their bicycles up the ramp alongside, then stood on the top step and looked back. The railings were high. It would be hard to fall into the water. Or even to be pushed. And it was the latter possibility that had risen by degrees to the surface of both their minds.

At the bridge over the Westelijk Marktkanaal they had to wait. The bridge was up so that a couple of large boats could pass. The dull, grey sky that had hung low over the city all morning began to darken, sink deeper. The first breaths of a breeze fluttered at Merel's hair.

She checked her phone.

'The bus goes quite a roundabout way,' she said. 'I figure that whether he walked or took the bus, he would have ended up here at about eleven.'

Once across the canal, they went down the short flight of steps to a path that ran down one side of the Kop van Jut, beside the water.

'Well, this is where he lived, in one of those blocks over there,' said Posthumus, but he had to repeat himself as trams thundered over the metal bridge just above their heads.

'I don't know about my journalist's instincts,' said Merel, 'but my woman's antennae twitch here. I wouldn't like to walk down this path at night. The back wall of the college . . . and those are just bathroom windows from the apartments. Nothing really overlooks this stretch, and you can't see it all that well from the street, wouldn't notice it really. And look, one of those lamps has been smashed.'

She pointed further down the path, to a street lamp beside some gnarled old willows, its glass shattered by vandals, the pole daubed with graffiti. Merel gave a short, high-pitched gasp, grabbed Posthumus's elbow, but immediately laughed.

'Sorry,' she said, 'this is all making me a bit jumpy.'

Posthumus followed her glance. Just a few feet away, the tarpaulin covering one of two small boats moored near the bridge was writhing. The boat rocked. There was an odd, belching sound. A corner of the tarpaulin lifted. Eyes. Eyes and hair, and a wheezy giggle.

'Little lady get a fright?'

The boat bobbed and lurched dangerously now; the cover was pushed further back and a large head pushed its way out, beard and hair matted by dirt into a mane of brown-grey dreadlocks, skin a painful-looking red, eyes blue, but tinged with yellow.

'You's in my garden.' More wheezy laughter. Merel took an unconscious step backward.

A man emerged from the boat, and – somewhat unsteadily – took the short step on to the grass verge. The bank of the canal was low along this stretch, barely a foot above the water.

An overwhelming odour preceded him. Sweet, stale alcohol mainly, over a deeper, darker smell of sweat and grime that Posthumus recognised from some of the apartments he'd been to. The man turned, and muttered something back to someone, or something, in the boat, but nothing moved. Again the laughter, as if he was transported by some secret, internal joke. He looked into the crate on Posthumus's bicycle.

'Picnic, is it?' he said, fingering the brown paper bag with the olive oil. 'Something for a thirsty man?'

'Not unless you drink olive oil.'

The man guffawed. 'Not unless I drink olive oil!' he said. 'Had worse, had worse.' He shouted something incomprehensible back to the still, silent boat. A name, maybe?

Perhaps it was a dog in there, thought Posthumus. The man was standing too close. Posthumus was holding his breath, conscious that he was leaning backward at an odd angle, but too embarrassed to take a blatant step back to join Merel. He could not hold out, and covered his retreat with: 'Do you live here?' As he said it, it sounded absurd. Almost as bad as 'Do you come here often?'

But the man simply said again: 'You's in my garden.' Then with a nod back at the boat: 'House and home, boat and home, house and boat, houseboat, boathouse, housey-boatie,' he said, chuckling to himself, then repeating: 'Ladies and gentlemen, ladies and gentlemen, ladies and gentlemen.'

Posthumus wasn't quite sure whether this last part was addressed to him and Merel or not.

'Any spare change?' the man said.

'Perhaps you can help us,' said Posthumus. 'Are you here every day? Did you see something strange just over a week ago? Someone fall in the canal? A young Moroccan man who lived here. Wearing traditional dress.'

'In my garden,' said the man, and began again with the wheezy laugh.

'Ten days ago. Monday before last,' Posthumus prompted.

'What day is today?' said the man.

'Saturday.'

'Saturday-Sunday, Monday-Tuesday,' said the man, then, turning again to the boat, 'ladies and gentlemen, ladies and gentlemen, laaydeeeees and gentlemen, gentlemen, gentlemen, gentlemen yes, gentlemen dress.'

This was useless. Posthumus turned to Merel to leave.

'Just a minute,' she said. She looked at the man. 'Gentlemen dress?' she asked. 'A gentleman in a dress? Gentle*men* in dresses?'

'Dresses yeses! Gentlemen in dresses. Dresses and hats, dancing like gnats.'

'What were they doing, these gentlemen?'

'Dancing like gnats in dresses and hats. In my garden.' He was laughing again, and muttering something back to the boat.

Merel hesitated a moment, then reached out and put a hand on his arm. 'Please try to help us,' she said.

The man stopped. 'Pretty lady,' he said.

Then abruptly he stepped back, closed his eyes. He began swivelling from side to side, rocking, his hands miming playing a guitar, singing softly to himself.

'Bom-titi-bom titi-bom titi-bom, *ballroom blitz! Ballroom blitz!* And the man at the back said attack tacky tack. Ballroom blitz! Was like lightning, everybody was frightening, and the music was soooothing and they all started moving. Ballroom blitz.'

Merel persisted. She spoke gently, but her voice was firm, interrupting his song and giving weight to each word.

'What happened next?'

'Took a swim.'

'Took a swim?'

'In the canal.'

'And there were two men?'

'Gentlemen dancing, *ballroom blitz*, one took a swim, jumped right in.'

Posthumus stepped forward.

'What do you mean, took a swim?' he asked. 'Did he fall in? Did he get pushed? Did he come up? Two men you say? What were they doing? What happened to the other one?'

The man was silent. He stared at Posthumus. Sullen. Then he turned to the boat and began shouting. Yelling something incomprehensible. They waited a while, but it was clear to them that they were no longer in his world.

'Come,' said Merel to Posthumus, 'I think we'd better go.'

'I'm sorry,' Posthumus said, when they were back up on the street. 'That was my fault. We could have learned more from him.'

Below them, the man was still ranting. Standing on his own on the grassy verge, shaking his fist at the boat.

'Quite a bit to think about, though, isn't there?' said Merel.

'Yes. Look, do you mind if we skip lunch? I'd like to sort through all this a bit.'

'You going to the police?'

'To tell them what? About a crazy old drunk going on about gnats and men in dresses, and singing Ballroom Blitz? They've already given Mohammed pretty short shrift. And besides, I have a built-in antipathy to the police. I'd like to sort this out for myself a little more first.'

'Are you going to Mohammed, then?'

'No. No, not yet. Not until things are clearer. But I think the time has definitely come to speak to this Najib.'

11

It was a lads' day out in Amsterdam. Off the marital hook. Train in together from The Hague around lunchtime, wide-screen rugby at Downunder Sports Café (plenty of beer), a *rijsttafel* (more beer), and a night in the sleazier bars of De Wallen. They hadn't done it for a while, but it was a tradition that dated back a good few years – back to when Mark Koning was a young press officer in the Amsterdam police communications department, and Onno Veldhuizen was with Organised Crime. Koning had on his 'Soccer is for Sissies' T-shirt. Veldhuizen, though a good ten years older, was dressed like an adolescent – or his take on an adolescent – in baggy jeans and a hooded sweatshirt.

'*Vat hom Fluffy!*'

Downunder erupted as the Bulls' Bjorn Basson bore down on the Stormers winger minutes away from the final whistle, grounding him just before he crossed the line to score, saving the game for his team and propelling the Bulls towards the final. The roar released a wave of warm beery breath through the bar. Men – many in knee-length shorts, most with bellies that boasted a good taste for the brew – crowded the room, facing the screen. Super Rugby: the premier championship for exclusively southern hemisphere teams.

'These guys really know how to play,' said Koning, as the final whistle went, 'a fucking world away from your Euro-wimps.'

'I win, drinks on you,' said Veldhuizen. They always had a bet on the outcome.

'Going to be an expensive day,' said Koning, getting up to go to the bar. 'Dinner's on me too – as a "thanks, mate" for that spin on the Amsterdam Cell. You see the story in *De Nieuwe Post* yesterday?'

Veldhuizen nodded.

'My guys are very happy with that,' said Koning. 'And not only that, but I have a hot little blonde journalist lapping at my ankles. Thought she was just going to get an interview, and ended up with plutonium. A surprised and grateful little blondie. And now that I know what she looks like, I'll be answering her calls pronto.'

He joined the thrust of men around the bar. Expats mainly. Aussies, South Africans. By the time he was back, the rugby had flicked over to a news channel, sound off. Civilians being shot at, followed by a still of Colonel Gaddafi, filling the screen to the accompaniment of Johnny Cash.

'Next episode of the Arab Spring, I see,' said Koning, nodding to the colonel as he put down the beers. 'Evil bastard. Can't your boys do something about him?'

'It's your boys that are fucking it up,' said Veldhuizen. 'Too much political pussyfooting.' He knocked back a mouthful of beer. 'I know what I would do.'

Koning raised his eyebrows and made a gun-shape with his fingers.

'Best way,' said Veldhuizen. 'Some situations demand firm action, and firm action is not always politically correct. Or squeaky clean. It can't be. Mossad and the CIA know that.'

Koning looked at his drinking buddy across the table. Veldhuizen looked quite capable of doing something like that himself, Koning thought, and it probably wouldn't be the first time he had taken someone out.

'Meanwhile you've got the Amsterdam Cell to play with,' he said.

'*This* time I'm going to nail them,' said Veldhuizen. 'Don't you worry, I'm going to win this one.' He tipped his glass towards Koning in salute. 'I always do.'

Posthumus paced his apartment. He had hoped to make Saturday afternoon something of a substitute for the disrupted morning, but he could not settle. After a few minutes he phoned Merel.

'Hi, I've been thinking,' he said. 'I really want to speak to Najib soon, without Mohammed being around. If you do meet up with Aissa again, is there any way you could somehow get her to arrange it? Do you think you'll be seeing her?'

'Yes,' said Merel. Her voice sounded odd, strained. Her responses so far had been muted. 'Now.'

'At the moment? You're with Aissa now?' said Posthumus. He could hear dishes chinking in the background.

'Mmm.'

'Sorry, sorry! But if you can, I'll be in De Dolle Hond tomorrow. All afternoon. Bye!'

Posthumus continued to pace. He did not put down the phone, but gripped it, agitating it as if he were trying to shake something out of it. Then he placed it neatly on his desk, beside his landline handset. He checked the screen on the handset. He'd forgotten to do that earlier. A missed call, while he was out at Mohammed's. Posthumus dialled Voicemail.

'Cornelius here. I'm doing a clean-up. Those copies you gave me of the Bart Hooft poems. The music of his soul, sayeth Voltaire. Or in our young man's case, rather the silver key that opens your heart, but also fits your bike lock.' The voice rolled momentarily into laughter, then: 'That's our very own Nico Scheepmaker. Anyway, do you want them back, or can I chuck them? Let me know.'

Posthumus pressed Call Back. One ring.

'Barendrecht.'

'Cornelius, it's Pieter. I've just got your message, and actually, yes, I would like them back. Perhaps we can meet up somewhere? I could come round, or a drink some time? Anna has a sort of informal open house in the café on Sundays.'

'Sounds good.'

'You pay for your drinks, of course,' Posthumus added hastily. 'It's more a case of friends dropping in for a chat. And I'd like to talk to you about the poems. Whether you think they're worth publishing; that's if I can trace his family of course.'

'Still obsessing about him then?'

'I feel . . . an obligation,' said Posthumus. 'But there's no need to go into that. I was also wondering whether you had spotted any clue as to where he might be from. In the poems, I mean.'

'Apart from the States, you mean?'

'America?'

'The English poems had good old US of A spelling. I remember a "color" with no "u", and at least one "gotten". Dreadful word. Even to a foreigner. You might have noticed *that*.'

'I hadn't. Thank you. That's helpful. Look, I'll see you tomorrow perhaps. Or give you a ring and come round.'

Posthumus hung up, and walked across to the front window. He stood looking out over the canal for a long time. Then he turned and picked up his mobile. He owed Alex a call, anyway. He had said he would phone. No answer, it clicked straight over. Posthumus left a message.

'Alex. It's PP. Can you give me a ring? Things have become complicated. I've agreed to help Mohammed Tahiri, that's the owner of the furniture shop, look into that canal death. And I'm beginning to have very serious concerns about it. But can you ring before you get into work on Monday? I want to ask you a favour. Something that is . . . well, it's not *exactly* illegal, but it's not a hundred per cent above board, either.'

'Thanks for the lunch, and the chat . . . everything. I'm glad I phoned,' said Merel.

She unlocked her bike from the railing outside Aissa's house.

'Me too,' said Aissa. 'I'm glad we sorted things out.'

'Shall we do it again some time?'

'I hope so. Maybe you'll meet the rest of the family next time.'

'That'd be nice.'

Merel waved, swung up on to her bike, and cycled off towards Bos en Lommerweg. The breeze that had picked up earlier was whipping about sharply now. The sky was a bruised black-grey, with an almost metallic sheen. Merel shivered and buttoned up the thin cotton jacket she'd put on that morning, turning up the lapels to cover her throat. She cycled alongside the stretch of wasteland between Aissa's house and the high street. Tall weeds bowed in the wind, catching flying scraps of paper. The first drops of rain hit her cheeks.

In the underpass that ran beneath the ring road, on the edge of the wasteland, a scooter started up. Its rider had watched Merel as she waved goodbye to Aissa. He picked up a small black backpack and put it on, back to front, over his chest, unzipping the top and feeling for something inside. He flipped the visor down on his helmet. Then he pulled out on to the bicycle path, turned and began to follow Merel up towards the high street. When Merel stopped at the junction, he slowed to a crawl. Another cyclist had pulled up alongside her.

At the junction Merel paused. To her left, the way back into town was windswept and barren, devoid of shops where it crossed the motorway, with a couple of gargantuan office blocks after that. Merel peered to her right, down the high street. At the far end she could see a greengrocer's, across on the other side. She decided to do her Saturday shopping there, hoping the weather would be a little better when she was done. She turned right, and cycled on down towards it.

Behind her, the scooter-rider frowned. He turned to follow her. The storm broke suddenly, just as Merel was nearing the end of the street. She pulled up under a shop awning and looked about her. The scooter stopped, too, a little way behind, its engine revving noisily. The metro station was just a few metres further on. Merel decided to give the greengrocer's a miss. She could take her bike on Line 50, she knew. She suspected she'd have to change somewhere, but she'd be able to get all the way to the centre. Dry. Well, mostly dry. Buy a cheap umbrella, do her shopping on the Nieuwmarkt, then she was meeting friends at three. Perfect. Hunched against the rain, she cycled as fast as she could the short distance to the station, scrambled for her pass, beeped it at the barrier, and pushed her bike into the lift. As the doors slid shut, the scooter sped away, its engine an angry snarl.

SUNDAY
12 JUNE 2011

12

De Dolle Hond drifted into the cosy contentment of another Sunday afternoon. Mrs Ting was long established in her position at the fruit machine, Marloes from the guest house next door (always in early on a Sunday) sat beside the fireplace with a rather hungover-looking young man; the Kesters who owned the tobacconists were there, the big apple tart had arrived from the Bakkerswinkel, and the smell of premium coffee percolated through the room. Paul de Vos sat hunched at his piano, absorbed in a vintage X-Men comic, his sole literary passion. The honeyed tones of Sarah Vaughan flowed gently out of the sound system. Anna was busy polishing glasses.

Posthumus took up his usual seat where the bar counter met the wall, beneath the display of old badges and medals. He made a mental note to go by the stamp man at the flea-market in the morning, to ask if he'd found out anything about that bird and star design. Sarah Vaughan came to an end. Posthumus looked across to Paul at the piano, and then at Anna. Had there been a repeat of that Saturday night? The two of them? Perhaps not. The musician had his back to her, and was looking sulky. Posthumus smiled, and hummed a little to himself. Bom-titi-bom titi-bom titi-bom.

'You seem cheerful,' said Anna, as she came over to put on some new music. 'Don't often hear you singing along.'

'I'm not really. But I've got this tune in my head. A crazy

drunk we met yesterday was singing it. Actually, it's been one hell of a weekend.'

'Well, at least your bump's almost disappeared. Feeling better?'

'Quite a lot, thanks. But, yow! What happened to your arm?'

'Burned it ironing. I *do* iron sometimes!' Anna said, noting Posthumus's surprise. 'In emergencies.' The task was usually left to the woman who came in to clean the café.

'Clearly not very efficiently,' said Posthumus. 'That looks painful. You can even see the marks of those little holes the steam comes out of. Are you sure it's OK?'

'Nothing that ointment and a bit of Nina won't solve.' Anna put on some Nina Simone. 'Now, with or without?' she said. Without asking, she cut him a slice of apple tart. Cream was his only variable. 'And then tell me all about this hellish weekend, while things here are still quiet.'

It took Posthumus a good ten minutes. Through to his second cup of coffee.

'I'm wondering whether I should have let myself in for all this,' he said, 'but now I've as much as promised Mohammed that I'll see it through.'

'And I know you,' said Anna. 'You'd never be able to let it go, anyway. Certainly not now.'

'I wish I'd got a better look at that guy who tasered me,' said Posthumus. 'I'm pretty certain it was Najib. Otherwise why did he run away when he saw me talking to Mohammed in the shop? And manage to evaporate again yesterday morning? He's trying to avoid me.'

'And you think he had something to do with Amir's death as well?'

'I don't know. Something isn't quite fitting. But I keep asking myself, what the hell was he doing in Amir's apartment with a *taser* for Chrissakes?'

'On a visit?'

'Come *on*. He broke in.'

'Or maybe it was someone else. Lying in wait. Perhaps it was Amir who was supposed to get blitzed, not you.'

Posthumus felt a little shiver down his spine. He stared at Anna across the bar.

'That's it! Ballroom *blitz*! Attack tacky tack. Men in hats, dancing like gnats. That's *it*!'

'He's finally lost it,' said Anna to Hans Kester, who had come up to the bar for more drinks. 'Knew it would happen some time.'

She looked across the bar as the door swung open. Merel came in.

'Perhaps you can help,' Anna said with a nod towards Posthumus. 'Your uncle's flipped. It must have been that bang on the head.'

Posthumus had leapt up from his stool. He barely greeted his niece, but grabbed her by the shoulders.

'I *knew* there was something I wasn't quite getting,' said Posthumus. 'That old drunk singing Ballroom Blitz and going on about men in dresses dancing. *That's* what he was remembering, maybe even trying to tell us. There was a fight. Two guys in djellabas. One of them at least making crazy movements. It was like lightning. Electric. Amir was *tasered*.'

As if working to order, Mrs Ting had a win. Even Paul de Vos seemed roused from his sulk by Posthumus's animation, and turned from the piano to listen.

'And I think we can be pretty sure,' Posthumus said to Merel, 'that whoever did that, and whoever tasered me in Amir's apartment, are one and the same person. It's too much of a coincidence.'

'Perhaps Merel would like a drink,' said Anna to Posthumus. 'And as for you, I'd go easy on the caffeine.'

Merel took the stool beside Posthumus. They both opted for wine.

'Lovely to see you gracing us with your presence again.' Paul had come over to the bar. Merel gave a non-committal smile, and angled herself towards Posthumus, away from the corner of the counter where Paul was standing.

'I was passing and just dropped in for a minute, because there's something I especially want to talk to PP about,' she said. 'And I don't have very long.'

'That's to the point,' said Paul. He looked over to Anna. She met his gaze, and slowly pulled down the draught-beer handle, filling a glass for a new arrival. Paul took out a cigarette, and sauntered outside.

Merel watched him go and was about to say something, but caught Posthumus's warning look, and his glance towards Anna.

'So what's all this about tasering?' she said.

'A possible scenario,' said Posthumus. 'In a way, Anna has just come up with it, talking about someone lying in wait for Amir. But she got the time and place wrong. Not last Friday in Amir's apartment, but that Monday night. And it was Najib. Waiting for him near his apartment, beside the canal. With a taser. We know he doesn't like Amir, maybe doesn't want the guy hanging round his sister. And I can tell you, tasers hurt! Perhaps Najib decides to teach Amir a lesson, rough him up a bit.'

'That tallies with something Aissa said.'

'How did that go? Sorry about that phone call yesterday, I had no idea you'd be with her.'

'When you left, I thought I'd give her a ring,' said Merel, 'and as I was still in the area, we met up. It was tricky at first. She thought you and I were somehow operating together. You can't blame her for not trusting journalists, given how many times people have been done over in the media.'

'But you sorted it?'

'Think so. She was fine about the piece I did on her, a bit less about the Amsterdam Cell story, but in the end she made me lunch, and we had a long chat. I think it's OK now. We even got down to a bit of girls' talk. Boyfriends and that.'

'But she said something about Najib?'

'Well, he was angry that she had spoken to me and not told him, but it's not just that. He's really jealous of her. Very protective. This new boyfriend she's got, Khaled, a friend of his, is the first one that he's ever approved of. Aissa said he's already going on at her to marry the guy! And this after he's always given her a really hard time about men before, even though he's younger than she is. He once put some sort of tracking device on her scooter, because he thought she was seeing someone he didn't know about. Questioned her about why she had been places. Can you believe it!'

'That is one very troubled young man.'

'And apparently there was a big argument that night over dinner. Najib really flew off the handle. A bit more than it seems Mohammed made out to you. So what you're saying makes sense.'

'And he left before Amir. So he could have gone to wait at the apartment, and tackled him again as he was getting home.'

'But why would he do it? Protectiveness over your sister is one thing, but we could be talking *murder* here.'

There, she'd said it. But somehow using the word made it seem less likely. More unreal.

'You're not still going on about that Amir guy,' said Anna, coming back to their corner of the bar.

Posthumus explained about Najib, his attitude to Amir, the taser. 'It was you saying "blitz" that did it,' he said.

'Aren't you getting a bit too carried away?' said Anna. 'If anything, it was probably just a tussle, a fight that got out of hand. An accident, and this Najib was afraid to go to the police.'

'And we don't even know that's how Amir ended up in the water,' said Merel. 'That crazy drunk is hardly a credible witness.'

'He could even have done it himself,' said Anna, 'and be spinning you some story. People like that are very good at picking up on what you want to hear.'

'And as you said yesterday,' Merel went on, 'you can't go to the police with a few lines from a song and some story about men dancing, so what next?'

'I still think I should talk to Najib,' said Posthumus. 'Now, even more so. Maybe not to mention Amir, but to confront him about tasering me at least.'

'Sounds crazy to me,' said Anna. 'Madness. The boy is dangerous.'

'Did Aissa say she could help set up something?' said Posthumus to Merel.

'That's what I came in to tell you. I couldn't really ask her. It seemed too calculating, too manipulative, just as we were patching things up. Building a friendship, rather than some sort of "I want something from you" relationship.'

'So, no go.'

'Well, not necessarily. Something Aissa said. Najib works in the shop on Monday afternoons, and he can't get out of that one because Karima's teaching Dutch, Aissa's at the university and Mohammed is on some liaison committee between the Moroccan community and the city. He does a lot of that sort of thing, apparently. So Najib has to be there, and he will be on his own.'

'So, tomorrow afternoon then. I'll have to swing something with work.'

'I still think you're mad,' said Anna. 'If it was him in the apartment, then he's already attacked you once. And now you're suggesting he's done something even worse than that.'

'At least the shop is somewhere public. And you two know I'll be there.'

'Well, I don't know, keep your phone handy, or ring me before you go in and leave it on,' said Anna.

'I saw him, you know,' said Merel. 'And he doesn't look very dangerous. He was leaving as we arrived for lunch. Skinny, about nineteen. Didn't look very strong. Quite nerdy, in fact. Aissa says he's a computer buff, a bit of a techie genius, according to her.'

'What was he wearing?'

'No black and gold trainers, if that's what you're thinking. But he was in a djellaba. Oh, and that's the other thing, I almost forgot. That Monday was the first night he started wearing traditional dress. It sounds to me like it was some sort of family crisis. Najib went upstairs after the argument and got changed. Mohammed was shocked, apparently.'

'They didn't mention anything about that to me yesterday.'

'Maybe it didn't seem relevant. Or do you think they're hiding something?'

'Can you trust this Mohammed?' said Anna. 'Or the Aissa woman?'

'I'd say yes, to both,' said Posthumus, after a while.

Merel nodded.

'Besides,' Posthumus went on, 'Mohammed would hardly ask for my help if he thought his own son was involved. No, I think talking to Najib has to be the next move.'

'And you're right. You needn't mention anything about Monday and Amir,' said Merel. 'Call his bluff. Tell him you know it was him who tasered you in the apartment. Ask him why he was there.'

New arrivals – the English couple who ran the snack bar

near the Dam – interrupted the conversation, as Anna went off to serve them.

Merel got up. 'I must go,' she said. 'I've got friends coming round to my place in a few minutes.'

'But we'll be in touch? That meal, some time soon?'

'I promise,' said Merel. She gathered the shopping bags she had brought in with her, gave a wave to Anna, and walked to the door. As she left, she crossed Paul de Vos coming back in.

'Bye. Don't take it personally,' she said, and went over the street to unlock her bicycle, propped against the wall opposite.

De Dolle Hond dawdled on through its Sunday afternoon. Posthumus had another glass of the Sauvignon Blanc, and listened, quietly pleased, as Paul grumbled about the inscrutable ways of women. Cornelius came by, sans Gabrielle, to drop off the poems, stayed for a genever or three, and a chat about the quality of the work. The Kesters, as always, grew a little pinker in the face and began bickering. Anna played a few opera aria favourites, and Marloes from the guest house persuaded Paul to accompany her, and gave them 'Op de Amsterdamse Grachten' and 'Johnny Jordaan'. Cornelius surprised all, and had the place in stitches, with a wickedly funny poem – rapper-style, off the top of his head – on the virtues of Anna and her ineptness with an iron.

It was just before five o'clock when Posthumus's phone rang. He spoke for a few minutes, then put it back in his pocket, grim-faced.

'Problem?' asked Anna.

'Merel,' he said. 'She's in hospital. She was knocked off her bike by a scooter, just as she was getting home.'

MONDAY

13 JUNE 2011

13

'I'm fine, really I am,' said Merel. 'Nothing broken. They thought I'd fractured my shoulder, but I haven't. I feel much better this morning. Just a bit stiff and sore.'

Posthumus was walking to work, talking on his mobile as he went. Merel's line had been busy all morning, and the night before had been answered by the friend who had phoned him from the hospital. An off-putting young man who seemed to have everything under control, and implied that Posthumus was not needed.

'I'm back home, even going into work later today,' Merel went on. 'Daren't miss a trick these days.'

'What happened exactly?'

'A guy came from behind, really fast, overtook me, and I think something must have got caught, 'cos it felt like I was being pulled along for a while, then, thwack. Hit the ground.'

Posthumus felt his gut tighten. A grip that squeezed up to the throat. 'You've spoken to your mother?'

'Not yet. I didn't want to worry her. I was slurring a bit, apparently, full of painkillers. I sound OK now, though?'

'Fine.'

'I'll ring her after this.'

'Those scooters should be banned from cycle paths. They're a menace.'

'And he was really motoring. At least they should crack down on that.'

'Did he stop?'

'Not a bit of it. Round the corner and gone.'

There was a pause.

'Do you think it has something to do with . . . all this?' said Posthumus.

Merel did not answer right away.

'I don't know,' she said at last. 'I didn't see him. People said he was a young Moroccan guy. But then people pretty much always say that. No one got a registration or anything.'

Posthumus had reached the steps that led down to the flea-market on Waterlooplein.

'You say anything to the police?' he said.

'I was flat out on the pavement. Didn't speak to them at all. And what's there to say? We've got nothing concrete. And besides, accidents with bikes and scooters happen all the time.'

'I just couldn't face it if I was somehow putting you in danger.'

'Now you're being melodramatic. Look, this was most probably an accident, and if there was any dodgy business it's far more likely to be connected to my piece on the Amsterdam Cell than anything to do with Amir. So I would have brought it on myself.'

'Still . . .'

'PP, stop being silly. Now I really must go. I'm a bit slower with everything this morning than I should be.'

Posthumus walked on through the market, glad that Lotti was up the other end with her trolley, and he didn't have to cope with her banter. He reached the City Hall.

'You there! Don't you want to know about this?'

Posthumus had forgotten the stamp man. He was sitting at his stall. Same tweed jacket and greying white shirt that he'd been wearing a few days before, Posthumus could swear it. He was holding up the scrap of paper Posthumus had drawn the bird and star design on.

Posthumus doubled back.

'Thank you, my mind was elsewhere,' he said. 'Good morning.'

The man shrugged. 'It's not worth much, if that's what you were hoping.'

'So you know what it is then?'

'Some sort of military training medal. Syrian. Two a penny. I doubt that I'd be interested.'

'No matter then,' said Posthumus, taking the drawing from him. 'But thank you for your help, all the same.'

The man seemed momentarily taken aback. 'On the other hand,' he said, 'that other medal you had. Now that's something different. I might well be interested in *that*.'

He noticed Posthumus's reluctance.

'On a commission basis?' he added.

'I'm not sure,' said Posthumus, smiling politely. 'But I'll ask my friend.'

He pocketed the scrap of paper, and walked on across the bridge to the Staalkade.

Maya was standing at the reception desk when he came in, talking to Alex. He greeted them both. Alex caught his eye, and gave him the briefest conspiratorial nod. Posthumus walked upstairs, and went to fetch himself a coffee while his computer booted up.

An email from Alex.

'Shit!' said Posthumus, out loud. A house-visit that afternoon with Maya. That was his one chance to speak to Najib, and he had hoped to sneak out early. He mailed back:

Can't Sulung do it?

The answer pinged in as Maya herself came through the door.

Sulung sick again. (Am worried about him . . . anything seriously wrong do you think?)

'Any chance of doing that house-visit this morning instead of after lunch?' Posthumus asked Maya as she passed his desk.

'Impossible,' she said. 'I have a funeral. I sorted a last-minute slot for that old lady from last week. The one with the long-lost niece – she wouldn't pay for her aunt's funeral, but she's imploring me to be there in person. Touching, isn't it?'

The sour cow almost snorted, thought Posthumus, as Maya, tight-lipped, sat down at her desk. He looked down at his screen, as another mail pinged in from Alex.

Good news is, I hit the jackpot with Amir's computer. First shop I phoned. Having the name helped. They were a bit reluctant at first, but you were right, and it turns out I'm good at lying. I told them we needed it urgently to trace his family, and in the end they were OK about sending it to the department address. Told them they could verify that on the city website. So it's coming by courier, should arrive tomorrow afternoon.

All very wicked and fraudulent and exciting. You are leading me astray.

Please eat this email.

Ax

'Sulung's off sick again,' said Maya, while her computer chimed to life. 'Strange how that so often happens on a Monday or Friday.'

'Last time he was off during the week, and came *back* on a Friday,' said Posthumus.

'Well, it still doesn't help with the Personal Effects backlog. He was going to sort that this morning.'

'I'll see what I can do with it,' said Posthumus.

None of them liked working on Personal Effects. Deciding what to do with the contents of those brown envelopes that arrived from the undertakers was (apart, perhaps, from winding up bank accounts) for all three the most tedious part of their job. Each item had to be individually logged: watches, phones, wallets, jewellery. Selecting what to ditch, what – if anything – to send to auction, in order to add tiny sums to minimal estates. Posting things on, if any relatives had been traced. And then there was the stuff that had nowhere to go: the single cheap ring, the trashy necklace, once beloved of somebody perhaps, but now simply a bother – ridiculous to send to auction, but somehow wrong to throw away. Those all went into a large carton, despatched to the auctioneers once a year, the proceeds going to a cancer research foundation. Sometimes it was hard to tell – things that might well be valuable, but didn't look it, or vice versa – and some internet trawling was needed before deciding. It was bitty work, troublesome, and – Posthumus was sure that even Maya felt this, though she would never admit it – a little depressing. At busy times, the office got behind with Personal Effects. And the past two weeks had been busy.

Posthumus brought the pile of eleven, no, twelve brown envelopes to his desk. For once he didn't mind doing this. It would give him some time to think. An excuse to be on the computer without Maya shooting him questioning glances. First envelope. He called up the computer file: a homeless person, named, but no relatives. Sulung's case, originally. He spread two strips of paper kitchen roll on his desk, and emptied the contents of the envelope on to them. A particularly filthy wallet, and an odd glass object on a neck-chain.

Slowly he put on surgical gloves from a box beside him, pausing as if he were contemplating the glass pendant, but with his mind segueing to medals and Syria. *Syria?* So the design of Bart Hooft's tattoo was probably Syrian. But what on earth could Bart have to do with the Syrian military? Was it like the tattoo-parlour man had suggested? That the tattoo came from someone he had met on the internet, a 'master'? Or was it something to do with Bart himself? Had he grown up there perhaps, as a foreigner? The American spelling in his poems the result of an education at some sort of international school? Posthumus picked up the wallet between thumb and forefingers, rested it on the kitchen paper and gingerly prised it open. And if Bart's father was the one that Gusta mentioned, the son of the pen dealer – Posthumus had still not quite given up on that fountain pen as a dead-end – if he was the son who had emigrated, 'some sort of academic', Gusta had said, could he have gone to Syria? An engineer? Something in Arabic studies?

The wallet released an odour of mildew and human sweat. It was empty, apart from a few foreign coins, and some three or four euros in change. Posthumus tipped the money into a charity collecting-box on his desk (the usual receptacle for any coins), binned the wallet, put the pendant in the general auction carton, noted all this on the contents sheet that came with the envelope, placed the sheet to one side for filing with the Case Report, and with a sigh reached to pick up the next envelope.

'Can I get you another coffee?'

It wasn't so much Maya's voice that startled him, but the offer itself. It was rare that Maya fetched coffee for anyone but herself. She must be feeling guilty about his uncomplaining taking-over of the Personal Effects pile.

'Thank you,' he said. 'Espresso Forte, the dark green one, double.'

Maya handed him an envelope. 'Another one, I'm afraid. I noticed it under some other stuff on Sulung's desk.'

Maya seemed unabashed in admitting she had poked about on a colleague's desk. It wouldn't have been the first time, Posthumus knew. His desk, too.

Posthumus read the name on the envelope. Amir Loukili.

What on earth was Amir's Personal Effects envelope doing on Sulung's desk? He peered inside. The little passport photos he'd shown to Mohammed, some loose change, the soggy notebook, now dried out and swollen, a train ticket. He saw that Alex had added the gory photograph that had come from the police. Posthumus closed the envelope again, and before Maya came back he slipped it into the bottom drawer of his desk. No need just yet to send this stuff on to Mohammed. He wanted another look at it first, and he wanted to speak to Najib.

Posthumus sipped his second coffee, and looked out of the window at the row of gable tops across the water. Ordered but varied. All a similar height, but with subtle changes in rhythm. A bell gable, a step gable, a flat cornice. Three neck gables in a row. A pattern, then a surprise. Something in Posthumus's mind was feeling for a pattern. The mind that filled the gaps, that made the stories. The mind that ranged over bookcases and music collections, looked at pictures on walls and into wardrobes, that came up with a life, a personality to fill a five-minute funeral oration, a final ceremony with an individual touch, this mind was groping, carefully. Feeling its way blind, not quite seeing what there was to see. Posthumus recreated for himself an image of Amir's apartment. White, plain, few variations – the snake of the abandoned laptop cord, one or two Arabic texts on the wall. But empty. Similar in its austerity to Bart Hooft's room, except—

'Something interesting going on out there?'

It was Maya. The coffee moment had been too good to last. Battle had clearly recommenced.

'I really should keep my eyes from wandering away from my own desk,' said Posthumus, and looked back from the window to his work.

He emptied out the third envelope and turned to his computer, but instead of calling up the appropriate case record, he went to Bart Hooft's file. To the section where the photographs of the apartment had been downloaded from the department camera. The walls were not entirely bare. A poster: Rothko. He had told Cornelius about that, and the books, the absence of music, to help him with the poem. What had Cornelius's line been? 'Weariness, solitude, and the far flight of music.' Something like that. But the poster. Yes, he remembered correctly. It was for an exhibition, and yes – Posthumus zoomed in on it – in the US. The Snite Museum, Notre Dame, Indiana. He'd never heard of it. Google. And yes again. The museum was part of a University of Notre Dame. Pretty big league by the looks of things, the sort of place that would attract foreign staff. So maybe not Syria after all. Not for Bart's father, anyway, maybe he went to work in the States. And there couldn't be many Hoofts in Notre Dame, Indiana. All he needed was a staff register or an online phone book. It didn't explain the tattoo, but at least he could speak to the parents, sound them out, tell them about Bart, send them the poems if it seemed the right thing to do.

'Having trouble calling up the file?'

God, that woman! Didn't she ever let up? Posthumus simply smiled at her, and returned to examining the contents of the envelope. Then he ploughed on through the rest of the pile. If he managed to finish, it would free him up later in the afternoon. Tracking down Bart's parents could wait. There were more pressing things to see to. Maya would be off to that funeral soon, and he certainly didn't want her around for what he wanted to do next.

'Can I have a word? Something's come up.'

Rachid intercepted Lisette just as she was getting to her office door. He was about to say more, but checked himself.

'Are you feeling OK?' he asked instead. 'Is now a good time?'

No, she wasn't and no, it wasn't. Not at all. But now of all times was not the time to show that.

'I'm fine, come on in,' she said, punching in her code on the door lock, glad that Rachid looked aside and did not notice her hand shaking slightly, the fury she had been suppressing for the past hour still gripping her body.

Lisette had spent the weekend rehearsing her attack, building a force of moral and psychological argument, and reinforcing it with cold logic. She had asked to see Veldhuizen first thing in the morning. And he had simply crushed her. Ridden straight over her, like some tank in a war movie, not flinching from its path as its metal tracks ground over the bodies of fallen soldiers.

First he had kept her waiting for an hour. The old tactic. She had expected that. Remained calm, quietly running through what she was going to say. He had not invited her to sit, simply fixed her with those eyes, the barest movement of a brow beneath that bald head querying why she was there. Lisette had argued ethics, and the instability created by the team not knowing about the agent, the way in which it was deflecting their focus from what mattered. She had pointed out the irregularity of what Veldhuizen was doing, and said it was making her job impossible. A mistake, that. He leapt at it and threw the book at her. Implied state interests she had no access to, leaks she had no control over. He demolished her skills as a manager, dismissed her as inept, threatened her position. It was a sustained and skilful blast. And she had capitulated. Caved in. The man knew his stuff, she gave him that; knew how to get what he wanted. And he deployed a sort of latent brute force that crouched just short of actual violence. Lisette suppressed a shudder. It sounded stupid, to anyone who had not witnessed it, and he kept it well controlled. A panther: large, dangerous, quick. And clever. That was the worst of it. She felt outsmarted. Not wrong, but outmanoeuvred. She hadn't lasted the course. And the reason she had finally given in was not so much that she agreed with him, or felt it was for the ultimate good of the service, but that she wanted to protect her job. It wasn't Veldhuizen she hated at this moment, it was herself. That was where the real betrayal lay.

Lisette walked ahead of Rachid into the office, quietly taking a long breath, smoothing her palms down the sides of her waist, looking about the room and drawing some comfort from the familiar, the lie of the desk, the picture on the wall – inert objects, solid, known, reliable. Rachid followed, and shut the door behind him.

'So, what's up?' asked Lisette.

'Last Friday after prayers,' said Rachid. 'Big Brother House. I didn't get to listen to it before the meeting. There's so much; this backlog is impossible.'

'I know, I know,' said Lisette. She tried to sound sympathetic. 'But after prayers?'

'I'm not sure what it is, and I'll have to listen to the weekend tapes, but it sounds like something's up. So I thought I'd flag it up to you right away, rather than just send it on to Ingrid.'

'Slow down, who is doing what?'

'It wasn't clear – just that Najib Tahiri seems to be learn-ing something he should say. Rehearsing it in Arabic, which I think could point to suicide video. Some phrases put me on the alert. And talk of holding big iron, which could mean getting some sort of heavy weaponry to show off on film. But I'll have to listen to the weekend material to be sure. Alami and El Mardi are also in the room, by the sounds of things. Here, look.'

He handed Lisette a few pages of transcript. 'A lot of this stuff is in English. The conversations, I mean, with the new guy Khaled. You don't need me for that. Couldn't somebody else at least help out by taking over the English?'

Lisette edged Rachid on with a nod.

'It's this Khaled who seems to be organising it, I think. I'm not sure, but it's him helping Najib with the Arabic on the tapes. I told you he was one to watch.'

Lisette felt herself go cold. Cold and calm. Now was her chance. She gestured to Rachid to sit down, took her own seat behind the desk. Now. Come clean. To Rachid? Veldhuizen's accusations echoed, as if she were still hearing them, some-where behind her head. She looked across the desk at Rachid for a long while, then lowered her eyes to the transcripts.

'Go on,' she said.

Together they leaned over her desk, reading through the texts.

'See . . . here,' said Rachid. 'Not just the usual stuff about despots of the West, but a personal reference to his parents. And then later this bit about the language of the sword. That sounds like the words of a suicide tape to me. Something more than just polemic. And here, all this about crusaders. Also, there's talk between the two of them of Tahiri's sister and Khaled. Marriage. It's a long shot, but I think maybe that could be part of the deal. Tahiri's boasted about it before, to the others, that he's going to sort out this marriage between his sister and Khaled. It could be something personal between the two of them – Tahiri and Khaled, I mean. Like some sort of guarantee to look after the family if Tahiri blows himself up.'

'And the family is the sort to arrange a marriage? Traditional, I mean?' said Lisette.

Rachid shrugged. 'Could be,' he said 'I don't get much on them, you'd have to check with Ben.'

'Or it could even mean that she's involved,' said Lisette. 'Try to get more on what Tahiri says about it exactly. "Married" has been used as a codeword for martyrdom, hasn't it? Does Ben have anything from his guys on this?'

'He's out meeting with an asset at the moment, I believe. Probably be back around lunchtime. By the way, the fuss with the Tahiris Ben heard about on Friday, it's because their cousin died. The one who arrived a few months ago from Morocco.'

'I thought he was in Brussels.'

Rachid shrugged. 'I don't know. Seems not. But I don't have any more, it was just something Tahiri said, complaining about his father. As I said, there's a lot to listen to.'

'Any more here?'

'Bassir,' said Rachid, returning to the transcript. 'He had an odd conversation. One-sided, his phone rang after prayers. That's one of the reasons the Tahiri texts are so patchy. Bassir was talking in the same room, so it was all going on at once. It was hard to hear properly. He seems to be talking about football, but it is odd somehow. Have a look.'

Lisette read the transcript. Part of a conversation about Bassir's support for the Amsterdam team Ajax, of someone who wanted to join. It was seemingly harmless, but Rachid was right, it didn't quite ring true. Phrases that sounded odd: 'he has no view to playing a game, at the moment for training only, in the first area'. Questions that didn't make sense in the context: 'Did you tell him about travelling to the picnic?'

'Football or Ajax for "jihad", do you think?' she said.

'That and the fact that we know from earlier tapes that Bassir was born in Rotterdam and is a Feyenoord supporter. So one of those must be dodgy. He'd hardly support two arch-rival teams.'

For another twenty minutes they discussed Rachid's take on the transcripts, on the Cell as a whole.

'You're good at this, I know,' said Lisette. 'And I do know that you're frustrated in audio, that you'd be brilliant as an analyst. But Ingrid is good, too, and at the moment there are so few people who could fill your shoes where you are now.'

'I know how these guys' heads work,' said Rachid. He did not use the InSec jargon 'targets'. 'I grew up with kids like them, I worked as a mentor when I was a student, a sort of street coach. I know what they're about, see things you guys just don't get. I know when something's coming.' He looked down at the floor, scuffed the toe of his trainer against the leg of her desk. 'And I know how to try to stop it. How to help.'

Lisette tapped the pages of the transcript together, and locked them in a drawer in her desk. Now it was Mick Waling's voice, not Veldhuizen's, echoing at a point behind her head. 'We are observers, not participants.'

'I'll speak to Coco about co-opting someone to take the English transcribing off you, at least,' she said. 'As for the rest, I'll see what I can do. I promise.'

They stood up at the same time.

'Meanwhile,' she said. 'I think we both deserve a bit of a break. Café Minus will be open by now, how about an early lunch?'

* * *

Ben was already deeply occupied with an extra-large portion of moussaka when they walked in, having worked his charm on one of the girls behind the food counter.

'Yo peeps. What's up? The queen croaked or something? You two look like your puppy just got squashed.'

They fetched some lunch and joined him. Lisette let Rachid fill Ben in briefly.

'Video's a new one on me,' said Ben. 'Amir, I just heard about. Drowned in the Prinsengracht. Remember seeing those reports of an unidentified body a couple of weeks back? I guess that was our man. The Khaled Tahiri-girl thing, that's been bubbling up over the past few weeks or so. Cousin Amir was on that scene briefly, but didn't get a look-in. The girl didn't go for him, and skinny Najib didn't approve. Bit of an asshole younger brother, it seems.'

Ben took another mouthful of moussaka, and went straight on: 'I don't know if we're quite ordering wedding cake yet, but the girl *is* all dewy for Khaled, and the man gets the Najib stamp of approval. Problem is Daddy doesn't like it. Or wouldn't, if he had a glow-worm's glimmer it was happening. It's all been mousey-mousey secret so far, but Najib's been boasting he's got it all in the bag. According to the skinny man, D-day's coming up soon.'

He swallowed his moussaka, and slugged back some Coke.

'Loves his gossip, does my go-man. And his sister is buddies with Aissa, and has been getting the whole tra-la about what a glory boy this Khaled is.'

'So "married" isn't a codeword, then,' said Lisette. And on top of it all, if this is for real, Veldhuizen's agent is guilty of unprofessional conduct, she thought. Lisette looked across Café Minus to one of the large, colourful Gauguin prints on the wall, seeming to gaze through it, as if the subterranean room had a window.

'Poor girl. I wonder if she knows what she's letting herself in for,' she said.

'The go-man's been following our Khaled on his late-night jaunts,' Ben went on. 'Remember? He was seen going out in Western dress. Walks in the park, it seems. And more. My man's found out what he's been up to, but couldn't tell me. Had to scarper. Said I'd get a surprise, though. I've just downloaded the pics, I was having a look when you came in.'

Ben tapped the tablet in front of him out of suspend mode, and a series of thumbnails came up on the screen, clearly taken in the dark with a night-vision camera.

'Hi-tech, your man,' said Rachid.

'This little lady,' said Ben, slipping a black box, barely larger than a cigarette packet from his top pocket. 'Zoom, the works. Only downside is the stamp-sized screen on the thing itself. But the next generation will even have thermal imaging.' He cradled the object gently in his palm. 'It's a beauty. Absolute state-of-the-art. Got it special, from my contact at i-Spy, you know, the shop near the Kolenkit? Sells all sorts of surveillance stuff, a lot of it better than we get!'

'This isn't Service equipment?' said Lisette. 'Ben, you're *already* on a warning for Desk Offences.'

'Uh-oh. You didn't hear that. Didn't see it,' said Ben, putting the camera back in his pocket, carrying on clicking through the thumbnails. 'Well, well, well. Look at this!' He angled the screen further towards Rachid and Lisette across the table. 'It seems even terrorists have their little secrets.'

Rachid looked at the screen and grimaced.

Lisette wiped her mouth with a paper napkin, scrunched it up and dropped it on her empty plate, stood, and picked up her tray to leave. As she did so, she leaned over and removed the camera from Ben's top pocket.

'I think I'd better have that,' she said.

As soon as Maya left the office for the funeral, Posthumus picked up his phone. He hadn't wanted the flak that would come if she eavesdropped on him asking his doctor about tasers. And she would. He knew, too, that it wouldn't be the sort of call he could slip into the confines of a coffee break. Not with that harridan of a medical receptionist who guarded the portal to the hallowed Dr Bentinck. Even phoning with an ailment he would be subject to the third degree – symptoms, details, duration – before she would deign to dispense an appointment. He wasn't wrong. In the end he resorted to: 'It's an urgent, extremely personal matter and I would like to speak to the doctor on the phone as soon as possible.' The looks he would get the next time he was in! She begrudgingly agreed to transmit the message to Dr Bentinck, and have him phone back when he was available.

Posthumus put down the phone and, opening the bottom drawer of his desk, he took out the Amir Loukili envelope, emptying it out in front of him. He picked up the swollen black notebook. Most of the pages formed a papier-mâché lump. He tried to prise a few apart. One or two gave way, but only partially, tearing along a jagged fault line that left patches of legibility, obscured by raised islands where the previous page – or pages – still clung fast. And all in Arabic. He thought for a moment, then – leaving the landline free should Dr Bentinck phone back – he took out his mobile.

'Cornelius, it's Pieter Posthumus.'

'So I see. And now hear. And how is my dear Charon? Is there another passenger in your ferry across the Styx?'

Posthumus laughed. He was beginning to get used to Cornelius Barendrecht. And after yesterday afternoon in De Dolle Hond, even rather to enjoy his company.

'No. No lost souls today,' he said. 'This is something else. On the off-chance, really. You don't happen to know anyone who can read Arabic, do you?'

'I can a bit myself, as it happens,' said Cornelius. 'I did a year at SOAS in London, as part of my chequered and somewhat haphazard academic career. A long, long time ago, though, and I haven't really kept it up. Depends what you mean.'

'It's something I need deciphering. Handwriting, in a notebook.'

'A man of intrigue and an actor dark. I might be able to help. If not, I'm sure I could rustle up someone. When?'

'It's not very much. Just a few words by the looks of things . . . but as soon as?'

'You're near the City Hall, aren't you?'

'Practically next door.'

'I have to be there in an hour. Wedding. Could drop in on the way, but it would have to be fleeting.'

'Fleeting is good. I don't want to do this if there's anyone else in the office, and that's only the case till around lunchtime.'

'Deeper and darker. Give me forty minutes.'

Posthumus replaced the contents of the Loukili envelope, except the notebook, and put the lot back in his desk drawer. Then he addressed himself to eroding the Personal Effects pile further, until Alex buzzed up that Cornelius was at Reception.

'Send him up,' said Posthumus, and met the poet at the top of the stairs.

'Let's have a look,' said Cornelius, as the two sat down at Posthumus's desk.

Cornelius turned what pages of the notebook he could with a long middle finger.

'Hard to tell,' he said. 'Especially with freehand rather than print. And I'm rustier than I thought. Could I take this away?'

'If no one sees you.'

'It's also that they're fragments out of context,' said Cornelius. 'And that things are often more elaborately expressed in Arabic, so a literal translation doesn't always get you anywhere. Take this, for example.' He indicated one of the more intact patches. 'It's oddly phrased, but the meaning is something like "my memento", "something to remember me by".'

Perhaps if he hadn't been looking at the photographs of Bart Hooft's apartment that morning, the phrase would have meant nothing to Posthumus. Or at most rung just a faint bell of familiarity. As it was, the unwelcome image of the dildo they had found buried in Hooft's sock-box flashed immediately into his mind. 'Something to remember me by.' Wasn't that what was written on it, below the drawing? The same image as Bart Hooft's tattoo. Posthumus realised with irritation that they hadn't photographed the object, had left it lying where it was. He said a rather distracted goodbye to Cornelius, and was walking him back to the stairs when Dr Bentinck returned his call.

Posthumus made it to his desk just before the phone went to voicemail.

'Pieter, what's all this about?' said Bentinck. He sounded concerned. Posthumus had been with him for years, since Bentinck had opened his practice just off the Nieuwmarkt.

'Sorry to ring alarm bells,' said Posthumus. 'But I really do need to find out something before this afternoon, and your assistant can be unyielding, to say the least.'

'It's her job.'

'I'll be quick. This is work-related. But it is something that might interest you.'

Bentinck was a crime-story fanatic. He sometimes drank at De Dolle Hond, and enjoyed nothing more than demolishing medical aspects of the latest TV series.

'I don't know how much you know about tasers,' said Posthumus, 'but I was wondering, could you kill someone with one?'

'The short answer is "no".' The doctor paused a moment. 'But there is quite a lot of controversy about them. Heart attacks and so on. There've been a couple of hundred deaths in the past few years, but it's hard to pinpoint cause and effect. What's all this about, really?'

'I can't go into that. Not yet, anyway. At the moment it's only a thought.'

'Basically, they just disable you for a few seconds. Your standard half-second zap will cause muscle contractions, spasms; two to three seconds would floor someone; five seconds or more . . . well, then you're possibly talking some danger. Breathing difficulties and the like. But you can't do that. Not with the latest models, anyway. They have an automatic cut-off. The older versions didn't have that.'

'And if you tasered someone in water, or next to water, so that they fell in?'

'Well, then maybe you're in business. Hey, just what *is* this? You're not thinking of knocking someone off, are you? I can tell you it's pretty difficult to get away with.'

Posthumus laughed. 'No need to worry about that,' he said. 'And I hope some time I'll be able to tell you all about it in De Dolle Hond, but not quite yet. You're busy, anyway.'

But by now Bentinck was going strong. 'Well, if you did give someone the five seconds plus,' he said, 'even if less, the first reaction is to yell, it's pretty painful.'

Posthumus was glad his doctor could not see his face.

'So you yell, then inhale deeply. Bit like a baby howling full belt. Your muscles are all over the place, coordination shot to ribbons. Dazed. You hit the water. If it was a long zap your breathing could be erratic anyway. Lungs fill up. You're out of

it, don't really know where you are, can't control your limbs.
You'd probably lose consciousness pretty quickly. And drowning doesn't take long, you know. You might have something
there. Now whether it would actually be *murder*, or some sort
of what they call proximate cause, there you've got something
the lawyers would have a go at.'

'Thank you,' said Posthumus. 'That's all really useful to
know. I hope to tell you more about it over a glass of wine
some day.'

He thought he heard Maya's tread on the stairs.

'Thank you very much for your time,' he said into the phone
as she walked in to the office, his voice a notch more formal.
'That will be of some help to us, I am sure.'

Posthumus and Maya left on the house-visit soon after lunch.
The visit itself did not last long. They seldom did when Maya
led them. Brisk, efficient, minimalist. The moment a will, bank
statement or funeral insurance was found, that was it. The
bare bones of family-tracing back at the office, case closed.
And this visit was further sped along by a file of the client's
papers put out for them on the dining table by an efficient
home-help. But the apartment was far out west in Geuzenveld,
and minutes after leaving the office Maya had been caught in
a classic Amsterdam traffic trap: a van immediately in front
of them had stopped to unload on one of the narrow streets
alongside a canal. Before Maya could reverse to find an alter-
native route, a queue of cars had built up behind them, each in
turn dependent on the patience – or impatience – of the one
behind to back up and unplug the stoppage, all trying to judge
by the nature of the van, and what they could discern of its
load, how long it might be there; most resigned simply to waiting, a few succumbing to futile hooting. The last car in the line
had proved to contain a driver of considerable forbearance, and

for a full twenty minutes Maya had raged, immobile and helpless. Posthumus sat calmly alongside her. It had taken an hour to get to the apartment. But that helped Posthumus in his plan.

It was after three thirty by the time they returned from the apartment to the car, the client's file and a few other papers in a salvaged supermarket bag.

'Shall I drive?' said Posthumus.

They would be going back into town along the Haarlemmerweg, and he was sure that Maya lived somewhere in the Haarlemmer Quarter. Anyway, it was worth the chance.

'It's going on for four o'clock,' he went on, 'and what with afternoon traffic, by the time we get back to Staalkade it'll be just about time for you to do a U-turn and head back home. You live somewhere along the way, don't you? Why don't I just drop you off near home?'

Maya regarded him sceptically.

'Who knows,' said Posthumus, 'we might get stuck behind a van again, *so* infuriating that!'

'Well, as luck would have it, my bag and jacket are still in the boot after the funeral this morning,' said Maya.

'No real need to go back, then,' said Posthumus. 'I can countersign on the visit for you now if you like, drop off this stuff at the office. It's all pretty cut and dried, nothing valuable, after all.'

'That would make sense.'

Fifteen minutes later, Posthumus was driving alone out to the Kolenkit Quarter, and Najib Tahiri. He parked across the street from Casablanca Sofas. Najib, he could see, was alone in the shop, sitting hunched over the desk in the corner, his arms resting on the surface, something small in both hands. Texting on his phone, thought Posthumus, and he locked the car, crossed the street, and without hesitating pushed open the shop door.

14

A buzzer sounded loudly as Posthumus entered the shop. Najib looked up from the desk, and jumped to his feet.

'You and I have things to talk about, young man,' said Posthumus. He remained standing by the door.

'What do you think you're doing here?'

'That's no way to talk to a customer.'

'Well, you aren't a customer, are you?'

'Now how would you know that?'

Posthumus did not move further into the shop, nor did he take his eyes off Najib, but turned slightly and reaching over his shoulder flipped the sign behind him to Closed. He remained blocking the door.

'What are you snoopin' around my family for?' said Najib. He reached towards a shoulder bag lying on the desk.

'Taser again?' said Posthumus. 'I wouldn't advise it, I'm in full view of the street. And there are plenty of people walking past.' He prayed this was still true, but did not move his eyes from Najib.

'Besides,' Posthumus went on, remembering for a moment something Anna had said, and wishing that *this* were true: 'Just before I came in I phoned a friend. The phone is still connected and it's in my pocket. She is outside and could be here with the police within minutes.'

Najib stood with his hand on the bag, but made no further move.

'Where did you get it?' said Posthumus.

'What?'

'The taser.'

'Who says I've got one?'

Posthumus said nothing, but looked squarely at the lad. It was the first time he'd had a proper sight of him, but that didn't help at all. The only clear image he had from the afternoon of the attack was of black and gold trainers, and even then he couldn't be sure whether the shoes, too, were part of the picture of a young man fleeing in a djellaba created by Sulung. The image came to him in the guise of a memory, but what was true recall and what belonged to Sulung's description, he could not in all honesty say. Damn Sulung for being sick, thought Posthumus. He should be here now.

'Why have you been avoiding me?' he said. He wished Najib would step from behind the desk so that he could see his shoes.

'How could I? Never seen you before, have I?'

'I think we both know that's not true.'

'Been told about you, that's what. Snoopin' around the family.'

'Your father has asked me to help.'

He needed to draw Najib out from behind the desk. Needed something concrete to go on, to help him decide where he was going to take all this. Something definite, provable, to his own mind, yes, but especially if he was going to have to go to the police – and that could mean allowing Najib to attack him again. Idiot that he was for coming alone. He tried a different tack.

'What did you have against your cousin?'

'What's that to you?'

'Your father is very upset about him, and your sister says the two of you didn't get on. I wanted to talk to you about him, that's all.'

'I don't care that he's dead, if that's what you're wondering. He was a *kafir*, an enemy of Islam, a partial Muslim, and that's worse than *you*!'

'From all I hear Amir was a devout, quiet young man,' said Posthumus.

'He was an ally of the devil, sent to lie to us, to deceive us!'

'How can you say that?'

'Him and everyone like him back in Morocco. Slaves of the king.'

'Amir wanted reforms?' said Posthumus. Just two days before, the Moroccan monarch's proposed referendum had hit news headlines. 'But that's good, isn't it? More democracy?'

'Allah rules, not men. Democracy is *haram*!'

'Who has been filling your head with this nonsense?'

'No one is filling my head with any nonsense! You think just because I'm nineteen I can't think for myself, right? Or maybe it's that I'm another dumb Moroccan? Treat me like shit, huh? Man, I've been treated like shit by you lot all my life, and tell you what? You want shit? I'll give you shit. Like you've never seen before!'

Najib was yelling. He stepped around the side of the desk. Black and gold trainers. But not quite of the design Posthumus had in his mind. Less gold. Much less gold.

Posthumus could see a temper like this flashing out that night beside the canal on the Kop van Jut, though. He should cool the situation a little.

'What does your father think of all this?' he said, and then more pointedly: 'What if he finds out what you get up to? It would crush him. Look around you. Look at all this, what he's done with his life, what he's given *you*.'

Posthumus heard a disturbing echo of his mother's voice, admonishing him some thirty years ago.

'Abraham was rejected by his family, and in turn he rejected his father,' said Najib, but he lacked some of the conviction of earlier. He sat behind the desk again, subdued.

'My father don't understand *nothing*,' he went on quietly. 'You're all too old to understand. You've forgotten, and you've had different lives. I've got my own mind. And it's *my* life now.'

Posthumus looked across the room at Najib. He could hear himself speaking at that age, to his own father. Suddenly Najib was like so many other hurt, confused, angry adolescents. Posthumus felt an odd surge of sympathy for the boy.

'Or, at least, I have my own destiny,' Najib corrected himself, his eyes downwards, 'and that is known only to Allah. He will not test me beyond my ability, but the devil lies in wait. I must make my choices, but they must be *mine*. Allah blesses me with a free will.'

Posthumus took a step towards the lad. Najib looked up, not at him but beyond him, over his shoulder. Posthumus was aware of a shape moving behind him. How, he did not know – a subtle change in the light, a sixth sense. He swung around, as the door buzzer went.

'You're not really closed, are you?'

A young couple, coming in to the shop.

'We said we'd be coming around this afternoon, to see the new upholstery fabrics.'

'This customer was just leaving,' said Najib, standing up.

Posthumus hesitated. There was little more he could achieve now. He turned to Najib. 'Think on what I said. About your father,' he said. He nodded to the new arrivals, and left the shop.

Posthumus drove erratically, deep in thought. The way back to Staalkade took him past the Kop van Jut. On an impulse he stopped the car, and parked. Perhaps if he tried again he might be able to get some sense out of that crazy drunk. But from the bridge he could see the little boat was empty, its tarpaulin slack and hollowed. He made his way not on to the footpath, but back across the canal, to the strip of park on the other side, sat on a bench and stared across at the Kop van Jut.

Posthumus was troubled by his encounter with Najib. There had been something almost heroic about the lad at the end, in a sad sort of way. But it was hard filtering out what Najib really believed from arguments that he was merely mouthing. A little like the way in which his own memory of his attacker was a cloud of somebody else's description and what he imagined to be true, thought Posthumus, with a wry half-laugh. He sighed. And those trainers had not looked quite right. But they were near enough. Yes, it was Najib who had tasered him, all right. All his instincts told him so. Even more so, now he had seen the boy face to face. And that in all likelihood meant Najib was involved in Amir's death, too – though Posthumus had been careful, he thought, not to give Najib any firm idea of his suspicions. But now what? If the boy had indeed got wind of what Posthumus suspected, he could panic, disappear. Should he give Najib the chance to go to Mohammed? He should certainly speak to Mohammed himself. If it had been an accident, a fight that got out of hand, and Najib admitted it, maybe he could get off with a lighter sentence. He would speak to Mohammed. Tomorrow. But what if he were wrong? And what if Najib wouldn't admit it? He doubted that possession of a taser would mean much. The doctor at the hospital had said they were common, a weapon of choice in some quarters. Evidence. He still needed hard evidence, whether that was for his own peace of mind before upsetting Mohammed, or for the police.

Posthumus leaned back on the bench and gazed disconsolately across at the Kop van Jut: the dull brown bricks of the apartment blocks, the clump of willows, the blank rear wall and back door of the college.

'I wonder,' he said, so loudly that a woman walking past through the park turned to look at him.

Posthumus crossed the bridge.

Twenty minutes later, he was on the phone to Merel.

'Merel. Are you still at the paper? Good. I think I may have found something.'

15

The image was grainy, washed in an orange light, certain colours standing out stark, too bright, like in an old movie.

'Where did you get this?' said Merel.

'I told you, the college has CCTV,' said Posthumus, 'and they've been having break-in trouble recently, so they had the OK to hang on to the footage.'

'You know that's not what I meant. How did you get your hands on the disk?'

'I lied.'

Merel turned from the screen to look at him.

'You really don't want to know,' said Posthumus. 'My work ID card helped, though.'

'You're mad, you could lose your job.'

'I need to *know*.'

'Still . . . we'd better get a move on.'

It had taken Posthumus over an hour to drop the car back off at the Staalkade and get across town to *De Nieuwe Post*, but newspaper offices never sleep, and the building was still busy.

'Luckily Jerry owes me a favour, and I know my way around this thing,' said Merel, making images flit fast across the screen, 'but we've only got about twenty minutes.'

'There's not much. I was hoping to get footage of the after-noon I was tasered too, but they only kept the after-hours files. The disk's got files from two different cameras, both nine till midnight, but I reckon if you fast-forward till about ten forty-five, eleven . . . there, stop!'

Merel had already frozen the screen. A small figure in white on the right-hand side.

'OK, normal speed.'

The figure began to move across the screen, walking along the canalside path behind the college.

'Bugger, bugger, *bugger*!' Posthumus hit the desk with the flat of his hand.

The camera was focused on the path along the side wall of the college, and on to the small bicycle park. Beyond that, the canal footpath just edged in to the top of the frame. The white-robed figure crossing the top of the screen was headless.

'The other file, the other file!' said Posthumus. Someone passing in the corridor looked in at them quizzically.

'No, wait a moment,' said Merel. 'Let's see what happens.'

A second figure. Walking behind the first. Also in a white djellaba. Also headless. Getting closer. Near the clump of willows. They stop. The first one turns. One raises an arm, the other jerks manically, collapses twitching to the ground and slides from view.

'Twenty-one, twenty-two, twenty-three . . .' Posthumus counted out seven seconds.

The remaining figure disappeared from the screen the way it had come.

'Ballroom Blitz,' said Posthumus, his voice very quiet. 'Dancing like gnats, or one dancing like a gnat, anyway. Let's look at that other file.'

The second camera was focused on the back door of the college, the porch, and the paved rear yard, leading back up to the street. In the top left-hand corner, one half of the stairway that went up to the bridge was visible.

'Sloppy,' said Merel. 'Not strictly legal, covering public space.'

'Let's just pray,' said Posthumus.

The first figure: descending the stairs. Half off the screen but for a moment full frontal, just edging into the top left-hand corner.

'Can you get in closer?'

Merel clicked the mouse a few times. The face zoomed larger.

'That's Amir,' said Posthumus.

Nothing. Ten, twelve seconds.

Second figure. A little further on screen. Descending. Body. Face.

'Stop!'

Merel was already zooming in.

Posthumus stared at the young man on the screen in front of him.

Merel leaned back in her chair.

'That's not Najib. No way is that Najib.'

For a long while, neither said a thing.

'Now what do you do?' said Merel eventually.

'Well, certainly not go to Mohammed with accusations against Najib.'

'The police? To get them to reopen the case?'

'With a headless video? They'd just laugh.'

'It's more than that. There's enough here, surely.'

'Not really. These wouldn't be the only two guys walking around in white djellabas in the area. There could be a good argument that there's no definite connection between the figures in the two videos. And I'd have to explain how I got the footage. My main reason for this was to have something to take to Mohammed, to make Najib come clean.'

Posthumus, absorbed, stared at the screen, and made a

slight rotating movement with his forefinger. Merel let the film run a little further, till the white figure slipped out of view.

'Can we see it again?' said Posthumus.

Merel dragged the film back a few seconds.

'You're going to try to get to the bottom of this yourself, aren't you? I can see you thinking!' she said.

Posthumus held up his hands, as if in surrender. 'You know,' he said, 'in an odd way I'm kind of relieved it isn't Najib. But I'm still certain it was him who tasered me. I could see it in his face, his reaction to me.'

'Then you're very forgiving!'

'This is just another strange piece in the puzzle.'

'And you're determined to make the full picture.'

Posthumus grinned. 'Can you make a printout?' he said, nodding towards the screen. 'A couple of stills from different angles?'

Merel nodded, clicked the mouse a few times, ejected the disk, and handed it back to Posthumus.

'Printer's this way,' she said. She winced as she stood up.

'God, I'm sorry. With all this I didn't even ask,' said Posthumus. 'How are you?'

'Knee and shoulder are still a bit sore, but otherwise OK.'

'I was worried.'

'Yeah.'

Merel walked in front of Posthumus to the other side of the room. At the printer she turned to him.

'I phoned my mother, just after I spoke to you this morning.'

'She's all right?'

'She flipped, if you must know. It took me half an hour to calm her down.'

Posthumus felt something grab his gut, something with a thousand needles in its claws. The sensation spread upwards to his throat. He could not avoid this now, not any more.

'She said I should ask you exactly how my father died,' said Merel. 'And about the time after the funeral in particular.' Merel looked troubled.

'Is there somewhere we can talk?' said Posthumus. 'Somewhere quiet.'

Anna had let herself in to Posthumus's apartment. For the first time in years, he had not made her a Monday-night meal. He had texted her around eight.

Can't do dinner. Don't want go out. Need speak. Can you get takeaways meet me home? Am turned inside out.

Turned inside out indeed, if PP was eating takeaways. Anna smiled as she put a pair of pizzas in the oven to keep warm. But when the front door opened and Posthumus walked in, his haggard look triggered a rush of concern.

'What's the matter? What's happened? Sit down!'

'I told Merel about Willem.'

'What about Willem?'

'Everything.'

Anna regarded her friend. He did not sit, but walked across to the open canal window, leaned against the wall and stared out.

'Sofa!' said Anna. 'And I'll get the wine.'

She returned with a bottle and two glasses.

'It was her bicycle accident that did it,' said Posthumus, sitting down. 'When she told Heleen about it, Heleen flipped. Said Merel had to make me tell her about her father. And she did, wouldn't let it go.'

'How much of everything, exactly?'

'*Everything.*'

Anna sat beside him and took his hand. Queen's Day,

233

1991. Sensible Willem, the loving father. Wild Pieter, living in a squat, doing nothing with his life. Willem lured to Amsterdam the night before, for what became a boys' night out – from party to drunken party in the revelries that preceded Queen's Day celebrations. Heleen was to follow with the girls next morning, for a more traditional family outing among the buskers and city-wide street market. Willem's promise to Heleen to catch a tram or cab if he'd been drinking. 'Hysteric Heleen' the others called her. Pieter persuading Willem to cycle. Late, late at night. The accident. With a taxi, as if by malicious irony.

'It should have been me,' said Posthumus. 'I egged him on to drink more than he wanted to, gave him a joint. He'd never smoked in his life, never even been really drunk. And I made him cycle home. Pissed and stoned as he was, he clung to his promise to Heleen. Or tried to. I told him his wife was a neurotic, and made him cycle home because I didn't want to have to schlep back across town in the morning with a hangover to pick up the bikes.'

He hadn't been like this in years. Unstoppable. Like he was in the confessional. As if talking like this would somehow bring him the means to purge himself of the guilt.

'You didn't *make* Willem do anything. I thought you'd stopped beating yourself up about all this.'

'Just because I don't talk about it any more.'

In truth, Anna had long tired of a tale that always ended in the same place, and for some time now had cut him short when he began. Posthumus turned to face her full on.

'I even spiked his drink when he tried to go over to Coke,' he said. 'What was in my head I just don't know. Jealousy, maybe. I loved him, but I was jealous. Golden Boy Willem who did everything right. I wanted to see him trip up. And, by Christ, he did.'

Anna let go of Posthumus's hand, leaned over and brushed a lock of hair from his forehead. This was a new one on her.

'You told Merel that?'

'Everything.'

Posthumus's wine remained untouched.

'It's not that much different from tasering someone,' he said, 'then watching them fall into the water and drown.'

'You've really got to get over this, you know, PP. Stop punishing yourself.'

'Seeing Merel brought it all up again. The whole thing with Heleen, too. It's hard to stop punishing myself when Heleen has been punishing me for decades.'

'Those little girls adored you.'

'Which is what made it so hard.'

'And Heleen was not exactly stable, even at the best of times.'

'That's unfair.'

Posthumus had been a bulwark to Heleen and the girls in the weeks following Willem's death. Had moved to Rotterdam for a while to be near them, become a surrogate father, stood by Heleen as her grief vented itself in anger at Willem for breaking his promise to her. For dying. And in the end Posthumus could take his sense of shame no longer and confessed. Told her that Willem had tried to keep his promise. Why he hadn't. And Heleen had blamed him not just for that, but accused him of betrayal. Of being there for the girls merely through guilt, because he had deprived them of a father. Her anger at Willem did not diminish. Instead she cut both brothers from her life, and took the girls to Maastricht.

'I thought I was over that part of it, that I had given up on family,' Posthumus went on. 'That like you I was fine without it. Merel coming turned all that on its head. I've been trying to avoid telling her.'

'How did she take it?'

'She was deathly pale. Distant. Said hardly anything while I was telling her. Then she said that it was all so confusing, that it was too much to take in at once. That she needed to get her head round it, didn't know what to say, to think, even. That she needed time. That I shouldn't call, she'd be in touch. Then she left . . .' Posthumus faltered. 'I don't suppose I'll hear from her again,' he said.

'Give her time.'

'That's what you said about Heleen.'

Anna leaned over, picked Posthumus's full glass off the table, and put it in his hand.

'It's pizzas, I'm afraid,' she said. 'But I can knock up a salad if you like.'

Anna didn't go back to De Dolle Hond that night.

Some Mondays she didn't.

TUESDAY
14 JUNE 2011

16

'Results,' said Veldhuizen. 'I said I wanted results.'

'And you're getting them.'

Veldhuizen's car was at the edge of a sprawling car park that served five different building-trade and DIY megastores, just off the Amsterdam ring road. No CCTV this far from the buildings. He'd checked. Already just busy enough at 8.30 a.m., with trade custom, for them not to stand out. Veldhuizen stared straight ahead, one wrist resting on the steering wheel. Wraparound shades. Speaking as if on a hands-free. The side window down. Not a car in the space beside him, but a scooter, its rider hunched over, apparently sorting some problem with the handlebar.

'I told you I had an idea,' said the young man.

'Maybe you didn't hear right. I said *result*, not *idea*.'

Veldhuizen took a sideways glance at Haddad's smart-arse son. The so-called 'Khaled'. That scooter had not come cheap. It was payback time.

'I don't need to remind you what I could do to those scraps of crap you call your official papers,' he said. 'Or what waits for you back home. And don't kid yourself. I've got plenty of other assets in djellabas who could step into your stinky slippers at the click of my fingers. *Results*.'

Veldhuizen's week had not started well. First the fucking Lammers woman, then a deeply unpleasant call from The Hague. The assholes. But he'd been full of promises, and now

239

he had to deliver. Or, rather, young Haddad had to deliver. The boy kick-started the scooter to life. What the hell was he thinking? Now they would have to yell at each other. But Haddad leaned over. Almost put his head in the window.

'I've made you a movie, old man.'

Veldhuizen did not budge. His eyes checked the mirrors. Nothing.

'Got them all hyped up, falling over themselves to impress me,' Khaled continued. 'Dared them. We made you a nice little "Goodbye, infidels, I'm gonna blow you up" job. Identifiable. Just one star, but two others in the background. Enough to get your boys going on them. Missed my vocation, I did. Director, scriptwriter. I even got you some lovely AKs in the background, for dramatic effect.'

'You *what*?'

'Don't worry, they're not real. And they're not at Mansouri's house any more, so the police won't know that. I left a few other handy little clues lying around, which they'd have to be blind not to find. And tell them to check his computer, but I guess you do that already.'

Veldhuizen remained expressionless. Not a bad move, he thought. The little tosser had grown cocky of late, but he knew his stuff. Had his father's style.

'So, only three directly implicated?' he said. 'Which?'

'Najib Tahiri, mainly. Alami and El Mardi knocking about, too, holding the AKs. I tried to get Bassir in on it, but he wouldn't bite. Too sharp by half, that one. I backed off,' said Khaled.

'I don't want you taken in with the rest of them. I'll sort something.'

'Sure you will.'

'What about Mansouri?' said Veldhuizen.

'There'll be more than enough on the computer to make

the police happy. And enough at the house to draw him in. Believe me. That's if your boys know what they're doing.'

'The video.'

'Got it. Right here.'

Khaled held up a memory-stick.

'Don't be an idiot!' Veldhuizen turned to look at him. 'Post it. *Today*. Anonymously. To InSec. And meet me tomorrow. Not here. I'll drop details in the Draft box.'

But he barely got to finish the sentence. The boy revved the scooter, bumped over a grass verge, and shot off along the bicycle path.

'Chief's late, I see,' said Ben, watching from Lisette's office window as Veldhuizen's Lexus ducked down the ramp into the InSec parking garage. It was after nine thirty. 'So I'm not the only naughty boy around here.'

'Ben, this is serious,' said Lisette. 'Leaving Post-its on your computer screen is one thing, using unauthorised hardware, having an *asset* use unauthorised hardware, is quite another. There was nothing on it?'

'Brand new. I gave it to him from the box. Didn't even have a go at it myself.'

He had the grace to appear subdued, Lisette noted. She couldn't help liking Ben. And she had to admit, it was precisely this maverick streak of his that worked so well for them in what he did.

'And the pressure is on,' said Ben. 'We did want to know what our man was up to, going out alone in civvies after midnight.'

'Well, yes.'

'Though I didn't expect it to be snogging blond boys in the Vondel Park!' Ben gave an impish giggle, but was immediately serious again. 'You . . . didn't look at all of them, did you?' he asked.

'I didn't download anything, and as you said, the one disadvantage of this thing is its stamp-sized screen.' She took the camera from a drawer, and placed it on her desk.

'That's OK, then,' said Ben. 'It's just like, some of the later ones, they're pretty rough. I mean, I knew gay guys went cruising in the Vondel Park, but I didn't think that anyone got up to *that* sort of thing. Anywhere. Except in movies perhaps. You shouldn't have to look at that sort of stuff.'

Lisette smiled. Suddenly cheeky Ben was all old-fashioned gentleman.

'Look,' she said, pushing the camera back across the table. 'I'm not going to take this any further. But you must delete everything on this, and anything you downloaded on to your tablet. Totally.'

'Ta,' said Ben. 'That's good of you, boss. And, yeah, sure. I will.'

'And don't use it again.'

Ben nodded glumly.

'You make me feel like such a schoolmarm!' said Lisette. 'But tell you what, I'll have a word with Hans in Equipment. See if we can't upgrade a bit, buy one for ourselves. Or if not, whether there's some way we can register and authorise this one.'

'Fat chance,' said Ben. 'But thanks again. Really.'

'Besides,' Lisette went on. 'I don't think it's Khaled we should be focusing on.'

'Not? He seems quite a stirrer to me.'

Lisette paused. Yesterday Rachid, now Ben. But coming clean to Ben would not be a good idea at all. Not at all. Mick, perhaps, but even then . . . No, it would have to be all of them at once, or nothing.

Ben was waiting for a response.

'It's the girl that bothers me,' said Lisette, after a while.

'Aissa?'

'Not Aissa herself, but what she's getting into.'

'You mean the tapes? That her brother's arranging for her to marry that creep?'

'Could be more.'

'We've got something on her?'

'Absolutely nothing that links her to the targets' activities. Not knowingly. Mick and Rachid are sure of that. You heard anything?'

'Just wedding bells, if skinny Najib is to be believed. Haven't heard it from anyone else, but she does see a lot of Khaled.'

'Then she's walking into this blind, whatever the set-up. Or worse, being blinded. I wish we could do something to open her eyes. But . . .'

Lisette took in a deep breath, and straightened her back in her chair, an indication the meeting was at an end.

'As Mick said the other day,' she went on, 'we are observers not participants. Sadly, sometimes.'

Ben got up, and walked to the office door.

'Gotcha, boss,' he said softly, turning to her as he left. 'And again, thanks.'

'It's good to see you back, anyway,' said Posthumus.

Sulung gave a shrug. Maya had left the office to get her mid-morning coffee; her snide parting comment about Sulung's Monday absence and his frequent cigarette-breaks still soured the air.

'You're sure you're OK?'

'I'm fine. It was just a check-up. There was a last-minute cancelled appointment. Then I had to sort out something at our mosque.'

An all-day check-up? And the mosque? Posthumus hadn't

thought Sulung was religious. He waited, but that was all Sulung was offering.

'Well, you know, if you ever . . .' Posthumus began.

'Sure.'

'There was one thing I did want to ask.' Posthumus shot a quick glance at the door. He could hear Maya talking to someone at the coffee machine. 'That guy who tasered me. Can you tell me again what sort of shoes he was wearing?'

Sulung rolled his chair back from his desk, as if to get a proper view of Posthumus.

'You are an odd one,' he said. 'Why?'

'Long story, but I think I might have tracked him down.'

'What the hell have you been up to while I wasn't looking?' Sulung gave a look of mock horror. 'I don't know, it was all so sudden. Trainers. Black, I think.'

'With gold on them? I thought I remembered you saying something about gold.'

'Yes, you're right. A sort of flash on the heel. Like a speed stripe.'

'It's funny. In my head I have lots of gold.'

'No. No, just a stripe. But, hey, it was a snapshot. Memory plays tricks.'

'Would you recognise him again?'

'Don't know. Depends, I suppose.'

'If you had the time, if I took you to see someone, you'd be OK doing that?'

'Well, yes, OK.' Sulung frowned. 'But what is all this? Have you been speaking to the police?'

'Not yet. As I said, long story.'

Posthumus thought for a moment, then reached into the slim leather briefcase he sometimes took to work with him.

'Was it this guy?'

He walked across to Sulung's desk, and handed him a

couple of photos – grainy CCTV shots, printed on A4. As he did so, he heard Maya walk into the office behind him. Sulung glanced at the photos, and looked up at Posthumus, his face expressionless. He shook his head, then flipped one of the A4 sheets over, and without a word gave them back, printed surfaces facing together.

At his desk, Posthumus slipped the photos back into his briefcase, placing it on the floor beside him. He turned to his computer as an email pinged in.

Hard to say. Was all over in a flash. But guy I remember much skinnier than that. Younger, too.

But, hey, maybe Maya's right. Maybe you're getting too deep into this. Time to back off.

S

Posthumus nodded to Sulung, and turned to get on with some work. Faxes to the Probate Office. A new client. He overheard Maya taking another case, too. Another drowning by the sounds of things, in the red-light district. Monday was usually the busy day, not Tuesday – weekends being what they were, and the two-day build-up of course. But yesterday had been quiet. His case was a tourist. Alone and dead in a two-star hotel. Heart attack. Passport on him, and the hotel should have his address, so it was straightforward. But never easy. Especially if there was a wife back home who thought hubby was away on business, had no idea he was in Amsterdam. That had happened before. His telephone rang.

'Piet, it's Cornelius. Used your landline. Cheaper.'

'And how can I help you?' Posthumus tried to keep his voice neutral, businesslike.

'That notebook. Why did you want to know what was in it?

And just *who* did it belong to? Sorry, to *whom*?' said Cornelius, grammar not quite defeated by curiosity.

'I can't quite say at the moment.'

'Ah, of course – my secret, black and midnight friend. Well, I've had a look, and the fragments I can make out are, how shall I put this? Very nasty indeed. But also beyond my powers. I'm seeing an old associate later today who can help, but I did want to ask – would you be happy and at one with our separating more of the pages?'

'Absolutely.'

'Bravo. Know you're busy. Won't talk. Ring me this evening. Details then.'

The line went dead before Posthumus could even formulate a question to find out more.

He couldn't wait. Swiftly, he texted Cornelius.

Details?

An immediate reply.

Can't commit. Wait till later.

Now what? All these pieces that at times didn't even seem to belong to the same puzzle. Posthumus opened his desk drawer, took out the Amir Loukili Personal Effects envelope. It was the only one of that batch he had been working on still to be processed. With a swift glance in Maya's direction, he flipped open his briefcase with one hand and slid the envelope into it. In the Personal Effects section of Amir's computer record, Posthumus marked 'Sent to next of kin'. But not yet. There would be time enough for that after he got the notebook back. He wanted to get to the bottom of all this first.

Mechanically, Posthumus continued with the new Case

Report in front of him. Computer record. Notify Alex. Complete hard-copy file. To the inbox. He wanted to speak to Mohammed again. It was curious that the man hadn't rung him to ask about progress. Probably being reticent and polite. Posthumus's fingers flitted around his desk, neatening piles, brushing away specks. He tore off the top sheet from the small notepad he kept beside the phone, already written on.

Snite Museum, University of Notre Dame.

Bart Hooft. Might as well. It would help focus his mind. Google. 'Indiana Phone Book'. He found a White Pages site, and keyed in Hooft. Instantaneous. One entry. Dr J.W. Hooft. Bingo! He checked World Clock. Indiana was six hours behind; they would still be asleep. Posthumus noted the number. Under it he wrote: *Something to remember me by*. Another piece, but the *same* puzzle?

Drudgery was what he needed; something that required his concentration, but did not occupy his mind. Maybe that would help, allow a shape to shift in the background, fall into place. He took out some bank work. But it was no use. Cycling, sleeping, travelling in a train – those were the things that helped, Posthumus knew. Something would suddenly unclog, and the answer would be there. Bank work did not help. And he couldn't concentrate on it, anyway, was making mistakes. He went to the Public Transport website. Well, it wasn't a train, but there wasn't the time to cycle. Besides, his bike was at home. And this would help kill two birds with one stone. Tram 14 took him door-to-door to Mohammed.

'I'm going out a little early for lunch,' he said, picking up his briefcase and leaving the room before Maya had the chance to irritate him. Downstairs, Alex was on Reception.

'You're early!' said Posthumus. Tuesday mornings were one

of Alex's times off, for university classes. Posthumus disliked the temp who usually took her place on Tuesdays. She'd been there when he came in.

'What happened to what's-her-name?' he asked.

'Got rid of her,' said Alex. Then, catching Posthumus's expression, 'In your dreams. No, I simply offered to come in early.' She leaned forward over the desk, looked towards the stairs, and mouthed: 'Amir's computer.'

'No sign of the courier?' said Posthumus quietly.

'Not yet, but I thought it would be best to be here by noon.'

'Keep me posted . . . and could you cover for me if I'm a bit late back from lunch?'

'Developments?'

'Dramatic.' Posthumus held up his briefcase. 'But I'll have to fill you in later.'

Maya's voice echoed in the stairwell. Alex looked heavenward, and crossed herself. Posthumus hurriedly left.

'These beautiful new fabrics came in only yesterday, chosen especially for this range,' said Mohammed, handing the customer a book of swatches. He glanced towards the street. 'I'll leave you to it. I'm over there if you need me.'

He walked across to his desk in the corner. It was no use. His heart was not in it today. Pieter Posthumus was coming, he'd just taken the call, and really Mohammed had little to tell him. Three times he'd spoken to his cousin Hassan on the phone, but the poor man was so anguished, so taken up with arrangements for the body, that Mohammed had not had the heart to ask him too many questions about Amir, let alone divulge his suspicions about the death. And what was all that, anyway? Some old man's silly imaginings? Mohammed now wished he had never phoned Pieter Posthumus, that he had let all this lie quietly. Well, that would have been the easy way out. But Mohammed Tahiri seldom took the easy way out. Such routes were for the faint-hearted.

'Yes. Yes, the bolsters are included in the price,' he called across the shop, in answer to the customer's query. Mohammed sat down at his desk. What had he started? Now, even Aissa was upset with him. Najib had complained to her that Pieter had been around at the shop yesterday, harassing him. The boy had told his sister, Mohammed noted, not him. Najib hardly spoke to him these days. And now Aissa was taking Najib's side, asking her father what he thought he was doing, letting this man interfere with family. Mohammed slumped a little. His children were floating away from him, moving into another world. It was as if they had outgrown him, like they used to outgrow their shoes (so fast!) when they were young. This notion of his about Amir was making it worse. And he felt guilty about Karima. He had never before kept secrets from her. Yet now he felt Karima herself was holding something back, something she shared with Aissa. A man? A prospective husband? He should know about such things, meet the man. He felt excluded. 'All in good time,' was all Karima had said when he pressed her.

'At the moment they're intended only for the Atlas range,' said Mohammed, getting up in response to a further query, and crossing back to the customer. 'But if that's a fabric you really like, and prefer one of the other sofas, I could have a word with the factory.' The sound of the door buzzer cut across the room. Pieter Posthumus.

'Excuse me a moment,' said Mohammed, and walked over to shake his hand, exchange formalities.

'I am very sorry, but I have not been able to speak to Amir's father,' said Mohammed, as they took their places at his desk.

'Don't worry, this is a really quick visit. I've come about something else.'

'Well, we have spoken,' Mohammed corrected himself, 'but not about the things you wanted to know. All I learned was that Amir was in Brussels not for business, but to attend a clinic, a doctor of some sort. More than that I could not ask. The time was not right.'

'A doctor?'

'I do not know why. There was so much else to talk about. Apparently it takes a while to go through, this repatriation. They are deciding whether to come and have a funeral here.'

'I'm sorry. I realise it's hard. Maybe next time, if you can. But in the meantime something has cropped up. Something I couldn't do by phone.'

Posthumus kept his eyes focused on Mohammed's face, as he pulled the CCTV photos from his briefcase. 'Do you know who this man is?'

Mohammed considered both photographs.

'No. No, this is not someone I know. Who is he?'

Posthumus continued looking at Mohammed. He believed the man was speaking the truth. He would have to trust him – he had gone too far, anyway, now that he had shown him the photographs. Briefly, he told Mohammed about the crazy drunk, the CCTV taser images, how he thought Amir had died. Mohammed's face was ashen.

'We should now go to the police?'

'Personally, I think not. But I understand if you feel that it's something you have to do. Theoretically, I shouldn't even be involved in this, anyway. Also, there's a bit of a problem about how I got these photographs. I would rather not use them unless we have to. My own advice would be to wait a few days, to try to establish a little more. At least to find out who this man is. Amir is still here, at the funeral parlour? Should it be necessary for the police to . . . reopen the case?'

Mohammed nodded.

'Well then, I would suggest we wait until we have something more concrete to take to them. Would you agree with that?'

'They laughed at me the last time.'

Agreed, then.

'Whoever this is should on no account get even the slightest idea we are interested in him,' said Posthumus, indicating the photos.

'I could ask Aissa,' said Mohammed. 'She knew Amir best. I would be discreet, say that it is something to do with one of the mediation groups I work with, a minor incident at the sports centre, something like that.'

Posthumus was about to nod his assent, when he remembered Merel.

'Do you mind if I hang on to them for a day or two?' he said. 'They're the only copies I have. I'm not sure I still have access to the equipment to print others, or if I can manage it on a normal computer.'

Mohammed held up his hands in a 'don't look at me for help on that one' gesture.

'I'll post them to you as soon as I can,' said Posthumus, 'or maybe photocopies, if the quality is any good.'

He didn't mention Amir's notebook. Simpler to hold back on that till he'd heard what was in it.

'I'd like, anyway, to speak a little more to Aissa herself,' he went on. 'About what she knew of Amir. Could you tell her, or could I perhaps have her number?'

Mohammed hesitated. 'There is a problem. I must confess that earlier today I was about to give up on all this, it is causing such disruptions in my own family. Aissa, I think, is angry with you. I did not know you were here yesterday, talking to Najib. He told her you were harassing him.'

Mohammed waited for an explanation. The concerned father.

Posthumus looked back at him steadily. He had thought that he would not bring this up.

'There is something else I have to tell you,' he said eventually. 'The day before we first met, while I was in Amir's apartment on a regular department visit, I was attacked with a taser. I'm afraid that, though I have no direct proof, I am certain it was Najib who attacked me. That was why I was here yesterday. Until I came across these photos – yesterday evening, after the visit – I also suspected Najib had something to do with Amir's death. You can understand why.'

'The taser.' Mohammed looked grave.

'I am relieved the photos show otherwise,' said Posthumus. 'But after speaking with him yesterday, I am even more certain it was Najib who attacked *me* . . . I'm sorry.'

'You are going to the police?'

'I have no proof. Yet.'

'Please, no. I cannot think Najib would do such a thing. But I shall speak to him myself about this,' said Mohammed.

'Do you know if he owns a taser?'

Mohammed slumped even lower in his chair. He seemed to have aged in the past few minutes.

'I would not know. My children are slipping away from me. I have no control any more.'

Posthumus felt a surge of sympathy. 'I suppose it happens as they grow older.'

'This is more.'

Posthumus retrieved the photos, and replaced them in his briefcase.

'And Aissa's number?' he asked quietly.

'Will you forgive a father?' said Mohammed. 'I cannot. A matter of her trust, you understand? But I will ask her to contact you.'

'There is one more thing,' said Posthumus. An off-chance. 'Does the name Bart Hooft mean anything to you?'

'Nothing.'

Mohammed sat up straighter in his chair. The customer.

'Sorry. If I could interrupt?' The man was hesitant, polite, standing just behind Posthumus. 'I've made my decision, when you have a moment.'

Posthumus rose to leave.

'Business is business,' he said, with a half-smile to Mohammed. 'And I must get back to work, too.'

Out on the street, he tried Merel's number. She did not answer. The phone rang for a long time before going to voicemail.

'Merel,' he began, but dried up. 'I can't do this,' he said, conquering his silence, 'not on a machine.' But he took a breath, and went on. 'I know you said not to call, but . . . please, please try to understand. Don't think this hasn't been with me every day for twenty years. Don't disappear. Once was bad enough.'

He was about to continue, but disconnected. A minute later he rang again. This was impossible. He really wanted to speak to Aissa, and wasn't sure Mohammed would ask her to phone, and even if he did, whether she would agree to. This was the only way through it he could see. It had to be done. Voicemail, as he expected.

'Look. I know this will make you think even worse of me, but quite apart from everything I need your help. To get in touch with Aissa if you can arrange it, to see if she knows what that guy had to do with Amir. And to get some more copies of those photos to give to Mohammed. I . . . help . . . please . . . sorry.'

He ended the call abruptly, put the phone back in his pocket. He felt like chucking it in the bin.

It was after two o'clock by the time Posthumus got back to the Staalkade. The tram ride had worked no miracles with his thought processes, but clearly Alex had managed a little of her magic – not a murmur from Maya when he walked in late. He texted Alex.

Maya an angel. How did you do it?

Alex had been busy on phone when he came in. The reply took a few minutes.

Trade secret. No sign of computer yet. Things a bit hectic down here, but come tell me all, when you have a mo.

Posthumus returned to the bank work he'd abandoned that morning. He waited until two thirty before he made the call. Eight thirty in the morning, Indiana time. Not too early, he hoped, but he wanted to catch them before they went out anywhere. And bugger Maya. This was official. Sort of.

'Is that Dr Hooft?' he asked, in English, when a male voice answered. 'Hello. My name is Pieter Posthumus, and I'm phoning from Amsterdam. This might be something of a difficult call . . .'

Ben connected his tablet to a printer. The work alcove in his apartment was a grotto of glinting screens, odd electronic equipment, boxes of cables with differently shaped plugs. He moved aside a couple of mobile phones and a curiously weighty Marlboro box on the desk to make space for the tablet. He would delete all the files. Securely. He had given his word, and he had his standards. They might not be everyone's standards, but they were firm. But the boss hadn't said anything about printing a few pics off, first. Just three, four photos. None of the really heavy stuff, those Black Tulip shots. Ben hadn't known until now that the Black Tulip existed. Certainly not his scene, nor anyone he knew. A small cellar bar down one of those corridor-sized alleys in the red-light district, apparently. How the fuck the go-man had managed to get photos in *there* without getting busted was a friggin' miracle. The man was good! And what didn't go on in there! Ben thought that sort of thing only happened in hardcore movies, not in real life. And he didn't consider himself naïve. So, no, not those. He was glad the boss hadn't taken a gander herself, when she took the camera off him – at least, he hoped she'd been spared from seeing the heavy stuff. But he'd print off enough. A couple of those shots in the park, that would do the job. He'd teach that Khaled creep a lesson. Help the girl out, too, in the long run. Ben had more than a touch of knight-in-shining-armour chivalry, when it came to women.

From a box on a shelf above his main computer screen, Ben took a pair of latex gloves. A large envelope, fresh from a new cellophane pack. He slid the photos into the envelope, and sealed it with Sellotape. No need to *give* away DNA. He already had the stamps, self-adhesive. Ben sat at the computer to make out an address label. He had been going to send it to the father, but his go-man had just confirmed that the father still hadn't met the guy. Straight to home base then. Ben keyed in *Aissa Tahiri*, and the address he had memorised from the files.

He was in time for the six o'clock post.

Anna, off camera, gave Posthumus a thumbs-up, and quietly left the room. He was connected.

Bart's father had taken the initial news calmly, but said he wanted some time with his wife before talking further with Posthumus. He had asked if Posthumus had access to Skype, because he hated telephones, talking to someone he could not see, especially for something like this. He had it himself, he said, to speak to his elder daughter and grandchildren in Alaska. Skype was new territory for Posthumus, but he knew Anna was connected. And it suited him better to be out of the office, conducting this conversation from De Dolle Hond. He had left work a little early, and was at the café just after five. Late morning in Indiana. This time they spoke in Dutch, though Jan Hooft's accent was odd, unaired, and he frequently resorted to English. He seldom came back to the Netherlands these days, he said.

'It is the worst thing of all for a parent to have to bear,' said Posthumus. 'Especially Bart's going in the way he did.'

They had already been through the circumstances of Bart's death, the funeral, and the reasons the call to Indiana had come so late. Posthumus knew, on this call, his role would be something of a counsellor.

'In a sense, we feel we lost him a long time ago,' said Bart's father.

Jan Hooft appeared to be in his late seventies, perhaps eighties. Thin, spruce, but with a sadness in his voice that seemed to have a permanence to it, one that went beyond the current conversation.

'We always blamed ourselves, you see. I suppose parents do. But we had no idea . . .'

He tailed off for a moment, then told Posthumus how they had emigrated when Bart was six, how – taken up with the star academic post he'd been offered – they hadn't realised how isolated the little lad, who couldn't speak English, was at school.

'We reckoned kids were resilient creatures, that he'd learn quickly, and he did, but he was singled out. Different from the start. And in a sense he felt it all his life. The depressions started some time in his teens. On and off. Later, it was always there. As if it were some sort of animal, lurking, ready to spring, and he had constantly to be on his guard.'

Posthumus nodded. Jan Hooft needed to talk, he could see, and he was prepared to listen.

'I think there was only one point when he conquered it, I mean felt that he had *really* defeated it. Just once. Maybe twice. That was when he met Rick. We . . .'

Jan Hooft looked to one side, where Posthumus had the impression his wife was sitting.

'We didn't approve of Rick. We knew Bart was gay, of course, but there were aspects to Rick's personality that were . . .'

He seemed to be searching for the correct word.

'Unhealthy,' he said.

Posthumus sat, responded quietly, as he was told of Bart moving to live with Rick in San Francisco, of Rick being involved with drugs. Dealing. Disappearing suddenly. Turning up in Amsterdam.

'Soon after he left, the apartment got raided. Bart wasn't there at the time, but he couldn't go back. He left everything and followed Rick. But Rick, it seems, had somebody else in Amsterdam. And he was arrested, anyway, soon after Bart arrived.'

There was an odd note of relief to Jan Hooft's tone. Posthumus suspected that this was a story kept tightly bound up, that Bart's father had not told it to many before.

'Bart panicked,' Jan Hooft went on, 'thought he'd be impli-cated and went underground. We heard from him less and less. It was as if he closed down. Pushed us away, too. He changed his address. Disappeared. We don't have family there any more. I came over myself once, but . . .'

He was silent for a long while, looking away from the camera. But Posthumus sensed he wanted to say more.

'You said there was a second time you thought Bart had conquered his depression.'

'He got in touch again. Suddenly, out of the blue, about a year ago. He wanted his birth certificate because he was going to apply for a passport. He'd let his old one lapse, you see, was living without any ID because he was still frightened. After more than a decade. Said he wanted to put his life together again. He wanted to travel, had met someone over the internet apparently. Even said he would come home . . .'

For the first time, Jan Hooft's voice faltered

'But this new man was like Rick in more ways than one,' he went on, clearing his throat. 'He simply disappeared, after just a few weeks. From one day to the next, gone. Bart stopped answering emails, changed address, went under again. I suppose . . . that could have been behind it all.'

Jan Hooft fell silent, and looked towards his wife again.

'Bart wrote some rather beautiful poems,' said Posthumus, stepping in to the gap. 'Quite poignant, many of them. Moving.'

Jan Hooft looked back towards the camera. 'Somehow, that doesn't come as a surprise.'

'Part of the reason I persisted in trying to contact you is that I think they might be good enough to be published. Should you want to do that, of course. For something of Bart's life to survive.'

'That is very noble of you, Mr Posthumus.' Jan Hooft smiled.

'The poems deserve it.'

'They're in Dutch?'

'Quite a few in English, and others in Dutch. The two are very different, as if they came from two contrasting sides of his character.'

Posthumus hesitated.

'But a number, I should warn you, are extremely graphic. Some might call them obscene. If you preferred, I could send a selection, and leave it at that.'

'I understand. Please, Mr Posthumus, send them all.'

A few minutes later, Posthumus had closed down the computer and was crossing the landing to the stairs that led down to the bar. They had moved on to trickier issues of funeral costs, of how the family would have to reimburse the city council if they wanted to claim any inheritance, and what to do with the Namiki pen (which had, indeed, once belonged to Bart's grandfather), but which luckily had not yet been sold to defray expenses. Posthumus nodded a greeting through the open door of the spare room, where Anna's cleaner was busy with a pile of ironing. More adroit than Anna herself, he hoped. Pausing for a moment, he opened his briefcase, took out his phone, and turned it back on. He hadn't wanted to be disturbed while talking to Jan Hooft. No missed calls. So Merel had not rung. Nor Aissa or Cornelius. A text message, though. From Merel. Posthumus was surprised to note his hand shaking slightly as he opened it.

Send me disk. Will make copies and post them to you. For Amir's sake. Don't know about Aissa.

  M

Non-committal. But something, at least. Posthumus tried Cornelius's number as he descended the stairs, but the phone was switched off.

'We rented bikes all day today, it was like *so* fun! Like you felt you were going to *die*, but . . .'

At the table beside the connecting door, a young American woman in a startlingly pink sweatshirt was regaling fellow travellers with her day's adventures. Posthumus edged past them, and made his way to the bar. Anna was busy with the beer pump at the other end. It looked like a round for the big American group.

'Wine?' she mouthed across to him.

He nodded. She'd bring it when she had a moment. Posthumus tried Cornelius again.

'Pieter. Hello. My erudite Arabist friend has just left. I was about to give young Lukas here a chess lesson. Wait a moment.'

Posthumus could hear Cornelius talking to his son, then apparently leaving the room.

'Still there? I'll be brief. There isn't much. It's all fragments. Pages kept tearing, or sticking together. It appears to be some sort of a confessional. The Arabic's good. Literary. The man was educated. But what he's writing *about*, now that's quite another matter. Pretty grisly stuff. Whipping with a hosepipe. Electrocution. That sort of thing. Electrodes on the soles of feet, on the genitals. And some other sort of dreadful violation. A lot about shame. A penetrating shame – that's his image – before family, before others, before Allah. I've made some notes. I'll get them to you. Now I must go back to Lukas. I abandoned the little man all afternoon for this.'

'Just one thing,' said Posthumus quickly, before Cornelius could disconnect. 'That page you read in the office. The one with the bit about a memento, "something to remember me by". Anything more on that?'

'Oddest of all, that one. Some sort of synaesthetic experience. Pain again, but described in the abstract, in terms of smell. Charring. Singeing. And all in the context of a farewell gift, or at least some sort of parting shot. I don't know what this young man was up to. Working on a novel, perhaps? In the manner of the wicked Marquis.'

Posthumus frowned as he put down his phone on the bar

counter. Distracted, he reached for a wine glass that was not yet there, shook his head, and picked up his briefcase. He had felt a little guilty that he had not let on to Mohammed about Amir's notebook. He didn't now. But he'd have to bring this up somehow. Or perhaps the laptop might throw some light on things. It still hadn't arrived by the time he had left the office.

Opening the briefcase, Posthumus slipped out the Personal Effects envelope he should have given to Mohammed, checked the contents. He took out the gory photograph of Amir's corpse that the young tosser of a policeman had included. He hadn't really bothered with it at the time, things had moved so fast after Alex's first call to Mohammed at the shop. He could spare Mohammed having to see that, in any case. He replaced the envelope and closed his briefcase, the photo still in his hand.

Posthumus looked at the image with distaste. In a band across Amir's stomach and chest lay a series of slash marks where the propeller had bitten in to him. All about the same size, pointed at each end, red and gaping in the middle, like partly opened mouths, or the pinking on a doublet in an old painting. The skin between them was flayed raw, and violent red; if there had been any taser marks, the tiny dots had surely been devoured by the course of the blade. He looked more closely. Then, rapidly, he moved the photo under the stronger light of the lamp above the till, and bent over it. 'A birthmark or something' the terrier copper had said – his excuse for sending the photograph. Posthumus could see it. Just below the collarbone. Reddish brown, with a darker centre. Slightly raised from the skin. Cancerous, almost. More of a scar than a birthmark, and though the edges were not sharp, they made an identifiable shape: a five-point star, the darker spot within it appearing blurred, as if out of focus, but a little like a bird.

Amir Loukili was scarred with something that resembled a military medal. And one of Bart Hooft's tattoos.

'For God's sake, PP! Customers!' Anna, bringing him his drink, stared appalled at the photo under the bright light on the bar counter.

'Sorry, sorry,' he said, turning it face down.

Anna reached her arm across the upturned photo, and handed him his wine.

Last week's iron-burn was healing – discoloured, slightly raised. Posthumus clutched her wrist, held it fast for a moment.

'Pieter Posthumus, what the hell's got into you?' Anna pulled her arm away, furious.

'Just a minute!' said Posthumus, with a glance at the wall clock. 'I've got to phone Rob Mulder at the morgue. He works until six, I might just catch him.'

Too late. Or Rob wasn't taking any last-minute incoming calls. Voicemail.

'Rob, it's Pieter Posthumus. I have a question about that canal body, the one from a couple of weeks back. Propeller damage. Unidentified. Don't know if you remember it, or how good your notes are, but . . .'

WEDNESDAY
15 JUNE 2011

17

The Post Room sent it up to Rachid. A memory-stick, posted anonymously, with AMSTERDAM CELL on the envelope. Within seconds, Rachid realised what he had, and called Lisette. By ten o'clock the whole team was in a meeting room, watching the video.

'Skinny Najib. Would you believe it,' said Ben, as the first image flashed up on the screen.

The sound was turned low. Najib didn't appear comfortable, stumbled from time to time over the Arabic. Alami and El Mardi joined him towards the end. Rachid had hastily prepared a translation, and read along with the video. When it ended, the team sat in silence.

'This evidence is credible?' Veldhuizen's voice came from the back of the room. Somehow, he'd got to hear of it.

'The computer guys have checked it out. Nothing dodgy digitally. No manipulation,' said Mick.

'And it fits the profile? You had any idea of it?'

'There are earlier audio matches from the weekend,' said Rachid.

'So you know where it was made?'

'The Mansouri house, most likely,' said Rachid.

'Then move on them. Now!'

'Surely we should—' said Lisette. She did not turn to look at Veldhuizen.

'You want blood on your hands?' he said. '*Now*. Those AKs

will still be there. And you've got new evidence on the rest of them, surely, as well as this Najib?'

'A lot of suspicious activity on Mansouri's computer recently,' said Mick. 'Someone's been posting in a jihadist forum.'

'Then *go*. Let's get this to the DA pronto. We'll have them nailed by the end of the day.'

Veldhuizen left the room.

Lisette stood up. 'Just a moment,' she said to the team.

They turned to her. It looked like she was about to give a speech. But she said nothing.

'Boss?' said Ben.

'It's just . . .' Lisette began, then seemed to find what she had been wanting to say. 'Whatever happens, I want you all to know how deeply I value everything you've done. All of you.' She caught Rachid's eye. 'And Mick, I'd like *you*, please, to write the report. As the chief said, pronto.'

'Thank you, Lisette.'

'And Rachid, get on to audio. Kill the taps.'

'Go go go! We got 'em!' Ben punched the air. 'Yeah, boss? Drinks all round after work? And not in Café Minus?'

Lisette smiled at him. She flicked a stray strand of hair back behind her ear, and gathered her papers. She did not say yes.

'Let me know if there's anything you need,' she said to Mick as she walked out.

'Ta ra-ra rum pi *pah*!' Alex followed her fanfare into the office, holding up a courier's parcel. Sulung and Maya had just left on a house-visit. 'Can you believe it? It came yesterday. Bloody Sulung had it!'

Posthumus appeared not to hear. He was standing at the window, staring across the canal. He had just taken a call from Rob Mulder at the morgue. A *brand*? Of course Rob remembered that corpse, he'd said, and the mark. The scar below Amir's collarbone was a brand.

'PP?'

'Sorry. Miles away.'

'I've got the computer. *Hello!* Amir's computer? Apparently it came after I'd gone home yesterday. Sulung was still around, just leaving. Had that moment shut the door, he said. Anyway, he signed for it, didn't want to open up again, so he took it with him. And then forgot all about it and left it in his car. Honestly, that man!'

Alex brought the package over to Posthumus's desk.

'It took me most of the morning,' she said. 'Phoning the computer company, tracking it with the trace-number, disputing its "Delivered" status with the couriers, finally getting the name out of them of who'd signed for it . . . just in time to collar the culprit as he left. And of course Maya was with him, so I couldn't exactly say "What have you done with the computer that PP and I semi-illegally had couriered from Brussels?" could I now?'

'Let's have a look.' Posthumus did not sound very enthusiastic.

The wrapping had already been opened. Alex slipped out the laptop and flipped up the screen.

'The repair company said we wouldn't need a password,' she said, as she turned it on. 'Start-up security deactivated.'

'Well, at least it's not in Arabic,' said Posthumus as the Desktop came into view. 'How's your French?'

'*Parfait.*'

'Good. Looks like we'll need it.'

'Shall we try that first?' said Alex. 'It's a diary program.'

Posthumus left the navigation to her.

'That's odd,' he said.

Patches of daily appointments, then long stretches of

nothing. Most of the appointments simply marked E, and a time. Some with further initials. E. BH, E. EvT.

'Go to the thirtieth of May. That's when he died.'

No appointments on that date. Another patch of E entries soon after.

'Hang on a moment,' said Posthumus.

He opened his briefcase, took out Amir's Personal Effects envelope, and checked the date on the train ticket.

'The appointments begin again the day he would have got back to Brussels,' he said. 'Can you go back a bit?'

Alex paged back, week by week.

'All the appointments are in Brussels, none in Amsterdam?' she said.

'Could be. Mohammed said he was seeing a doctor of some sort.'

Back to the first entries. Not too long ago. March. There, E became EXIL. With an address.

'I'll google it,' said Alex.

She linked the computer to the office wireless network.

'His search history's been deleted, by the way,' she said after a few clicks. 'And the only bookmark is for Muslim prayer times in Brussels . . . Here you go. EXIL.'

'Some sort of asylum centre,' said Posthumus.

'More than that,' said Alex, opening a website and scanning the French. 'Medical and psychological support for victims of violence and torture.'

Posthumus frowned. He told Alex about the brand. About what Cornelius had found in the notebook.

'Maybe it was some sort of therapy technique,' said Alex. 'You know, he had to write out his experiences. Like sometimes you have to note down your dreams, or describe situations that have angered you.'

'But why Brussels? Why not here in Amsterdam?'

A voice echoed up the stairwell.

'Hello! *Hello?*'

'Yikes. Someone at Reception. I'd better get back,' said Alex.

'I'll look around a bit more,' said Posthumus. 'See if there's anything there. I'll give you a call if I need any help with the French.'

He was alone in the office. Before he went on with the computer, Posthumus walked across to the Closed Cases shelf. Bart Hooft's hard-copy file.

'A *brand*?' he said again to himself. He removed the photograph of the tattoo on Bart's arm, put a Post-it note in the file to that effect, and slipped the photo into his briefcase.

Posthumus returned to the laptop. There didn't appear to be an email program. He was about to open Word, when his mobile rang. Mohammed.

'Pieter, I have this minute been talking to my cousin Hassan.' Mohammed sounded subdued. Grave. 'I have found out something about Amir.'

'Go on.' Posthumus had an idea what was coming.

'Last year, Amir went to study at the University of Damascus. I did not tell you this before. We did not know it ourselves. Amir said nothing to us about it. It seems that earlier this year, some friends of his there were arrested. Amir, too. The friends had become involved with a group that wanted to overthrow the government, but one of them was an informer with the security police. Hassan has connections. He managed to get the boy released. But the others, the others, I don't know. I think maybe some were killed. And they did terrible things to Amir before they released him, the security police. *Terrible* things. Some, he would not even tell his father, he felt such shame. His father said Amir changed completely after that, he was never the same.'

'I . . . I do now have some idea of this. Amir had a notebook . . .'

'Please destroy that book. I have no wish to know. I have promised Amir's father that no one else shall hear of this. For Amir's sake. He felt such shame. Hassan wanted to take some action, he comes from a powerful family. But Amir begged him not to. He did not want this to be known. He wanted to cut it from him, to be able to forget it. That's why he was in Brussels, for treatment. There is a special centre there, with very good doctors who speak French.'

'Amir's computer arrived this morning. I have seen the appointments.'

There was a silence at the other end of the line.

'Please,' said Mohammed. 'The notebook, and this computer. I do not want to see them. Amir's father will not want them. Amir wanted this to be private. He did not want to stay in Morocco with people he knew, did not even want to live in Brussels, near the treatment centre. Where people might know. That is why he came here, whenever he could. Where the only family was us, distant family who had not seen him for years, who did not know of his past.'

Again, a silence.

'I am very sorry to learn all this, about Amir,' said Posthumus. 'And it must be deeply upsetting for you. But it does make it doubly important now to find out what happened that night.'

Mohammed's voice, when he spoke again, sounded choked.

'Amir would want to be left in peace,' he said. 'He begged his father to do nothing, his father has begged me to remain silent. For his sake. I have failed my family once, and I will not fail them again. And what is this, anyway? Some old man's imaginings, with no facts.'

'That's not entirely true any more.'

'Please, Mr Posthumus. You said yourself when you came

to my house – the police have closed the case, your department has closed the case. Now Mohammed Tahiri is closing
the case.'

Mohammed said goodbye politely, and hung up.

There was a text waiting from Merel.

Am about to meet Aissa. She is OK speak you. Just. Café at
OBA. 13h00. Will you?
M

Najib came downstairs from his bedroom late. Mohammed
had long since left for the shop, Aissa was at the university,
and Karima was out giving a language class. The morning's
post already lay on the hallway floor. He picked it up. Three
envelopes. One unusual. Large, addressed to Aissa. Najib
turned it over. No sender address. The flap was taped shut.
Najib scowled, and let the other envelopes flutter back on to
the floor. Not for the first time, he opened his sister's mail.

At first, Najib did not take in the dark-haired figure in
Western dress in the photographs. The images came as too
much of a shock. He thought the photos were some sort of
sick trick to offend Aissa, a mistake even. He was about to
tear them in half, when he recognised Khaled. Even then, it
took a few moments for each element of what he saw to fall
into place. Khaled! This was disgusting. Khaled, to whom he
had poured out his heart, told his own secrets. Khaled did
this. Najib felt the hollow sinking of betrayal. All the struts
removed at an instant.

Of all the group, Khaled was the one who had befriended
him, said he understood, who guided him. Khaled, who he
looked up to as an example. Who he had wanted to marry
Aissa. Khaled! Najib kicked at the flimsy table in the hall. A
vase rocked, crashed to the floor. Tears pricked his eyes. 'So

he thinks he can deceive her, mock her? Humiliate her?' Najib spoke aloud, and kicked again at the pieces of vase. He did not pick them up. 'And he thinks I'm stupid.'

Najib opened the front door. He would have to be quick, he thought. Khaled would still be at home. He had to catch him before he left for the study-group, he didn't want the others to see this. But he would get Khaled. Chuck this photo in his face. Make him admit it. And apologise to Aissa. To them both. Make some amends. On the path, Najib stopped. Who had sent these? he wondered. Who else knew? And what if it *was* a trick? Or if Khaled said that it was, that the photos weren't real. He looked at them again. Where was this, anyway? A park? Najib turned around, went back inside and ran upstairs. He had a better plan. He'd find out, all right. Find out who this was, if this was true. Maybe even catch Khaled at it. Get some proof. So that he couldn't deny it.

'Stupid, am I?' he said to himself, as he flung open his bedroom door. 'I'll show him stupid.' He grabbed a screw-driver from the old lunchbox beside his computer, dropped to the floor, reached under the desk and began unscrewing. Too tight. He pulled at a thin slat of wood, splintering it but releasing a small, flat backpack that had been secured under the desktop. Things no one else knew about, except Khaled. The taser, the gun. Both from Khaled. Then there were the things not even Khaled knew about. Najib reached into the bag, and pulled out a black case. He heard his mother come back home.

'Najib? You still up there? What's happened here?'

He heard her picking up the pieces of the vase.

'Did you hear me? Come down please.'

Najib tried to put the bag back. The splintered wood wouldn't hold. He heard the lid of the dustbin snap shut, his mother sweeping with dustpan and brush. Tape! He scrabbled in his desk drawer. Nothing. He'd have to try the hall cupboard. His mother was coming upstairs.

'What are you doing up there? I'm going to do a wash. Can you bring me your sheets?'

No time for that, or to put the bag back again. Najib's eyes darted around the room. Nowhere to hide it. He had a box-bed, flat on the floor. She'd come in, take the sheets, look around for dirty clothes. Probably check the wardrobe, too, knowing her. No time. He shoved the black case back into the bag, shouldered it, hurried downstairs, and shouting a quick greeting to his mother, ran out into the street. He knew what he had to do.

He was outside Khaled's apartment in under ten minutes.

Posthumus hadn't visited the new public library before. The café was on the top floor. He remembered once overhearing Sulung going on about it. One of the best views in Amsterdam, he'd said. Seemed the place was a favourite Sulung hang-out. Posthumus took the zigzag of escalators to the top floor, and looked around him. The café was big, busy. A balcony terrace gave a view over the city. He could not see Merel, or Aissa. Posthumus walked towards the area at the back, where clusters of easy chairs helped fill a no-man's land between the café and the foyer of the library theatre. Empty – save for Merel and Aissa. They were sitting a little apart. Posthumus went up to them. Aissa looked pale, ill.

'I'm glad you'd see me,' he said, to Merel rather than Aissa.

'I thought it would be better if it was me who explained things to Aissa, not you,' said Merel. Her expression was grim. 'And I showed her the photos. The copies I made for you.'

'And?' Posthumus glanced at Aissa.

'It's her boyfriend. Khaled.'

'Oh Christ.'

Posthumus walked over to Aissa. She turned her head away from him. He sat down.

'What can I say?' he said to her quietly.

Aissa did not respond.

'There might be an explanation,' he said. 'Is Khaled a jealous sort? It could simply have been a fight that got out of hand, we've always said that. Perhaps we can get Khaled to go to the police? It would be much better that way.'

Aissa turned back to look at them both.

'I've been trying to phone Khaled all morning. Before I spoke to Merel. He's not answering,' she said.

Done a runner, thought Posthumus. But surely not, how could he possibly know?

'Besides,' Aissa went on, 'Khaled knew what I thought about Amir. He knew there was nothing there. He joked about it, he didn't care – he'd never even met Amir.'

'He didn't know Amir at all?' asked Posthumus.

'I don't think he'd ever even *seen* him,' said Aissa. Then she stared at Posthumus, as if he had said something truly dreadful. Glanced at Merel, as if for support. Back to Posthumus.

'Except once,' she said, almost inaudibly. 'Except once. On the night Amir died.'

It didn't sound like Aissa's voice at all.

'He came to the house. To call for Najib.'

'Your father said he'd never seen Khaled before,' said Posthumus.

'Najib answered the door,' said Aissa. 'Khaled didn't come in. I remember being glad of that, because things were just starting with him then, and I thought it would be embarrassing, with Amir there, and my parents hinting about weddings. So I was glad he didn't come in. But I knew he could see Amir, so next morning I mentioned him to Khaled. We hadn't spoken of him before, but I told Khaled that there was nothing to worry about, that Amir was a distant relative and that, besides, he just didn't do it for me, there was nothing between us, and my parents were not the sort to force anything, anyway. And Khaled acted really odd. Denied he had seen Amir, which I knew couldn't be true. He was more concerned about whether Amir had seen *him*, said anything about *him*. It seemed strange at the time, I remember, but I told him Amir hadn't even mentioned him, and he dropped it, changed the subject, started joking . . . But I suppose, by then, Amir was dead.'

Something in Aissa cracked, shattered. She turned her face to the back of the chair, pressed it into the cushioning. Sobs jolted through her like electric shocks.

'I'll deal with this,' said Merel. She went to sit beside Aissa.

Posthumus hesitated. He felt sickened. Merel held his eye.

'I'll ring you,' she said firmly.

Criss-crossing floor by floor down the escalator, Posthumus took out his phone.

'Is Sulung back yet?' he asked Alex.

'They got back soon after you left, but Sulung has gone out again. Look, there's something I need to tell you about Sulung.'

'Later, please. And I can't face Maya now. Could you tell her I've gone home with a temperature or something?' said Posthumus. 'This . . . this is all getting out of hand. I'm going to have to sort it out.'

Back outside, he turned right along the quay and headed to De Dolle Hond.

Najib stopped a block away from Khaled's door. He recognised Khaled's scooter, parked in the street. He knew that Khaled could not see it from his small apartment at the back of the building. Not until he got right outside. Najib reached into the backpack for the black case. He opened it, and took out the tracking device he had bought when he suspected Aissa was secretly seeing a man. Before, he'd used it against Aissa; now, he thought, he'd use it for her. Najib made certain that the clip and magnet he had fitted on to the tracker were still firm. He activated the device and its microphone, checked the link to his smartphone functioned. He worked quickly. And he knew from the time he had attached it to Aissa's scooter exactly where to put it.

Najib walked swiftly down the street. He barely paused as he bent, passing Khaled's scooter, to clip the tracker under the right rear mudguard, and strode on. It seemed just seconds later that he heard the sound of a scooter starting behind him, and turned to look over his shoulder. He had been just in time. Khaled was about to leave for the study-group, he'd be coming past any minute. Najib stopped suddenly, and swung round. For a moment he thought he'd made a mistake. That wasn't Khaled's scooter. Someone else was on it, about to ride off. Then he realised. No mistake. And not somebody else. It was Khaled. With his beard shaved off, and a duffel bag slung across his back. And not in a djellaba but wearing the same shirt as in the photograph. Najib slipped into a doorway and pulled out his mobile. Called Khaled. To check. To be sure. The figure was securing the duffel bag to the chrome carrier on the back of the scooter. He took out a phone, appeared to look at the screen. Did not answer. Najib heard the line go to voicemail. He disconnected. For a minute the figure did not move. A text beeped in to Najib's phone.

cu rang. am sick staying home. bad. Not ansring door

Najib watched as Khaled set off, heading not to Hassan Mansouri's house but in the opposite direction. Najib felt a spike of anger. Where to? What was he up to now? He would find out. He would not be far behind.

Onno Veldhuizen was late. A taut morning. He had had to up the pressure a bit. But, by this time tomorrow . . . Veldhuizen grinned as he cut the Lexus across three lanes of traffic to the slip road. He felt the satisfying sensation of his thumbs pushing down on the jugular. It was all go. The DA was on top of it. The Hague was happy. Only Haddad's boy to sort out. But he'd be waiting. Had no option.

The Lexus sliced along straight, almost empty roads in the business park on the southern edge of Amsterdam. Not quite high-rise. New buildings: sharp, mediocre, glinting with reflecting glass, computer architecture for nondescript companies, struggling to survive in bad economic times. Fading 'To Let' signs stretching entire floors. Veldhuizen veered suddenly off the street, down a ramp into the parking garage below a flint-grey, stone-clad block, newly completed. Empty. A victim of the downturn. Too few takers, and the developers defunct. A solitary security guard sat at the front desk, bored, beside a bank of dead CCTV screens. The entrance to the garage was round the back of the building, out of sight. Veldhuizen made it his business to know about such places.

Young Haddad was not there. Veldhuizen edged the Lexus down on to the first level, then backed up beside the ramp, just beyond the smoky-grey patch of light that seeped in from outside. His side window slid silently down into the well of the door. Expertly, he opened his phone with one hand, slipped out the battery and sim card. Water dripping somewhere. A clink of metal.

Najib ran along the street after the receding scooter, until he saw it turn left into Bos en Lommerweg, and head up towards town, out of sight. Now it was certain. There was no way Khaled was going to Hassan's house. Najib took out his phone and connected to Track. There would be a couple of seconds delay. But it was near enough. The Google map with a small, moving dot came up on the screen. Najib kept walking, fast, towards the Bos en Lommerweg. By the time he reached the corner, he saw on the screen that Khaled had turned into the Hoofdweg, and was speeding south. South and east. Same direction as the metro. Najib sprinted the few hundred metres to the De Vlugtlaan Station, beeped his card through the barrier, charged up the stairs, and offered a grateful *du'a* as a Line 50 train arrived the moment he hit the platform.

The dot on the screen was travelling parallel to the track, lagging behind as the train sped between stations, edging ahead when it stopped. Khaled was inside the ring road, out of sight beyond the Rembrandt Park. Najib checked his screen every few seconds, fidgeting, the fist that was wrapped around his phone hammering on his thigh, urging the train on, passengers in, the driver to close the doors and get moving. Go!

A long stop at Lelylaan. Najib watched the dot move far ahead, cross the Kostverlorenvaart and go on to the Amstelveenseweg. Getting out of reach. Where was Khaled going? Najib zoomed out on the map. The train started again. Najib noted that Amstelveenseweg crossed under the metro track, a few stops further on, one station after Line 50 took a V-turn and headed north. He zoomed back in, and watched the dot go over the metro line and continue moving south, past the VU Hospital. The train took a sharp turn. Now he was travelling in the opposite direction to the dot. He would have to get out. He jumped up and stood at the door, moving from foot to foot, checking his phone constantly.

Najib sprinted out of Amstelveenseweg Station, barely

pausing to beep his travelcard, pushing at the gates of the barrier as they opened.

'Hello, sonny. And where are we off to so fast?'

Two police officers, out on the street. Najib froze. He had a taser and a gun in his bag. If they did a stop-and-search . . . it had happened to him before. For no reason at all. His eyes darted about frantically, saw the signpost.

'Please. I'm going to the hospital. My father has had a heart attack. *Please*, officer!'

The man looked sceptical. The woman with him shrugged, gave her colleague a nudge with her elbow.

'Go on, then,' she said. 'Get on with you.'

Najib ran towards the hospital, turned a corner out of sight of the officers. Sweat was beginning to cling to his djellaba. He leaned against a wall, out of breath, and checked his phone again. Khaled was no longer on the Amstelveenseweg. He had turned left, behind the hospital and university, was heading back up in the same direction as the metro again. Najib turned his head to hide his tears from passers-by. But the dot stopped. Turned on to a road with tramlines, and headed out of town once more.

Najib hurried on, through the throng of students spilling out of the university. Waited at a crowded tram stop. And waited. Surreptitiously he checked the screen. Khaled was going fast now. Way ahead. Out to the city limits. Najib watched as the dot angled off again, left the road with the tramlines and hit the open countryside. He zoomed out on the map. Khaled was on the road to the village of Ouderkerk. Najib had no idea how to get there. He'd lost him. A tram came, but Najib did not get on. He leaned dejectedly against the shelter. Watching the dot as it crossed the Amstel river. He looked again. Khaled had not stopped in Ouderkerk. He had travelled around the outskirts of Amsterdam, and was heading back towards the far south-east of the city.

Line 50 doubled back again and ended up in the south-east. Najib was sure of that. It was the way to the Ajax stadium.

'Where's the nearest metro station?' he asked a student.

'Up there. Zuid.'

Najib ran. He'd have to risk any more suspicious policemen. At Zuid he checked the screen again. Khaled was still on the outskirts of the city, still moving towards the south-east. But going more slowly, it seemed. One minute to a train. Najib slipped on to the first carriage. A corner seat. He tried to slow his breathing. One or two glances his way. He shrank into his sweat-damp djellaba, turned his face to the window. Two minutes, four minutes. Still heading east. Another station. Six minutes. The train swept round sharply, now aimed back south, towards Khaled, train and dot converging on each other from opposite directions, the gap between them narrowing. Khaled wasn't travelling in long lines any more. The dot was darting in different directions, short spurts in a patch between the metro line and a motorway. Najib glanced at the train's route-display. Five stations between them. Four. The Ajax stadium, glinting, looming, like a newly landed spaceship. ArenA Station. A mall of superstores. The train emptied. Next stop. Again Najib waited right up against the door. The dot had come to a stop.

'Don't run, don't run,' Najib said to himself. A business park. He stood out even more in these empty streets. Moroccan, in his djellaba, the few figures moving between the buildings white, all in suits. Najib thought about dumping the bag. Just in case. He didn't want to be found with this stuff. But there was nowhere he could see, in this swept, tidied, ordered place. He dialled in to the microphone on the tracker, put the phone to his ear. Nothing. Bad reception. Just crackling. Then when it stopped, water dripping, footsteps, a rustle of movement near the mike. He checked the screen. It was hard to tell exactly where the dot had stopped. The streets in the map had no names, the layout didn't seem to match what he saw. Najib looked about. No sign of a scooter.

Veldhuizen shifted slightly in his car seat. His eyes, adjusting to the dark, made out the figure of Haddad, a bag slung over his shoulder, wheeling the scooter, coming out of the shadows from the left.

'How ya doin', old man?'

'Where the fuck did you come from?'

'Delivery ramp, round the side.'

'You're late.'

'Got lost, old man. And besides . . .' The boy leaned over and put a hand on the bonnet of the Lexus. 'You didn't get here too long ago yourself.'

Veldhuizen was silent. Young Haddad's new-found cheek was beginning to rile him.

'You ready to go?' Veldhuizen asked.

Young Haddad shrugged one shoulder forward to indicate his duffel bag.

'Get yourself to Brussels right away,' said Veldhuizen. 'There's a flight from there to Damascus tomorrow morning. Your father's sorted you a proper passport and a ticket. Business class.'

Spoilt brat.

'Both are waiting for you at the airline office. Keep the papers I got you till you get to the airport . . .'

'. . . but for God's sake destroy them properly once you're there.'

The cheeky little shit finished his sentence.

'I want you out of here right away,' said Veldhuizen.

He paused. Young Haddad pissed him off, but he had to give credit where it was due.

'You did good,' he said. 'They'll be arrested any minute, and this time they'll be toast. Mansouri, El Mardi, that skinny little runt you made the video with, the lot. But you are out of here *now*. When it happens I don't want there to be even a whiff of your little Syrian arse.'

Najib looked up and down the empty street. For a moment he faltered. He felt like turning around and going home. What was Khaled up to? Was he meeting that man? Najib's lip curved upwards in distaste. He felt a swell of pity for Aissa, which broke into a wave of hatred against his former friend. Where could Khaled be? Somewhere silent. With water dripping. He looked about him. Across the street there was an empty office block. There? A place two *flikkers* would meet? Najib saw a security guard at the desk near the door, reading a magazine. He crossed the street, walked past the building, round the back. A parking garage.

Najib listened again to his phone. Still only the rustle of movement, footsteps, then: 'How ya doin', old man?'

Najib stopped dead. He leaned up against the wall. Reception was clearer. He was close. He continued listening. Slowly, he walked towards the garage ramp.

Veldhuizen turned to look at young Haddad. 'Yeah, you did good. But I don't need to tell *you* the reasons to get out of here quick,' he said.

He let that sink in.

'Your father tells me Damascus is safe for you now,' he went on. One side of his lip curled. 'Sounds like you were getting up to the same sort of tricks there as you were here,' he said.

'With the same success. Eventually,' said Haddad.

'Not what I heard. You weren't so clever out there. Your father tells me your "friends" tumbled you, were after your blood.'

Bring the cocky little shit down a notch, thought Veldhuizen.

'Yes, *were*,' said Haddad. 'But my father is good at his job. There's none of them left to bother me now.'

'Except one.' Veldhuizen could not resist a smirk. 'Your father's still worried about that. I hear you . . . damaged . . . a young Moroccan, who turned out to be pretty well-connected back home. Perhaps you should be a little worried about that yourself.'

'You're not listening, old man,' said Haddad. 'I said *none* of them are left to bother me now. Or my father. Why do you think I came to Amsterdam, not anywhere else? Following a lead all of my own, I was. To make a nice surprise for Papa. Show him that his son has worth.'

'Your father doesn't need help from the likes of you.'

'Sometimes, yes, maybe he does. Like dealing with something that was too hot for him to touch, like a little smartarse shit from a powerful family. So I showed a bit of initiative. That I can act on my own. Effectively.'

Haddad drew out that last word, almost as a taunt.

'There *was* one nasty surprise waiting for me,' he went on. 'One night, at little Najib's house. But I'm good at thinking on my feet. I sorted out pronto what might have taken weeks. In a way I owe one to the little runt.'

He leaned forward until his mouth was inches away from Veldhuizen's ear.

'Oo, but that night! You don't know how close you were to having this whole story of yours blown to bits. *You're* the one who should be grateful. Lucky I'm a quick thinker.'

Veldhuizen recoiled. In the corner of his eye, he caught a movement. A change in shape in the shadowy grey light.

'There's someone on the ramp.'

Haddad straightened up. Looked towards the exit.

'Nothing,' he said. 'Getting paranoid, old man.'

'Just get the fuck out of here,' said Veldhuizen.

He started the car. Then he remembered. Shit. The telephone. He turned back to Haddad.

The boy was standing with the phone Veldhuizen had given him in one hand, sim card between thumb and forefinger of the other, a grin on his face.

'Forgotten something?' he said. 'Losing your touch, old man. Here, catch!'

He chucked the phone in at the window. Flicked the sim after it.

'Something to remember me by!'

Najib's head was swimming. He couldn't hear that last bit. After Khaled also called him 'little runt'. He stopped, pressed the phone to his ear. The other voice again: 'There's someone on the ramp.'

Najib took a step back. Turned and ran around the side of the building. A delivery entrance, Khaled had said. Najib didn't want them to know he was there. Wanted to see who this man was, what was going on. The police? The bits of what he'd heard spun around in his mind as he ran, trying to make sense of it all. The side entrance. Najib slowed down, and very quietly descended the ramp into the darkness. He wanted to know more. Whatever it was, Khaled was betraying them. Not just Aissa. This was different. Betraying them all. The video! That had been a fake. Just for kicks, Khaled said. A horror gripped Najib as he began to see what had happened. Hurt. Fury. He could see them now, in a patch of grey light across the garage floor – Khaled beside his scooter, the man in a car.

'Here, catch!' Khaled was saying. 'Something to remember me by!'

The car pulled away. Roared up the ramp.

Najib ran at him from the darkness.

'Little runt. I'll show you little runt!'

He plunged his hand into his bag for the taser. Got the gun instead. So what. Khaled turned, silhouetted against the light.

'I'll show you,' Najib screamed, and squeezed the trigger.

18

'*Now* will you sit down and tell me what is going on?'

Anna's voice was firm. De Dolle Hond was empty save for the two of them, and Mrs Ting. Posthumus had darted in after lunch, announced that Amir's killer was Aissa's boyfriend Khaled, and had gone straight upstairs to Skype. He was back. Bright-edged, filled with a tense energy, but pent-up. Like a top-quality rapier, thought Anna, or a hunting dog pointing at prey. She hadn't seen him like this in years.

Posthumus sat at the bar. He took a medal from the collection on the wall, and placed it on the counter. Anna walked up to join him. The fruit machine clunked out a handful of coins. From his briefcase, Posthumus produced three photographs: Amir's gory corpse, the CCTV picture of Khaled, an arm with a tattoo. He laid them on the counter with the medal, arranged them, straightened edges so that a line around all four objects would form a square.

'I've just been talking to Bart Hooft's father,' said Posthumus. 'He told me Bart had met someone over the internet, that he was getting his life together and wanted to travel. This was last year. Before the Arab Spring. So Syria was a possibility. But his master pulled a disappearing act, and Bart didn't go.'

'You are going to have to help me,' said Anna. 'You're clearly way ahead.'

She knew this mood of his. Knew what she had to do. Posthumus didn't appear to be listening. He stared at the objects on the table. Rearranged the order, so that the medal was in the centre, the photos arrayed around it. Anna waited.

'At last the pieces all belong to the same puzzle,' said Posthumus. He seemed to be talking to himself.

'What do we know?' he went on 'The tattoo on Bart Hooft's arm had something to do with Syria, with the military. There's a Syrian medal rather similar to this one that matches it. All his other tattoos were related to bondage, discipline, S&M. This one was probably the mark of his "master". That's borne out by the fact that it also was drawn on to a rather unsavoury dildo we found in his apartment.'

Anna raised an eyebrow. Was it her imagination, or did Mrs Ting also pause at the fruit machine?

'I didn't tell you about that,' said Posthumus, momentarily back to earth. 'And you didn't read the really heavy poetry. S&M stuff. Or BDSM to be more precise: bondage, discipline, dominance, submission. A very specific scene.'

He moved the photo of Bart's tattoo a little further from the rest.

'What was not on Bart's arm, but was on the dildo, was the phrase "Something to remember me by". That phrase also appears in Amir's notebook.'

'*Amir* was into S&M? Surely not. Or are you thinking Bart was also murdered?'

Posthumus considered a moment. 'No. No, I don't think so,' he said. 'Unless it was a sex game that went wrong, but there was no sign of that. I think he saw a pattern in his life was repeating itself. He felt deserted, and the depression he thought he had conquered was rearing up again. The last few poems bear that out.'

'There was no note.'

'That's not uncommon. Not when someone has completely given up. There doesn't seem to be any point.'

He moved Khaled's photo above the medal.

'But there is a link here. Somewhere, there's a link,' he said. 'Bart's tattoo design is taken from a Syrian medal. Amir was arrested in Syria, probably tortured. He has a brand . . . yes, a *brand*, with the same design as the medal.' Posthumus pointed to the mark below Amir's collarbone.

'So, you got through to Rob Mulder? After attacking my arm yesterday,' said Anna.

Posthumus looked a little sheepish, but Anna laughed.

'I'm sorry, I can get carried away sometimes,' Posthumus said.

'What friends are for,' said Anna. She leaned over the counter and ruffled his hair, but he was poring over the photos again.

'I think Bart's "master" and whoever branded Amir are one and the same person,' he said. 'Same phrase, same image, same mindset; the brand just further along the spectrum. But who is it?'

With a fingernail, he tapped the photo of Khaled.

'You think so?' asked Anna.

'I don't know. Just don't know. Why? What's the connection? Khaled killed Amir. I think we can be sure of that, but apart from the headless CCTV moment, there's insufficient proof . . .'

'Nothing watertight.'

'*Anna!* Really! But let's run with that for the moment. Khaled and Amir are connected by Aissa and Najib. And Khaled saw Amir at Aissa's house the night he killed him. He used a taser. From the CCTV footage and the old drunk's description, I think we can be sure of that, at least. My doctor confirms that someone tasered in water, or who falls in immediately, could drown.' Posthumus frowned. 'Najib used a taser on me, in Amir's apartment,' he said. 'But I'm not sure where that takes us.'

He sat back on his stool, and looked up at Anna. 'Still too many questions,' he said. 'Why would Khaled kill Amir?'

'Jealousy?'

'Could be. But it seems extreme. And Aissa had told him he had nothing to worry about. But what was *that* all about, anyway, if Khaled was into gay BDSM? And then what's the medal connection? And where does Najib fit in?'

Posthumus picked up the medal.

'Is it OK if I hang on to this?' he asked, patting the photos into a pile, and placing the medal on top. 'Gives me an object to focus that line of thought on. The man at the flea-market seems to think it's valuable, by the way.'

Anna nodded, straightened up, and gave the bar a wipe, as Posthumus slid medal and photos into his briefcase.

'I had put on the good coffee for you,' she said. 'But I think what you really need is a drink.'

She poured out a glass of his favourite New Zealand Sauvignon.

'On the house,' she said. 'And then I think it's time you phoned the police.'

Najib was out on the street. On Khaled's scooter. As fast as it could go. He did not even think about cops, about speeding. Or where he was going. He was drenched with sweat, his breaths were short, staccato. He reached the edge of a park. Stopped. Took out his phone. His hands were shaking. Ahmed! Ahmed would know what to do. First name on the list. Ahmed Bassir. Long rings, then an answer.

'I've killed him, I've killed him, I've killed him!' Najib's voice was choked.

'Calm down,' said Bassir. He spoke firmly. Quietly. 'Try to get a hold on yourself. Tell me what has happened.'

Najib gulped in air, but the sound of Bassir's voice subdued him. He explained what he'd seen. What he'd heard. What had happened.

'I thought that little *kafir* was up to something,' said Bassir. 'Look. This is what you do. We have to get rid of the gun. Come to me. *Now*. Don't go home, don't contact anyone. Not your parents, not Aissa, not any of the others. We can sort that out later.'

'We must warn them!'

'*No one*. Got it?'

'Got it.' Najib could barely speak.

'Where are you?'

'I don't know.' Najib's voice was almost a wail. 'I'll check my phone.'

'No. Keep talking. Look around you.'

'Tafelbergweg. There's a park . . . and a golf course.'

'Wait a moment.'

The line went silent. Ahmed must be checking a map. Najib stifled a sob. He realised he had wet himself.

'OK.' Ahmed was back again. 'We do this. Don't come to me. I'll come and pick you up. Ride around towards the back of the golf course. Don't rush, don't attract attention. There's a big park. Wild land. Maybe you'll see a lake. The street is called Abcouderstraatweg. Got that?'

'Yes.'

'The bicycle path is separate from the road. With bushes. Wait there. Off the road. Don't do anything to make people look at you. I'm bringing my car. It's nearly two o'clock now, and there's stuff I've got to do first, but I'll be there by half past. Look out for me, and follow me when you see me.'

'Thank you, Ahmed.'

'But you speak to *no one*, understand? Telephone *no one*. Not even your family. If you contact anyone, you're on your own.'

A few late-afternooners had drifted in to De Dolle Hond. Posthumus was about to phone Sulung, then thought better of it. This needed to be face to face. He reread the text that had come through from Alex.

> Look whatever is happening you need to know. Sulung wife dying. Cancer. Bad. S crushed. Bottled it up. Felt couldn't tell us. Sad silly man. But this why absences and not always with it. Broke down to me earlier. Maya still not know. He needs yr support. Man 2 man. Ax

Posthumus sighed. This one could wait until tomorrow. He had too much else on his mind. The woman on the police phone-line had been polite. Perfectly. But he'd sensed the 'not another nutter' scepticism when he said he thought he had some information about a possible murder, a case already closed. He'd been palmed off with an appointment next morning. He looked at the clock. It was nearly four. The fish shop on the Zeedijk around the corner would still be open. He could knock up a quick spaghetti vongole in Anna's kitchen, and they could eat early at the bar, before the after-work crowd made it too hectic. He didn't feel like going home just yet.

He was on the Zeedijk when his phone rang. At first he thought Mohammed had pocket-dialled him. All he could hear was machinery and yelling. Then he realised it was Mohammed shouting.

'Hang on, hang *on*! What's that racket? I can't understand you,' said Posthumus.

He stood to one side on a little sluice-bridge, a finger in his free ear.

'What have you done?' Mohammed was saying. 'This is you! What have you done?'

'What's going on?' said Posthumus.

'Helicopters. Police. Everywhere. What have you told them?'

'Nothing! I haven't even seen them yet.'

It was barely half an hour since he had been on the phone to the police. This couldn't be that.

'They came for Najib,' said Mohammed. 'Turned his room upside down. Took his computer.'

'They've arrested Najib?'

'I don't know where he is. He ran out this morning, hardly said a word to his mother. Broke a vase, and something under his desk. He won't answer his phone. But they've taken his friends.'

'His friends?'

Posthumus turned from the street, looked down into the water.

'Aissa phoned the house where they meet,' said Mohammed. 'The wife. She says her husband was taken, and others. Police even questioned Aissa.'

'*Aissa's* been arrested?'

'No. No, they didn't want her. Just questions.'

A helicopter drowned out Mohammed's voice. When Posthumus could hear him again, he was still talking about Aissa.

'She told me about earlier today, in the library. Your photos and this man Khaled.'

'She's spoken to the police about that?'

'No. They did not ask her. Just about if she knew where he was, and Najib. But they were talking about terrorists. What have you *done*? My little Najib is no terrorist!'

'Look, Mohammed, this is nothing to do with me. I don't know what this is.'

'But . . .'

Mohammed hesitated. When he spoke again he sounded a little calmer.

'This morning,' he said. 'I didn't tell you this, when I phoned this morning. But yesterday, after you came to the shop, I spoke to Najib about the taser, and what you said. I made him talk straight, to me, his father. He admitted that was him. He said he panicked, thought you were police. But all this! And now with Amir and this Khaled! What did you *tell* them?'

'Believe me, Mohammed. I have an appointment with the police tomorrow morning, but that is all. This is not to do with Amir and tasers. This is something else.'

'My boy, my boy.'

No, not calmer, thought Posthumus. Mohammed sounded broken.

'Karima is crying. Aissa is crying.'

'You must see to them,' said Posthumus quietly. 'That is where you are needed now.'

'I will send them away. Now. I will find a last-minute flight to Morocco. We were going for Amir's funeral, but they must go now. To get away from all this. My boy, my boy . . .'

'Mohammed, I am truly sorry about this. Really. Go to your wife and Aissa. I'll phone you tomorrow. We can talk then.'

But the line was dead. Mohammed had gone.

Bassir was driving. They had just passed Antwerp. It was nearly five o'clock. The gun, the taser, the scooter and duffel bag were all at the bottom of the lake, near where Najib had waited for him. Najib's sweat-drenched djellaba had dried, but he knew he smelled of piss. The radio was on. He had stopped crying.

'There'll be something fresh for you to wear in Brussels.'

It was as if Bassir were reading his mind.

'Thank you, Ahmed.'

They rode on for a while in silence, the radio low, barely audible.

'Aissa, my family, they'll be so worried,' Najib began. Bassir had taken away his phone.

'Not now, not from Brussels, not even from Spain. You can write to them once we're in Pakistan, *inshallah*. We can't risk it till then.'

'And the money . . .'

'Don't worry. This is all funded. I was sorting it for two other brothers. It will just have to be us, instead. We'll have to wait a bit longer for the passports, that's all. But the house in Brussels is safe. And there'll be ways of paying back, *inshallah*.'

Bassir leaned over and turned up the radio. Five o'clock news.

Reports are coming in of a massive police anti-terrorist opera-tion in west Amsterdam . . .

'That will be our brothers,' he said quietly.

He turned to look at Najib.

'And very nearly us, too. If you hadn't phoned . . . But there will be ways of punishing them, the infidel. More, much more than that journalist. Real retribution. Avenging the brothers' arrest, and your family's hurt, and Aissa.'

Bassir looked back to the road.

'It's a good training camp, in Pakistan,' he said. 'You'll learn a lot. But I'd say you're already one step there. Dealing with an evil little *kafir* like Khaled. You're quite the hero, I'd say.'

'I . . . I'm lucky I phoned you, Ahmed.'

'It's not luck, it is destiny. The will of Allah.'

'Yes, Ahmed.'

Team C's celebratory drink was muted. Three arrested, three still at large. So, some cause to clink the glasses, but not enough for a jig in the big wide world, as Ben had hoped. In Café Minus, instead. Rachid had declined, Lisette had gone home early.

Mick, Ingrid and me, thought Ben. Big ball of fun.

'Boss OK?' he asked Mick.

'Said she wasn't feeling good,' said Mick. 'And I must say she looked pretty rough. And Rachid?'

'Going on about how if we'd listened to him, we'd have the other two *and* Bassir,' said Ben.

Ingrid gave a dismissive shrug. 'Well, at least the evidence we *have* is sound,' she said. 'This time it will go to trial.'

The double doors swung open, and Veldhuizen walked in. Ben's shoulders drooped. This was going to be a fine party.

'Drink, chief?' he asked, trying his sweetest smile.

But Veldhuizen looked grim. 'Where's Lammers?'

'Gone home sick.'

For a moment Veldhuizen just stood there. Hard. Blank. He turned to go.

'I'll phone her,' he said. 'I've just heard one of your targets is dead. The Syrian. Shot. He was found in an empty office car park by a security guard. Unconscious, died on the way to hospital.'

The chief left.

Ben felt a cramp grip his gut. Aissa Tahiri? Would she? Surely not. Not shooting, anyway. This must be something within the group. And she was clean of all that, they'd checked her out, had nothing on her. But he wished, now, that he hadn't sent the photos. Still, it was too late for that. At least she wouldn't be marrying the little creep. That's something that might cheer up the boss. She'd wanted to protect the girl from that. And if anything, those photos would help the girl get over the fact her hottie was now stiff and cold.

'Win some, lose some, I guess,' he said, raising a glass to the other two.

Even so, he didn't really feel like a party now. Ben drained his drink.

'I'll be going, then.'

In the parking garage below Café Minus, Veldhuizen sat in his car. What the *fuck* had happened? Who the hell had killed young Haddad? His Syrian misdemeanours catching up with him? And to have been the fucking last on the scene! The last to see the poor little shit alive. Veldhuizen felt a shudder of relief that he'd checked the place out first, knew the CCTV was cold. And that no one in the street had seen him come or go. But still.

Lammers didn't answer. Probably just as well. He needed to think. If she knew he was out of the office earlier, put two and two together, got a hundred and six . . . What to do? Sweeten her? Or threaten? He'd get his promotion, could see her good. But she wasn't the type to take to that. Threaten, then? She was just as implicated. Or at least he could make her out to be. But maybe it was best to lie low. Wait for her to move. See what she said. He could sort Lammers. He'd done so before. And maybe it was best young Haddad was out of the way. Dead men tell no tales, and all that. He'd been a slippery little shit.

For a moment, Veldhuizen felt a pang for his friend back in Damascus. It was the worst thing that could happen to a father. Even in their business. What would he tell Haddad, when his son didn't turn up home tomorrow? Veldhuizen's hands beat out a rapid rhythm on the steering wheel as he thought. The truth. He would tell the boy's father the truth. That he had sent young Haddad off to Brussels. Maybe edge the truth on a bit. That he'd seen the lad go. Offer his sympathies, do all he could to find out. Haddad wouldn't let it go at that, he knew. But what was there to go on? They'd found nothing on the boy but the fake ID. The scooter had gone. Even if Haddad did manage to make a link between 'Khaled' and his son, he'd surely think it was his Damascus adventure catching up with him. No, this was a win.

The parking garage was giving him the creeps. Veldhuizen flicked the Lexus to life, and roared up the ramp into the evening light.

Posthumus fumbled with his street-door key. He checked his watch. Just after eight. He'd stayed longer than he thought at De Dolle Hond, had missed the evening news. No matter. The late news would probably have a fuller report. He let himself in. There was a thick envelope inside on the floor. Hand-delivered. Addressed to him. As Posthumus picked it up, he heard Gusta coming out of her apartment. He stepped aside to let her come down the stairs, narrow, treacherously steep Amsterdam stairs. 'It's like the architect was going to put in a lift, then went for stairs at the last moment, in the lift shaft,' a friend visiting from England had said.

'Hello, dear. Sold that Namiki pen yet? Going to be a rich man?' said Gusta as she descended, a flurry of multicoloured silks, wafting her aromas of face-powder and tobacco smoke.

'Not mine to sell, alas,' said Posthumus, pressing back against the wall as they passed each other in the tiny hall, almost cheek to cheek. 'Actually, I discovered it belonged originally to Old Man Hooft. The one who ran the stall at De Looier market? It was inherited by his grandson, a very lonely man who hanged himself a few weeks ago. He used it to write poems.'

'Goodness gracious,' said Gusta, Posthumus taking her place on the staircase and beginning the climb. 'How did you find all that out?'

'Long story,' said Posthumus, as he turned the corner on the landing. 'I'll tell you all about it. Another time . . .'

Inside the apartment, he kicked off his shoes, put down his briefcase, and opened the envelope he had picked up downstairs. It was from Cornelius. Amir's notebook. And Cornelius had typed out a transcript of everything he and his friend had managed to translate. Kind man. Posthumus put the notebook beside the black, cloth-covered box on his writing desk – his ponder-box, containing the fetishes and mementos of unsolved cases from his Integrity Unit days. He dropped the translation on to the sofa, and walked to the kitchen to get himself a glass of wine. The doorbell rang. Posthumus sighed. Probably Gusta back again because she had reached her bike and realised she'd forgotten her door keys. It happened twice a month on average. He buzzed the street-door open.

'That you, Gusta?' he called down the stairwell.

'No. Me. Merel.'

'Come in, sit down. Some wine?' Posthumus offered, as Merel came through the door. She was smartly dressed.

'No thanks, I don't have much time. I need to get to Central Station. I just missed you at De Dolle Hond, but Anna said you'd come home. You've heard?'

'Mohammed phoned me. He sounded destroyed. I don't know any details. I wanted to watch the news, but I've missed it.'

'I haven't had a chance either. I've been on the move. But I spoke to someone back on the desk. Three members of the

Amsterdam Cell are re-arrested. And last I heard was that there was a warrant out for Khaled . . . and Najib. It must have happened soon after Aissa got back home from the OBA. I mean, *Najib*? Poor girl, on top of everything. I've been trying to get hold of her, but she isn't answering.'

'The police were questioning her, too, but she's OK, wasn't arrested, Mohammed said. You sure you won't sit down?'

'No, no. I really am pushing it time-wise. That's not what I wanted to talk about. And I wanted to see you, rather than phone.'

Posthumus felt a sudden spike of pins-and-needles below his sternum.

'There's a lot happened these past few days,' Merel went on.

Posthumus nodded. They both remained standing, near the door. He felt as if his mind were working on a delay switch, processing what she was saying a second or two later.

'It's all set me thinking,' Merel said. 'The whole thing with Aissa, *all* this. Look, PP . . .'

Merel gave him a cautious smile. She was all Willem again.

'Whatever happened that night with you and Dad,' she said, 'some things are too important to lose a grip of. Trust, for one. Honesty. Connecting. I appreciate you telling me everything you did. Everything. That took some guts. I admire that. I guess I hero-worshipped you when I was a little girl, and you were snatched away. Like Dad. It's good to have you back, even with clay feet. And whatever Mum is going to say about it, I don't want history to repeat itself.'

Merel seemed to run out of steam. She stopped. Posthumus was blinking, heavily.

'Friends?' Merel asked.

'Friends.'

'And, anyway,' said Merel. 'I think you blame yourself too

much. Clay feet maybe, not a whole clay torso. Maybe *you* should have a go at forgiving *yourself*.'

'Perhaps I can.'

'Dinner tomorrow night? A nice long talk?' said Merel.

'Done.'

'But it may have to be on you.'

'No problem at all,' said Posthumus.

'Because the other thing I've been having to get into perspective, is that I've probably lost my job.'

'What?'

Merel was at the door. She opened it.

'I stayed at the OBA with Aissa for a couple of hours after lunch. Didn't go back to work. Didn't answer my phone. Mark Koning – a big spin doctor in The Hague, maybe I mentioned him that night I cancelled dinner? He phoned. When he couldn't get me on my mobile, he phoned the office. Left a message to ring him urgently. Whatever it's about, if my editor gets to hear about it, which I'm sure he will given the happy politics at *De Nieuwe Post*, and he makes the link with this afternoon's events . . . *Chop*. I didn't even make it to the official press briefing.'

'Merel, I'm sorry.'

'Don't be. Being with Aissa was infinitely more important. Besides, Koning called again half an hour ago, on his way to or from something in Amsterdam. He agreed to have a drink. That's where I'm off to now. Bit of damage limitation. Café Eerste Klas at Central Station. Perhaps I'm going to get something after all. Let's pray for a miracle.'

She gave him a wave, blew a kiss, and was off down the stairs.

'See you, Meertje,' he said softly as he closed the door.

Posthumus stood for a while, his hand still on the door handle. Perhaps Merel was right. He had trouble letting go of things, he knew, but maybe it was time to try to stop blaming himself for Willem. Sure, it hadn't helped, what Heleen did, taking the girls away, but now that Merel was back? Someone who knew, who shared the experience. Even if she'd only been a kid at the time, she was *Willem's* kid. He crossed to the sofa. He'd realised long ago he couldn't keep burdening Anna with it all, but Merel was different. Involved. Family. Something else that he had pushed away these past twenty years. Time for a change? Posthumus sat down. Anna was family too, in a sense, after all these years. She meant even more to him in many ways, but without those intricate little strands of inter-connection and obligation of a blood tie. Posthumus gave a soft laugh. Blood tie! What a quaint old-fashioned term. He picked up Cornelius's translation of Amir's writings, cradled it in his hands for a few moments, then began to read.

When the last of the A4 sheets was face down on top of the others, on the sofa beside him, Posthumus got up and paced the length of his apartment a few times. Then he stood at the open window and stared a long while out across the canal. At ten o'clock he switched on the television for the news.

The news bulletin kicked off with a full report of the re-arrest of the Amsterdam Cell. Three suspects still at large. A photo of Najib. Posthumus felt an ache of sympathy for Mohammed. An earlier interview with government spokes-man Mark Koning. Wasn't that the man Merel was going to see? Posthumus didn't like the look of him. Smug bastard. Smirking on about new evidence, how the others would soon be captured, how this highlighted the need for stricter legisla-tion. A news flash. A body found in Amsterdam South East, linked to the terrorist case. Posthumus froze. But not Najib. A photo of Khaled, from an ID card. False identity, the police-woman was saying, but, according to the card, supposedly Syrian. An appeal for information. Distinctive jewellery found on the body. Posthumus hit Live Rewind, then Pause. A gold neck-chain. Hanging from it an old medal: a bird, set inside a circle within a five-point star.

By the time Posthumus returned to the news, it had moved on to protests in Athens. He switched off the TV, gathered the A4 sheets from the sofa, and walked around the spiral stair-case to his desk, where he picked up his ponder-box. He took the medal and photos out of his briefcase, and placed them on top. So, *Syria*. Khaled must have been from Syria. The miss-ing piece he needed. The part of Posthumus's mind that rifled through bookshelves, raided CD collections, scanned diaries, built up pictures of his clients, and gave shape and substance to his funeral orations for anonymous lives, played over this new palette. He began to paint a scenario. Khaled. Call him that, for want of anything else. Khaled – Bart's 'master', Amir's torturer. 'Something to remember me by,' said Posthumus to himself. Khaled was the link. Two mementos, one of love, or his version of it, one of hate. One mind, same spectrum.

Cornelius's transcripts had made dreadful reading. And that last bit, the bit about the branding. Synaesthetic, Cornelius had called it. The agony described in terms of sounds and smells. The reek of Amir's own burning flesh, the sound of a voice he knew, a pain of betrayal. Posthumus closed the box, but carried it with him, first to the kitchen, where he took a bottle of wine from the fridge, then to his front window, over-looking the canal.

Mohammed had said that one of Amir's group of friends in Damascus had been a police spy. The familiar voice? Posthumus reached the window, pushed it wide open. His mind continued to paint, filling the spaces between the pieces he had. Khaled the spy in Damascus. Khaled in Amsterdam. Back in Amsterdam. For another dive into Amsterdam's darker waters, into Bart's world? Or pursuing

Amir from Syria? Khaled associating with a group of terrorists. Khaled for some reason doing the same thing here as
in Damascus. But why? For whom? And did he know Amir
was related to Najib, seek Najib out especially? Or did that
come as a surprise, visiting Najib and recognising Amir? No,
the other way round. Khaled scared of *being* recognised, of
having his cover blown. That night at Mohammed's house,
seeing Amir when Amir could not see him. Dealing with it.
Posthumus shuddered, despite the early summer air. What
of Khaled and Aissa? All a fake? On his part anyway, the
poor girl doubly cheated. And Najib? Najib snooping for
some reason (why?) in Amir's apartment, caught at it by
two official-looking men, tasering one in panic. A taser given
to him by Khaled? After Khaled had used it on Amir. And
where was Najib? Had he tumbled Khaled somehow? Najib
the terrorist? Surely not. Perhaps.

Posthumus took a cushion from the sofa, placed it on the
floor in the open window, and sat, his back against the edge
of the wall, legs extended across the opening, his ponder-box
alongside him. He set the wine bottle beside the box, held
on to the glass. A swan slipped past on the canal below, and
disappeared beneath the bridge. The gabled houses, curtains
open, light glowing from within, looked like rows of lanterns
strung along the waterside. Dr Jansen from the ground floor
nodded up a greeting as he arrived home; the young sculptor
a few doors down was going out for the night. A rattle and
a clang broke the silence, as a woman unlocked her bicycle
from the bridge railing.

Posthumus poured himself another glass of wine, and
opened the box. The puzzles he refused to let go. Copies of
Bart Hooft's poems and a picture of the Namiki pen still lay
inside. He picked up the three photos he had brought with
him. Bart's tattoo, Khaled, Amir. One by one he dropped

them into the box. Then the transcript of Amir's notebook. Finally the medal. Pieter Posthumus took a sip of wine, stared out at the gables across the canal for a moment, then slowly closed the lid.

EPILOGUE
A LONELY FUNERAL

Five people followed the coffin from the chapel at St Barbara's Cemetery to the graveside. The cemetery director, the undertaker, Pieter Posthumus from the city council, the poet Cornelius Barendrecht, and a reporter, Merel Dekkers. Out through the pine groves and past the grander tombs, then the more modest headstones, and on to a barren, sandy patch beside the railway embankment, where only the occasional plaque marked a grave apart from anonymous neighbours. There were times when Posthumus, in the course of his duties, had walked alone behind the cemetery director and undertaker, but even on those occasions every part of the ceremony was conducted with the utmost decorum. The solemn choreography of the pall-bearers, the reverent air, the flowers from the City of Amsterdam placed on the coffin.

Posthumus should perhaps have expected that the case of the person known as Khaled Suleiman would land on his desk, but he had been momentarily taken aback by the call. He had made discreet enquiries, but Aissa was already in Morocco, and Mohammed soon joined her and would have nothing to do with it. Najib had not reappeared. There had been one phone call, a woman asking about the time of the funeral. She would not give her name. Police, Posthumus thought. Secret services, even. And indeed, there was a sixth person at the ceremony, the cemetery director quietly let on to Posthumus, in the little room adjoining the chapel from where the director himself sometimes observed proceedings through a discreet panel of one-way glass.

The police public inquiry had yielded no information about 'Khaled Suleiman'. It was as if he were a ghost, even before he died.

The coffin was lowered, as law dictated for unidentified bodies, into a shallow grave, 'Level One' in the jargon, to facilitate exhumation if the need arose. One by one the followers in the cortège stepped forward to sprinkle a spade of sand over the lid, then they turned to make their way back to the chapel.

'I thought your poem was admirable, given the circumstances,' said Posthumus to Cornelius.

'As you said,' replied Cornelius, 'even a killer deserves some sort of final marker. But it wasn't easy. Quite a story though.'

Posthumus had filled him in on what he had been able to put together.

'The police didn't want to take it further?' asked Cornelius.

'They noted it all down, but didn't seem particularly interested in theories about the past life of a dead terrorist.'

'And the poet chappie?'

'Bart Hooft? I decided in the end not to say anything to his father,' said Posthumus. 'Better that way. But he's going to try to get the poems published.'

Cornelius gave Posthumus a surprised glance.

'Some of them,' said Posthumus. 'The milder ones.'

They reached the chapel.

'Coming in?' asked the undertaker. The city council's customary cups of coffee were on offer in an anteroom.

'Not this time,' said Posthumus. 'We have friends waiting.'

Anna was expecting them at De Dolle Hond. Alex would drop in, too.

'You've been very quiet,' said Cornelius to Merel, as they walked to the car.

'Lots to think about,' said Merel. 'Contemplating my new freelance life for one.'

There had been no miracles. Mark Koning had simply wanted to get into her knickers. No way.

Posthumus put his arm around his niece's shoulders.

'You did the right thing, staying with Aissa that afternoon,' he said, as she opened the car door. 'You've done the right thing all along. And you're good at what you do. You'll get your story. One day, you'll get that big one.'

Still hidden, Lisette Lammers watched the little cortège disperse. She had waited until now. Waited to see if anyone connected with the Syrian showed up at the funeral. Curious to see whether Veldhuizen had the guts, or the ounce of goodness, to go. But no. She knew her next step.

She took two letters from her inside jacket pocket. One was a simple letter of resignation. Short. That one had been easy. The other was longer, and had been considerably more difficult to write. It contained no light matter. It would almost certainly kill the Amsterdam Cell case, and could well mean prison for her, for divulging state secrets. It was addressed to Merel Dekkers, the journalist whose details were on record after she began associating with women around the Amsterdam Cell. That letter outlined everything Lisette knew. About the Syrian, about Veldhuizen. It did not spare herself, or play down her role, but it laid out what she suspected about the new evidence, and exposed how it had been obtained.

On the way back into town, Lisette posted the letters in the first mailbox she saw.

ACKNOWLEDGEMENTS

We are extremely grateful to Bert Kiewik and Ton van Bokhoven of the TRUP department of Amsterdam City Council's DienstWerk en Inkomen, for their help in researching the background to the work of our (very different) 'Funeral Team'. Cornelius Barendrecht's poem is inspired by one by a real-life Lonely Funeral poet, F. Starik.

Our heartfelt thanks, too, go to our English editors, Ruth Tross and Morag Lyall, for their fine judgement and eagle eyes. A very special thank-you to Farid, Kate and Michiel, Mohamed, Pierre, Rop and Yassine for their individual and invaluable contributions to the book.

Pieter Posthumus will return in

LIVES LOST

MAY 2015

Pieter Posthumus is enjoying a quiet drink in his favourite bar when the owner of the guesthouse next door comes bursting in: one of her tenants has been killed.

The discovery of the body is just the first of many mysteries. How is this death related to another, years before? Why do some people in the neighbourhood seem so sure that Marloes, the owner, is guilty of murder? And why did the dead man paint one picture every year – a copy of a Dutch master, but set minutes after the original?

As Posthumus travels the old Amsterdam district of De Wallen searching for answers, he slowly uncovers a tragic tale of missed chances, regret and revenge.

Read on for an exclusive extract . . .

CHAPTER ONE

Pieter Posthumus had never seen so much blood.

'*Jesus*,' said someone behind him. He felt a hand nudge him in the back, pushing him into the room.

'You're used to it.'

'We don't usually see the bodies,' said Posthumus. 'Not like this.'

The night that Zig Zagorodnii was killed had begun quietly enough. June just over. The smell of linden blossom still hanging in heavy pockets in the air, catching you unawares as you rounded a corner. Muggy. It had been unseasonably rainy. Posthumus had cooked something Moroccan, a new direction for him – chicken and orange tagine. Then a glass or two of wine, sitting in his front window, looking out over the canal.

At nine he'd decided to go down to De Dolle Hond. The weather seemed to be holding, or at least it would for the ten minutes the walk would take him. There was always a lull between the after-work and post-dinner crowds, even on a Friday. The café would be quiet. He could sit at the bar and chat with Anna before things got too busy. They hadn't seen each other for a couple of days, had some catching up to do.

The Kesters from the tobacconist's around the corner were

there. (When not? thought Posthumus.) He nodded a greeting as he came through the door. A few other regulars. The English couple who ran the snack bar near the Dam. The woman from the new boutique down the alley, at the fireplace with a friend. Paul de Vos at the bar, saying something that made Anna laugh. Posthumus gave a sour smile. The Fox Trio didn't start till ten. He hoped that little fling of a few weeks back wasn't flickering into life again. What Anna could see in a man whose chief reading was vintage X-Men comics perplexed him.

'Howdy pardner,' said Paul.

His urban cowboy image extended from the tip of his tongue to the toes of his embossed leather boots. Posthumus gave a dry nod and joined them, taking his usual stool, where the bar counter met the wall.

Paul hung on talking until the rest of the trio arrived, then sidled over to set up at the far end of the café. A couple of tourists came in, surprised at finding a place like De Dolle Hond on the edge of the red-light district. They sat silent over their drinks, bright-eyed, the girl taking photos with her phone – the Delft vases, the carved heads along the wainscot, bric-a-brac that was a legacy of three generations of Anna's family. Leaning back against the wall, Posthumus settled into the cosy familiarity of it all. Anna poured him another drink, then went to serve a clutch of newcomers. Irene Kester nodded drowsily, almost in a doze. Paul began with a little riff on the piano, then turned on his stool to announce the first set.

'Hey there, dudes and dudesses, good evening. For those of you who don't know us yet, we are The Fox Trio . . .'

It was then that they heard it. Not so much a scream, as a wail. 'Anna! An*na*! *Anna!*'

Seconds later, Marloes from the guest-house next door was

outside, banging so hard on the window that she cracked the glass.

Posthumus was first out of the café. Marloes stared at him, as if he were a stranger.

'Zig. Zig,' was all she said.

There was blood on her cheek, down one side of her dress.

Posthumus ran. Past Marloes, past the painted-out street windows of the guest-house, and in the door. Straight up to the first floor, where the rooms were. He shot a glance around the small landing. One door open. On the right, at the back. He stepped over to it, and stopped dead in the doorway. A salvo of soles on wood, as others from De Dolle Hond followed him up the narrow stairs.

There was blood everywhere. A dark pool beneath Zig's head, where he lay half-on half-off the bed. A lopsided halo with a sticky sheen. More on the radiator at the back of the room, running down in dried dribbles to the floor. Splashes. Crimson smears on the walls, thinning into pale smudges. Scarlet sock-prints on the lino. Blood drenching Zig's T-shirt, soaked into the bedding. Posthumus reached for his phone. An odd sensation welled through him, a wave of weakenings, of internal stays giving way, as if he had been holding back tears and was about to break down. Someone behind him was gagging. Someone ran back down the stairs.

'He's got to be dead,' a voice was saying. '*Jesus!*'

'Shouldn't we check?'

'Maybe we can do something?' A nudge in his back. 'You're used to it.'

'We don't usually see the bodies,' said Posthumus. 'Not like this. I'll phone an ambulance.'

'I already have, and the police.'

It was Anna. She was standing behind the others, her arm around Marloes, who was making odd, strangled whimpering noises, still staring blankly. The little group crowded on the landing was hushed, and stood looking at the scene framed by the doorway as if it were unreal, on a screen.

'But maybe you should check . . .' Anna went on.

Posthumus nodded to her, paused, then turned and took a step into the room.

'We shouldn't touch anything. Don't they always say that?' came one of the voices from the landing.

Posthumus trod carefully across the lino, avoiding patches of blood. He had no real idea what to do, but if there was still a chance . . . The bed was against the left-hand wall, pushed up into the far corner of the room. Zig lay on his side on the floor, his head on the bed, facing out to the landing. With his marble skin and soft curls he looked like the broken figure of a cherub, crashed to earth from a church ceiling. He'd pulled off the bedding, maybe trying to use it to staunch the blood. Posthumus could not see a wound. It must be on the right side of his face or head, he thought, from the way the blood had pooled on the mattress, run in threadlike lines along its seams. He reached over to place two fingers on Zig's neck. But even before he touched the youth, Posthumus knew – the eyelids half-lowered, the mouth slightly open, jaw slack to one side. The sense of an absence, of something departed. He returned to the landing.

'I think it would be best if everyone went back next door,' he said.

'Come on, you lot,' said Anna. 'Let's do what the man says.'

They needed no encouragement.

Anna exchanged a glance with Posthumus, and said quietly to Marloes, 'Come with us. I'll make you a drink. PP will sort things here. There's nothing we can do. The police are on their way.'

'Police, yes.' Marloes was quieter now – glancing about her, but still not seeming to take everything in. There were tears on her cheeks. Her hair hung loose, grey at the roots. She moved to follow the others down the stairs, heavy, unsteady, hands gripping at the fabric of the baggy, home-sewn dress she wore.

'Zig, Zig, little Ziggy,' she said.

Anna followed her down, touching Posthumus lightly on his forearm as she passed.

Across the landing, the only other resident who seemed to be in remained swaying slightly at her room door. A skinny blonde girl, very stoned, the music in her earphones so loud that Posthumus could hear its sharp tsikka-tsikka from where he stood.

'It's OK, I'll deal with this,' he said.

The girl looked at him with glazed eyes, not a flicker of curiosity. One of Marloes's strange brood. It wasn't a guest-house, really, more of an informal refuge. A shelter for the lost and broken young souls Marloes took under her wing. And God knows there were enough of them around here. Zig had been one, some time back. He'd been a rent boy, Posthumus thought, from eastern Europe somewhere. He wasn't sure exactly.

'Go back inside.' Posthumus mouthed the words exaggeratedly as he spoke, pointing into the bedroom.

The girl shrugged, stepped back and closed the door behind her.

Posthumus heard a police siren, but it stayed distant. He checked his watch. Four, five minutes since Anna phoned?

They should be here by now. He stood outside Zig's doorway, facing the landing as if on guard. Who the hell would do something like this? Zig was such a pleasant young guy, hadn't been on the game for years, as far as Posthumus knew – had some sort of bar job somewhere, and helped Marloes out in the guest-house. He was really kind to her, came in to De Dolle Hond with her quite often for a drink. Posthumus shuddered away the feeling that Zig was staring at the back of his neck. He turned and looked again at the young man, crossing his arms tightly over his chest as he did so, as if trying to hold himself together, prevent his own life-force from flowing away so freely.

Zig's room was in compete disarray. Now that was something Posthumus *was* familiar with. Every week, he surveyed apartments of the dead, of the anonymous and abandoned, of the friendless and depressed, of people disowned by their families, sloughed off when they died to the care (and expense) of the city burials department. And far too frequently came the flotsam and jetsam of the underworld, leaving just such scenes of tumult. Posthumus's eyes darted about the room. Bedside table awry, broken reading-lamp, half-open sports bag with a pair of trainers poking out. An easel, knocked off balance against the right-hand wall, paint-tubes scattered on the floor. Posthumus glanced at the painting. A copy of a Vermeer, and not too bad at that. So the lad was an artist of sorts. More Old Masters on the wall – postcards, mini posters, pages torn from art books.

Sirens again. This time clearly converging at the end of the street. Posthumus took a step away from the doorway, with a glance back at Zig. This would probably end up being one for the Funeral Team. The call from the police in a week or two, even if they had traced family, handing his department the responsibility of finding someone to pay for the funeral, or of sorting it themselves. He gave Zig's corpse a sad little smile. Marloes might adore the lad, but Posthumus doubted she'd have five grand to spare. He would make sure the case landed on his desk. The others didn't care. Posthumus alone checked bookshelves, went through music collections, rifled among private letters to build up a picture of his 'clients', to give them a more personal send-off. His colleague Maya called him a macabre snoop.

Blue lights were flashing outside, flicking through the fanlight above the door on to the stairwell. Car doors banging. The doorbell rang. Posthumus went down to let them in, closing the door on the ground floor that led to Marloes's apartment as he passed.

Within minutes, police tape stretched across the road from either side of Marloes's house. Posthumus ducked under it and elbowed his way through the gaggle of gawpers standing on the other side. Anna had closed De Dolle Hond and pulled down the blinds. He tapped on the door. Anna opened it herself, just enough to let him in.

'What's happening back there?' she said. 'I've asked those who went next door to wait around a bit. I thought they should, until the police got here.'

Posthumus slipped inside. People pressed behind him, trying to peer over his shoulder into the café. He pushed the outer door shut, but stayed with his back to it, in the entrance area.

'They've called in forensics,' he said. 'I told the guy in charge we'd be here when they wanted us.'

He did not mention Marloes directly, but glanced around the café, recognising faces that had been on the landing, and a couple of stalwarts who had stayed behind anyway: Irene Kester comforting Marloes at a table near the fireplace, Paul and one of the other musicians from the trio dispensing coffee behind the bar.

'Someone will be over any minute,' he went on. 'Good that you got them to stay.'

'Those tourists left, said they didn't want to get involved,' said Anna, turning to rejoin Marloes. 'They didn't want their weekend messed up, and I couldn't do anything to stop them really.'

Posthumus remembered the young man had been on the landing. 'Can't force them to, I guess,' he said.

He walked up to the bar.

'No, no . . . I need a drink, some wine,' he said, as Paul slid a cup of coffee across the counter.

But he took a biscuit from the plate that had been laid out. It was bizarre, but the sight of Zig had made him feel hungry. Ravenous. For something homey, substantial – *hutspot*, the sort of food from his childhood he almost never ate now. What was *that* about? he wondered. Some weird sort of affirmation that he was alive? Instinctive preparation to fight, to strike out against whatever was responsible for that broken young body lying next door? Poor, cheery, laid-back little Zig. *Why?* He looked over to the table near the fireplace. Marloes seemed emptied, completely bewildered.

Posthumus picked up his wine, and another biscuit, and after a glance to Anna to see whether he should, went to join them at the table.

'What's for him in Berlin?' Marloes was saying. 'As soon as he's real, he wants Berlin. And now I have to clean. We can't stay long.'

She wasn't making a lot of sense. But then Marloes was a bit of an oddball at the best of times.

'Good, good,' said Marloes, looking up at Posthumus as he came closer. 'He doesn't like coffee. But not wine, beer. Beer.'

'Marloes and Zig were going to come across for a drink together,' Anna explained. 'That's why she went up to his room. When he didn't come down . . .'

Anna noticed Posthumus's glance. There was no longer blood on Marloes's face and hands.

'We helped her clean up a bit,' said Anna to him quietly. 'She was in such a state about having it on her. I think she went in there and cradled him when she saw.'

'Zig, my baby,' said Marloes. She was rocking slightly, backward and forward in her chair. 'We must help him. Are they helping him?'

Anna's face was creased with concern. She looked a little panicked, out of her depth. After nearly three decades behind the bar, she was adroit at dealing with heartbreak and disaster. But with Marloes, she seemed at a loss.

'Marloes,' said Posthumus, sitting down at the table. 'Something terrible has happened. To Zig. You know that, don't you? What you saw . . . Zig is dead.'

'He wants to go to Berlin. To leave. What's in Berlin for a boy like him?'

'Marloes . . .'

Posthumus waited until she made eye contact, then continued.

'Zig is dead, he is not going to Berlin. I know this is difficult for you, and seeing him like that was a terrible shock, but Zig is dead. I am sorry that this has happened to you.'

He realised that he was falling back on phrases from the

training course he'd gone on before joining the Funeral Team, and that they were failing him.

'The police are next door, and they will be coming here to ask people questions,' he said. 'They will want you to remember everything you saw.'

'No, not now, I am too tired. So tired. I want to sleep,' said Marloes.

Anna looked across at Posthumus. She had clearly been through all this already. She took Marloes's hand. She must have known Marloes all her life, Posthumus thought. What was Marloes? Mid-fifties? Not that much older than him or Anna, he suspected, though she looked more. And her family had owned the building next door almost as long as the generations of de Vrieses had been at De Dolle Hond. For a moment Posthumus pictured Marloes and Anna as children, playing together in the street. He wondered whether she had always been so odd. Certainly, as long as he'd known her – a local institution, in her gaudy home-made dresses and beads. Scatty. Her conversation always a bit all over the place. And the guesthouse. Taking those people under her wing, like a giant neighbourhood Mother Hen.

Marloes had fallen silent, just sat there shaking her head. Irene Kester patted her on the thigh, with a: 'There, there. He's in a better place now.'

Posthumus sighed.

The others who had been up on the landing sat talking quietly round a table in the front corner of the café. Paul was tidying up behind the bar while his fellow musician packed up on the podium. The old clock on the back wall ticked heavily. There was a rap at the window. Posthumus got up to let in the police.